The Adventures of Robina
by Herself

THE ADVENTURES OF ROBINA

by Herself

being the memoirs of
a débutante at the
Court of Queen Elizabeth II

edited by

Emma Tennant

faber and faber

LONDON · BOSTON

First published in 1986
by Faber and Faber Limited
3 Queen Square London WC1N 3AU

Printed in Great Britain by
Butler & Tanner Frome Somerset

British Library Cataloguing in Publication Data

Tennant, Emma
The Adventures of Robina
I. Title
823'.914[F]   PR6070.E52

ISBN 0-571-13796-2

Editor's Note

I met Robina on one of those summer nights in Scotland when the rain comes down so hard it turns to hail, and the cold makes you want a fire (but there was little chance of that, in the remote farmhouse where I was staying: the Farmer and his wife, an elderly couple, were tight-fisted and the Log Shed out the back was kept locked). I was there in a professional capacity: there was a Library that needed cataloguing; damp had already got in on the Eastern Wall; and as many of the books had been *in situ* for close on three hundred years, I had a busy enough time sorting out and putting aside those in need of urgent repair. Robina came to visit her Aunt and Uncle, to sign some document apparently, when I was indexing, re-shelving and, of course, reading such masterpieces as Defoe's *Roxana*, Smollett's *Peregrine Pickle* and the Journals of James Boswell. As the rainstorm grew more violent, turning to white stones that bounced off the windows of the old house and making a white blur of the hills and the belt of conifers beyond, Robina came and sat with me in the Library and told me the story of her youth. In the morning, before I woke, she had gone. I decided to write down her account of the days, in the late 1950s or thereabouts, when she had been presented at the Court of Queen Elizabeth. And I found, as I followed her adventures, that the ways and manners of a certain section of the society in which we live, are virtually unchanged since the early eighteenth century. Thus Robina came out on the page somewhat influenced by the language of those times.

I was born in *Cumbria*, near the border with *Scotland*, or so my aunt and uncle told me. My family in the last century had been yeoman farmers in *Ayr* and then gone to *Glasgow*, where there was a great fortune to be made from the manufacturing of chemicals to replace natural dyes; the fortune was then sown round the world in Goldmines, Industry and Railways and reaped an even greater harvest; but I was destined to see little of it, and to find my own way in the World.

My mother ran away when I was born, my father settled the sum of £25,000 on me and disappeared as well, leaving me an orphan in charge of my father's younger brother, a genial man whose land lay just North of the Border. It was his wife, alas, who made my life a misery. My aunt's stringent economies, with the income which should rightfully have been mine and which had been placed in Trust for me until I should reach the age of twenty-one, left me often hungry. Had I known then that my inheritance would be further withheld from me, I would not have wished to continue with my Life. Yet now, for all the strange adventures I have lived through and all the Crimes I have committed for the lack of Money, I give thanks that I was never the possessor of inherited wealth, the root of man's inhumanity to man.

Whether it was because I looked South over the Border so often in longing for the childhood I should have had with my father and mother in that beautiful country of mountains and lakes, or whether it was a result of the strained feelings between us, my aunt announced one day shortly before my sixteenth birthday that I was to go South to Oxford, to an Establishment for Young Ladies. The fees would stretch her own purse and my uncle's to the extreme, but an education in French and French History of Art was considered more important than the sacrifices which this programme would entail. 'You'll have no dress allowance,' *says my Aunt*, 'I have made these for you' – and she lays out a collection of items of which the description here would be too dismal, except that they were to figure largely in my new life and can be given a

1

brief inventory. (1) *A green baize skirt* was the most remarkable of these. It was cut in a circle and indeed I had seen my aunt going round on hands and knees on the floor with an old roll of baize – it was taken from the attic, she says, to explain she has not dipped into her funds for it, nor squandered the income from my Trust of which she and my uncle were the Guardians. (2) *A Black Top*, which my aunt says I may wear with the green baize if I am invited out at *Oxford*; and this is *off the shoulder* and was passed down from my aunt's sister's elder daughter, who had in every way shown greater proficiency and strength of character than I, and was shortly destined to go to *University*. Apart from two very plain dresses, also once the property of this remarkable niece of my aunt's (3) was a short *Fur Coat*: 'It is mine and only on loan to you,' *she says*; 'it means a great deal to me as it was my mother's when she was alive,' and so on. At which my uncle, coming in from a rough shoot at the time with his guns still on his arm, says he must try to guess the fur and he had shot some vermin very like it only that afternoon. Then my aunt says he knows perfectly well it is Musquash and goes out. This kind of scene was common between them, I am sorry to say.

My uncle then says how much he will miss me when I am gone and how I must take care at *Oxford* not to get into the Wrong Set and not to Drift. 'You'll enjoy yourself there,' *says he*, coming across to me and stroking the fur coat, which I still had on me, and asking me did I think the fur was squirrel, or did I think it could be Rat, and all sorts of fooleries. As he laughed he rubbed my back all the harder, until the fur bristled under his hands and he was so near me I could smell the Port which my uncle liked to drink with the other Farmers after a Shoot.

Then my uncle fell quiet and said how pretty I had got and how many Young-Men would be after me when I arrived in *Oxford*. 'Here,' *says he*, taking a bundle of notes from his back pocket. 'This is to start you off' – and he pulled me to him once more and went out of the room quickly.

2

So it was that the next day I went South by Train to *Oxford*, with £25 in Scottish banknotes rather than the £25,000 which was rightfully mine.

*

If I was glad to leave my aunt, I must say here that my uncle's kindness to me had always been exemplary; and that when, after a short time at the Finishing School I was sent forcibly North again, it was he who pleaded that I be given another chance, whereas my aunt, as might be expected, was set to pack me off at once to the strictest of Scottish boarding-schools. All this, however, is said too soon: I was entranced by the Train, and by my first journey to a Seat of Learning in the South; I had been at a village school, remember, and had known only the sons and daughters of Farmers.

As luck would have it, my aunt's *Fur Coat* was the cause of the beginning of my life of Romance, for which I blame myself continually and regret the impetuous actions which brought my Family into so much trouble.

The coat, at a sudden stop of the Train, fell from the rack and on to the head of an old gentleman; and the next thing I heard was the sound of laughter in the Corridor, where a Young-Man of great beauty and elegance was standing. He pulled open the door, this Young-Man, and helped remove the fur from the head of the Old Man, and soon we were talking together as if we had known each other always. Indeed, I believe the other passengers thought so too, and thought that we were lovers, for after smiling at the episode of the *Fur Coat* they looked tenderly away from us and out of the window, which gave my new Admirer the chance to be thrown up against me by the movements of the Train and to squeeze me hard before leaning back again.

All this was new and strange to me, I have to say, and I was made to feel all the stranger when my Companion told me that he was destined for *Oxford* as well; that he was a Student there and that we would meet often; and that he was by birth a *Russian Prince* – although the wars in his native country had

3

caused his family to suffer all kinds of misfortunes and to leave for *Paris*, where his father had had to endure a spell as a Cab-Driver. 'But we are rich now,' said Prince P—, as I shall for reasons of discretion call him. And he said that his stepmother, who had been an *Astor*, had houses all over the world, in *America* and *Mexico* and *Italy* and a famous collection of pictures in her house in *London*, which he cordially invited me to come and see, as I had told him I was embarking on an education in the History of Art. Prince P— was glad too to hear that I had never been to *London* and promised to show it to me thoroughly; – 'but first,' *says he*, 'I shall tell you that you are by far and away the most beautiful, pretty and charming girl who has ever been to *Mlle Weiss*'s Establishment' (for this was the name of the place) 'and as the young inmates there are set free only on Saturdays' – at which he threw back his head and laughed (and I own I had never seen a finer, whiter set of teeth, in a ruddy face with high cheekbones and very bright eyes, a deep blue, I think) – 'as the Young Ladies,' he goes on, 'as *Mlle Weiss* is pleased to call them, are set loose as I say only on Saturdays and then only up until eight p.m. I will call for you on Saturday morning at eleven.'

There is probably no moment in the life of a Young Woman that is more pleasing to her than when she hears for the first time of her Beauty; and, as I have told, although my uncle had begun to notice it, my aunt had done much to tell me that my hair, which was red and gold and bunched in curls, was Common; 'Scotch Hair', she would say of it, and that it came from my great-grandmother (the only ancestor of my Uncle's that my Aunt was prepared to acknowledge, because of her lowly origins). This was the first *Robina*, who had been a gypsy and lived only by 'Habit and Repute' as a Wife under Scotch Law, with her name and her husband's on a brass plaque on their front door in Glasgow, but no Certificate between them. My aunt said that my Character too came from *Robina* and that no good would come of it, for this Mysterious woman, before living with my Chemist and

4

Merchant grandfather, had borne three children, no one knowing from where or whom. And it was true I resembled her extremely. I was tall, but not too much so; my legs were (and remain to this day) long and shaped like a dancer's; my hair gold-red, Complexion fresh, and grey eyes made up the rest.

There was little time, however, for reflection on all this – or to wonder, which I must say I did later, as to how Prince P— came to know so much of the habits and inmates of *Mlle Weiss*'s Establishment – for my new Companion was both squeezing me and talking at such a rate that in order not to arouse the contempt or suspicion of the other Travellers I was forced to make a show of being well used to this form of Behaviour (which may well have been *Russian*, for all I know).

Prince P— told me a hundred anecdotes of his family on that journey, and he asked me several times to Marry him, saying that although the great Palaces in his homeland had been taken from them, they would be returned to the family again soon and we would live in splendour, with servants, and sledges to go through the snow in the streets, and we would dance in houses where the rooms were heated by furnaces inside the thick walls. He, Prince P—, was the eldest son, which meant we would have the Best Estates, and if I wished I should have my Uncle to stay with us, for he would find the opportunities for a Sportsman were excellent. As for me, I should wear White Velvet Gowns edged with swansdown and a coronet of diamonds and pearls in my hair, as suited a Princess of the Royal Blood, etcetera.

Whether this talk, which made the journey go extremely quickly – particularly as it was accompanied, as I say, by Prince P—'s hands reaching up under my skirt in sudden Dives (which put my blood up for the first time in my life, partly in Shame at the presence of the other Passengers) – whether this talk, as I say, was responsible for the Tastes I was later to develop – viz. a love of Gaiety rather than Duty, Pleasure rather than Sobriety, I shall never be able to say. But when I look back on all the Grief I was to occasion my Aunt (for I see now that she was a Good Woman, with my Best Interests at heart), I understand that she was aware from my earliest days of a love of Fancy and idleness in me, and saw she must put me up against the Real World as often as she could. That she had little degree of Success in this was certainly not for want of trying.

Prince P— now told me that we were coming in to *Oxford* and that I must be very Careful when I was there, seeing no one but him and refusing the invitations and advances of all the Students. 'They will be after you as soon as they see you,' *says he*. 'They will ask you to their Rooms but there will be no party when you get there. They will take you in Punts' – and here I had to ask what these might be – 'and you will find yourself stuck far Upriver' – and so on.

I was alarmed at all this, but not too much so; as some of the Passengers were now smiling openly at Prince P—'s talk. I asked him then if the other Young Ladies at *Mlle Weiss*'s Establishment ran these risks, and if so, how they survived their year at *Oxford* at all; but Prince P—, seeing I was not taking the matter seriously, threw both arms round me and with tears in his eyes begged me to take Care, and particularly when I met, which I was sure to do, a certain Lord E—. 'He seems quiet, and his good looks are the kind you don't see at first – no, no, don't laugh,' *says* Prince P— in anguished tones as the whole carriage bursts out laughing, 'he is from the oldest Scottish family, his charm is deadly – you ask me of the other inmates of *Mlle Weiss*'s, well I must tell you that in the last year three have gone down with it, and been sent down from *Oxford* too.'

'Sent down?' *say I*, for I knew very little in those days. 'Where to? To Hell?' I have to say, as I thought it was the only place you could go down to, and very often my Aunt had told me that was where I would go, for she had a dour background of Calvinist beliefs. 'No, no, to *Switzerland*,' *says* Prince P—. And he starts laughing with the rest of the Passengers (as I was to notice in him, Prince P— had great Changes of Mood and would laugh when others were crying, and cry his eyes out when something quite pleasant or amusing had just been said]. All of which was Slavonic Charm, no doubt, for the Compartment was thoroughly on his side by now and hoping I would not be flighty enough to disappoint Prince P— in his honourable expectations of me.

As I could not then ask further questions, or elicit the meaning of *Switzerland* as a place to which one might be sent after an acquaintance with Lord E—, I fell silent and made no struggle, despite the constrictions of Prince P—'s Bear Hug, which continued all the way to *Oxford* Station. But, as I now know, nothing is more foolish in this world than to warn a Young Woman of the dangerous charms of a Member of the Opposite Sex; and my thoughts, which seemed to all intents and purposes to be focused on the Russian Prince, were already far from him and inventing the outlines of Lord E—. I could say, even, that I heard nothing further that Prince P— said, although he spoke furiously for all the rest of the journey, except when it was time for us to disembark on to the Platform, and he was handing down the Fur Coat and wrapping me in it, and tangling with the feet of the other Passengers, for Prince P— was as Clumsy as a Puppy. 'Don't say my name to *Mlle Weiss*,' *says he*. 'I am such a favourite of hers that she would insist I come round to Dinner, and I want to see you alone first.' And he reminded me that he would come on Saturday, with a Ring, he said, for we were now Engaged to be Married.

So passed my first Train Journey; it was not the last, unfortunately, to land me in Trouble without the slightest misdemeanour on my Part.

*

Often in my life it has been my lot to form a bond of liking and Trust with another woman, only to find myself Betrayed. If Envy lies behind the kind words and flattering looks I have so often received from women I can only say I never considered myself more fortunate than they; and less fortunate certainly, in the case of *Annie*, an Inmate of *Mlle Weiss*'s, who received (she said) a large Personal Allowance from her Father and was very handsome too, with long, black hair and Green Eyes. It would have been hard then for me to know – with *Annie* coming out into the hall at *Mlle Weiss*'s and taking my bag – and saying to me that everyone was at dinner and I should come in too and join them – and all in the most friendly and open way – that this wretched Young Woman would dog my Steps and bring me Bad Luck wherever I went.

I followed *Annie* into the dining-room at *Mlle Weiss*'s and was greeted by the Stares of about eight girls and a very old man, whose shock of white hair and very dark eyes immediately proclaimed him as some kind of Genius (although I had not met any of these at my Uncle's Farm and thought at first that he must be Mad). 'Don't be afraid,' *Annie says* in a low voice in my ear. 'I am your Best Friend and will look after you. *Mlle Weiss* has gone out to tell Cook to bring in the Cauliflower Cheese and now here she comes along the passage.' And *Annie*, who I saw then, as I say, as my Saviour in this Terrifying Situation, announced that I was the New Girl down from *Scotland* and was late because my Train took such a time to cover the distance; and that I should find my seat at once. Again, as I say, I was only to discover later that *Annie* had purposely kept an empty seat for me next to the Old Man, the very place where I would find myself most ill at ease; and it was on my way there, pushing past the Chairs of the other Staring Girls, that *Mlle Weiss* came in – so I had given the impression, as, too, must have been well planned, of not caring to wait to be greeted by *Mlle Weiss* before making my way to sit down.

For all *Annie*'s plots and schemes, I must say here that it took a great many more of these to shake the Trust *Mlle Weiss* had in me – for we liked each other at once, much to *Annie*'s discomposure, no doubt; and besides that, *Mlle Weiss* had so kind and thoughtful and intelligent a face that all the love I should have had for my long-gone mother I felt mount up in me for her.

'You have missed the Soup,' *says Mlle Weiss*, who first had pulled me back from the row of chairs and stood holding me at arm's length and staring up with friendly curiosity into my face (for I was taller than she). Then, before sighing and pushing me gently back on my path to my seat next to the Old Man, *she says*, 'I have known your Family a long time and it is only for that that I told your dear Aunt that I would take you here, for we are Full Up. But you know you are the spit and image of your lovely great-great-grandmother –' and she goes on laughing to explain that she was not of that age herself but had worshipped always the legends and tales of that Extraordinary and Beautiful Woman of the Ancien Regime and now sees her again in me. '*Mon Dieu!*' *says Mlle Weiss*, as the door opened and a rough-looking Girl in Snow-boots came in, carrying the Cauliflower Cheese, as its very Strong Smell suggested, 'French and French History of Art will come naturally to you, *ma chère.*'

It may have been that *Mlle Weiss* had been talking of me as this Paragon who was expected at the Establishment (which was a modest-sized house in M— Street, just opposite M— College in the Centre of *Oxford*) for some hours before my Arrival and that there had already grown a feeling of Dislike toward me, of which *Annie* had made herself, so to speak, the Foreman; in any case, I saw angry eyes turned on me, everyone's in fact, except the Old Man's, who stumbled still through his Soup, and *Annie*'s, who gazed reverently up at *Mlle Weiss*. 'Eat,' *says Mlle Weiss*, smiling still and going on with her remarks of this wonderful Grandmother, though I could hardly think who she might be, as *Robina* the Scotch gypsy would surely have had little to do with French or French History of Art. '*Clarky*, you shall pass your soup plate to me now and this is *Robina* who is coming to sit by you.'

Of all the impressions and fears I was due to suffer that evening, the worst by a long way were my dealings with *Clarky*, or old *Mr Clarke*, as it appeared was his name. So frightful were the twisted veins in his head and the eyes set straight ahead of him so full of gloom and thunder that the whole tableful of giggling girls might be struck dead by the

Glare, that I could hardly eat at all; and I was glad, innocent as I then was, when *Annie* told me I should go upstairs with her and we would all sit and hear some Music before it was time for bed. '*Mlle Weiss* and *Clarky* like to drink their coffee in peace,' *says she*, 'and I must make you comfortable here while you tell me about yourself.' 'And your world-famous grandmother,' *says* one of the other girls, a tall, Dark Beauty, who had the angriest face of all of them.

Mlle Weiss saying she would soon come up to see me, I followed *Annie* up; but not before turning at the door and observing quite unexpectedly (to me, at least) *Mlle Weiss* run round the table and throw her arms most lovingly around the shoulders of old *Mr Clarke*. I wonder then if my Aunt had known the character of this Establishment; and was not certain whether to feel reassured that Prince P— apparently knew it so well; in short, I went up with *Annie* in my mind as my mentor and possible provider of Escape; and how right I was in some ways we shall soon see.

*

If I have to add here some details of my family, it is only because my arrival in *Oxford* was the first time in my Life that I was to learn the strange effect my Name was to have on so many people. As I have said, there had been a Fortune made, and Tales of the man who made it throwing down his gold pince-nez on the Map of India and there finding Gold; and Tales of his daughters marrying into the Nobility and breaking at last the centuries of sway of Landed Families; and Railroads and a House in Berkeley Square, which, what with other Estates and not excluding the West Indies, turned all equally to an ample state of Ecstasy or Rage. It was in vain – and always proved to be so – that I should speak of the Modest Life in Scotland of my Uncle and Aunt, for to speak of it was as if I had not spoken; and, as I was to discover more each day, it was the name of my Uncle's Elder Brother which was to prove the most exciting to my new acquaintances.

It was unfortunate, however, that I was, at that stage in my life at least, unable to satisfy anyone on the subject of my Uncle's Elder Brother. He and my Uncle had had a Falling Out years before, and his Name was never said in our house. I knew therefore a great deal less of him than anyone else; and within minutes of finding myself led into a small sitting-room all done up in Chintz I had proved a great disappointment to the other Young Ladies of *Mlle Weiss*'s Establishment. It seemed that this Elder Uncle had himself amassed a Great Fortune, as well as Inheriting; that the girls wanted to know if he really, as the Gossipers (they said) proclaimed, lived in a Palace made of Coral on his island by the Coast of Scotland and kept elephants and giraffes there, in a Private Zoo grown over with Tropical Trees and Flowers. They wanted to know too if he had Sons, this Elder Uncle, and whether or not they had married yet; but there again I was no good to them, and, at a disagreeable silence falling in the room, *Annie* rose and said I should come next door to her room, where she had a Record that I would very much enjoy hearing. But the Dark Beauty (whose name was *Susan*) first seized the opportunity of making remarks to me for all to hear and in order to derive a silent satisfaction. First, 'Your Family is without the slightest interest to me,' *says she*. 'We have heard enough of it and it is only because *Mlle Weiss* was employed by one of them that she carries this stupid attachment to the Name.' 'Yes,' *says Annie*, 'it was when *Mlle Weiss* was working with some Great-Aunt or whatever of yours that she eloped with *Clarky*.' 'Eloped?' *say I*, for all the girls are looking at me closely now, as if I have spoiled their Year at the Establishment by arriving as the instant Favourite.

Annie, in her guise, as I thought it then to be, of my Friend and Protector, now told the tale of old *Mr Clarke*, a brilliant mathematician and Economist who had been the adviser of many Governments and made and lost fortunes in Tin and other Commodities, being in hard times and taking the post of Tutor at the house of a Family which (and again I was ignorant of it, to my Shame) was closely connected with mine and Eminent; and at this the girls in *Mlle Weiss*'s sitting-room looked at me with even greater Loathing. '*Mlle Weiss* was governess in that family,' *says Annie*, and she proceeds to tell that even in their old age *Mlle Weiss* and *Mr Clarke* had fallen in love and run away together to set up a Finishing School in *Oxford*, where *Mr Clarke* could be with his famous collection of *Eastern Art*. I could hardly express my surprise (for surely my Aunt, with her Puritan views, must be unaware of the reason for the existence of this Establishment she had sent me to) before *Annie* goes on to say that *Mlle Weiss* is a kind woman but a Terrific Snob and the fact of my great-great-grandmother being some great French lady who had been the Mistress of a King had been told them all for many Hours before my Arrival. '*Mlle Weiss* decided to take you in here,' *says she*, 'even though there is No Room.'

I must say that these last words made me extremely uneasy, not only because I had never heard of the existence of these Great Ancestors (my Aunt, despising my Uncle's Scottish family and considering her own quiet origins to be more distinguished, had not told me any of its History) but also because I now wondered if I should be expected to sleep on the Floor in *Mlle Weiss*'s sitting-room, and, if so, how I should be able to learn French and French History of Art.

'Come,' *says Annie*, who was pressing me to go next door with her; and I was glad to follow her and without looking back at a Crew of Girls who seemed on the brink of Mutiny. '*Annie*,' say I, 'how am I to live here?' and I proceeded to tell her in a rush that I had made one friend already, or rather I was Engaged to be Married, to a *Russian Prince* I had met on the train; and that as I was so unpopular already it would be best if I ran away, and I was asking only that she, *Annie*, would help me in this and take me to Prince P—, for I had never been in *Oxford* before.

Annie burst out laughing at this. 'Prince P—?' *says she*, 'just wait till *Mlle Weiss* hears this.' And she laughed on, which left me time to look round the small but comfortable room where there was a dressing-table laid out with silver brushes and combs and two beds with a small table in between. 'Prince P— is well known to *Mlle Weiss*,' *says Annie*, when she can find her breath. Then, full of Concern, *she says*: '*Robina*, you will be happy here and I will tell the others to mind their Manners with you. I have by far the largest Allowance from my Father of anyone here. In the Holidays I ask some of the Girls to come to my Home where there is Riding and we own the land as far as the eye can see. I will make it quite clear that any girl who is rude to you in any way will not receive this Invitation.'

All this was said very grandly and I hardly knew how to show my gratitude. 'My allowance is two thousand pounds a year,' *Annie* goes on, before I had time to speak. (This was a great deal of money at that time.) 'And now you can tell me how much yours is as you know mine and I can give you my word I will tell nobody.'

It would give me pleasure to say that the years have brought me greater wisdom than I had then in the matter of discussing Money. But I find myself still as much at the mercy of the Inquisitive or Covetous as I was on that occasion at *Mlle Weiss*'s. It was true, though, that on that occasion I was tired from the Train Journey and the Arrival at *Oxford*; and thus even more open and foolish than I would be today. For Money is like the Plague and should be covered up and buried at dead of night; whoever puts the announcement of what they have on the Door will be shunned and taken advantage of alternately. The fact of it is that I told *Annie* that I had twenty-five thousand pounds, when the only wise course would have been to tell the immediate truth, which was that I possessed twenty-five pounds only, given me as a Leaving Present by my kind Uncle.

'Twenty-five thousand!' *says Annie*, and before I have time to explain the Trust and all manner of things that suddenly leapt into my mind (I was to discover too late, as with the protestations of the quiet Farming Life led by my Aunt and Uncle, that such facts are not heard, in the Rush for Information, when the subject is Money) *Annie* starts to yawn loudly and says it's time to go to-Bed.

'But my bags,' *say I*, 'I'll go down for them.' (For I imagined this must be a Curfew Hour appointed by *Mlle Weiss* and so was afraid to be caught in the dark without even having unpacked my Clothes.) 'Never mind,' *says Annie* with a different kind of laugh, that I did not much like the sound of. And she pulled her Cardigan off and then her Blouse. 'Do you think I need a Brassière yet?' *says she*, parading up and down in the small space before the dressing-table, where the Mirror with its two side panes threw back a dazzling number of Breasts. 'My mother says that as everyone wears one then so must I; but it's said the Shape will suffer –' and so on, as the Minx walked round the room and brushed up against me with her Breasts, so that I was nearly Fainting. 'Certainly I have the most Lovely Bust at *Mlle Weiss*'s,' *says she*.

If I could have prayed then for my Aunt, who had been Cold with me but always Correct, to rescue me from this strange Household (of which she most certainly could not have had the remotest Idea) I would have done so; but I was too afraid, even, to dream of Escape, when my Routes out were now so utterly cut off; and I stared at the two Beds, the one nearest to me having on the pillow a lacy Garment quite unlike, as will hardly need saying, the flannel nightgown my Aunt had made for me.

'Is this my bed then?' *say I to Annie*, pointing to the further one. And, 'Is it Time for bed?' and other fatuous sayings, to pretend I was well used to this Parade of Breasts between Girls and had been at Boarding School (where I imagined this to take place) all my Life. 'Now you must show me Yours,' *says Annie* with a wicked giggle, diving in to my Blouse and causing me to remember with Horror that she was not the first that day to do so, for Prince P— had already tried. 'You are wearing something, you are wearing a Bra!' the Wretch then says with a triumphant cry; and for all my pleas, while I must say that Tears ran down my face, which I could feel was hot and red, *Annie* pulled at the Garment I most feared and loathed and which my Aunt for some time back had made me wear, viz. a *Bust Bodice* as she termed it, of

14

a hard white cotton and machined up by my aunt from some pattern of Before the War. 'You are quite big,' *says Annie*, squeezing. '*Mlle Weiss* will give a Birthday Party for you soon, you'll see.'

I was too confused then to ask what might be meant by this, although I was to find out in due course. Besides, the Situation changed as suddenly as it had begun; all the lights went out, as I had feared, a Screaming went up from the Sitting-room next door and *Mlle Weiss* came up the stairs and into the bedroom with a Torch. 'What is this?' *says she*, in a tone of Fury. 'Annie, you were supposed to take our New Girl to her room an hour ago.' And *Mlle Weiss* looks at the further Bed, which I had thought to be mine, and goes over to feel if it is empty, which it is. 'And where is *Susan*?' *says she*, still angry in the extreme. 'You will be Gated on Saturday for this, both of you.' She glares at us both: 'Come with me now and I will show you across the Road,' *she says*. As I did not like to ask why I should go across the Road, nor to tell *Mlle Weiss* that I had an invitation to go out on Saturday from Prince P—, I went down the stairs and picked up my Bag in the Hall and followed *Mlle Weiss* out into a frosty night, with a bright Moon that helped us cross *The High*, as *Mlle Weiss* told me was its Name. She then opened a door and we were at the foot of a Steep, Narrow Stairs leading to the Flat belonging to Old *Mr Clarke*. 'I told your Aunt you would have to be here a Term, as we are Full Up in the House,' *says Mlle Weiss* in quite a matter-of-fact way as she climbed the stairs and showed me into a poorly furnished bedroom, very stuffy. 'It's Nothing,' she called out as a Groan came from next door, 'go to sleep, *Clarky*.' Then, as I was reflecting on how very much my poor Aunt must have wished me out of her home, to send me here, *Mlle Weiss* gave me a kiss on the cheek and went back down the stairs and into the street.

*

No sooner had *Mlle Weiss* gone and I had started with my Unpacking than it came to me that I must visit the Bathroom,

15

and that *Mlle Weiss* had failed to say where this might be. What with all the thoughts of the Day, the Proposal of Marriage from Prince P— and the boisterous friendship which *Annie* was set on making with me, I was doubtless half asleep already, for it didn't cross my mind that I should try the handles of the doors in the narrow passageway with extreme care for fear of disturbing old *Mr Clarke* behind one of them. Indeed, with my Mind puzzled by all the extraordinary happenings of the day, and a part of me, too, that looked forward with innocent Joy to the morning and my first lessons in French and French History of Art, I went quite naturally to the door across from my own Room, and, seeing a line of reddish light under it, let myself in.

Old *Mr Clarke* was dozing in a low tapestry chair by a lamp with a deep crimson shade. He leapt to his feet, however, as soon as he heard me, and he stood some time staring at me with his great, gloomy eyes, which gazed out from under his tuft of white hair so that he stood there like an Owl surprised in the middle of a long Sleep. If I find it hard to say that old *Mr Clarke* was clothed only in an ancient-looking Dressing-Gown of an Indian design and that it was insecurely fastened round him, it is because my Aunt, who would come up every evening at home to make sure I undressed in the Dark, for fear the Curtains in my room were not drawn and the Farmhands might look in, had brought me up to be very shy and modest, as my recent experiences with *Annie* have shown. 'Come in, my dear,' *says* the Old-Man. 'You have come to see my collection, I suppose.' '*Mr Clarke*,' *say I*, 'I am truly sorry.' And I went on to explain that I was searching for the Bathroom, that *Mlle Weiss* had brought me across *The High*, etc., for it began to be clear to me that no one had told the poor old man he would be sharing his quarters for a Term. 'Never mind that,' *says he*, 'and you are to call me whatever you like for I never pay attention to the Prattling of the Girls.' And he began to laugh, wheezing all the while, and the Dressing-Gown lapsing on him as he did so, and I could not fail to see how various Parts of him,

16

shrivelled and fragile enough already by the looks of them, trembled and shook as he gave vent to his Mirth. 'Come and sit here,' *says he*, going over to a window-seat, done up like the rest of the room in red Damask. 'I will bring you my Collection; and some of the Pieces, however much Money was offered me I would never part with – no, not even to Save my Life!'

I was quite amazed by all this, as can be imagined, and waited in great Fear while the old Mathematician went over to a chest of black, inlaid wood and pulled at a sheaf of sheets; but even by the time he had turned again towards me I had seen displayed on the Walls scenes that could never in a Life-time of Sin have been dreamed up; and it was impossible to conceive that there must exist depictions of the Human body even more profane, so they had to be hidden away from view in a Chest. 'You must go up closer,' *says old Mr Clarke*, and to prevent him from handing me off the seat I went to the Walls, where at least a hundred of these scenes, some brightly coloured, were framed and hung. 'They are very fine, are they not?' says he. And he goes on to say that they are *Indian*, that this one is *Seventeenth Century* and that one Earlier, and so on, although it seems to me that they are B—to—ks and A—es of whatever Century it may be, and all belonging seemingly to Acrobats who lay or cavorted on Carpeted Mats. 'These are *Late*,' *says old Mr Clarke*, guiding me to the Far End of the Room, and pulling aside a Screen upholstered in a deep red Plush. 'A Bastard Form by then, don't you agree?' And he goes on before I can get away, for I was by then in so much need of the Bathroom that I thought I might lose Hold of Myself, 'These are *Japanese*, and it's for that Sadistic Quality that I keep them hidden; the Cleaners have Complained about them, you know.'

I daresay if it had not been for old *Mr Clarke*'s last outburst of Laughter, which caused him to Bend Double in danger of Rupture (for he gave too a great Bellow of Pain) that I would have had to stay in that insufferable room and look at the *Japanese prints*. For a first Glance had been enough to show me the extent of Cruelty and Perversion of which Mankind is capable. I had no time then, however, to reflect further on this, and taking advantage of the Old-Man's Coughing Fit I ran from the room and found myself immediately in the Bathroom, which was all the time just one door along. And there I stayed, it must have been an hour or more, until the silence from old *Mr Clarke*'s room was so unbroken that I dared to Let myself Out and creep back into my own.

*

Whether *Annie* was at the root of all the misunderstandings and interruptions that dogged *Mlle Weiss*'s life and mine, I cannot say; but even at the time of my first morning in *Oxford*, when we were all gathered in the Chintz sitting-room and *Mlle Weiss* was beginning her very first Lesson with us, it would be hard to say that this new so-called Best Friend of mine was entirely innocent. The worst of it was that at the start of the lesson *Mlle Weiss* was in high spirits; I, who had hardly slept, was excited nevertheless at this new phase of my Life beginning; and the other Girls were more friendly, even *Susan* deigning to smile and to say in a low voice as we sat-down that I was invited by her father the *Bishop* to come and stay whenever I liked; and also that she, *Susan*, had a Brother who would show me their City and the famous Cathedral, for they lived in the Close, etc.

A pile of books lay on the table and on them were the words *Manon Lescaut*, for this was the name of the book we were to read in French. *Mlle Weiss*'s big old poodle, whom she named *Ras*, lay under the table, and he jumped up with a volley of Barking when the doorbell rang, for we were hardly one page into the book when this happened. 'What can it be?' *says Annie*, but smiling wickedly and demurely. 'I'll go and see,' she says, and she is down the stairs before *Mlle Weiss* can speak, so we are left with our mouths open over *Manon Lescaut*; and the dog *Ras*, even more enraged now, plunges down the stairs after *Annie*.

Soon *Annie* was back and we had none of us moved an

18

inch, as if we had been cast in Stone. 'A packet,' *says Annie.*
'But no one there, *Mlle Weiss.*' A giggling started up at this,
and I should have known then that some trick was afoot, or
that *Annie*, which was in fact the most likely, had said my
name silently with her lips when she came into the room
behind me. 'And who is it for?' *says Mlle Weiss*, reaching out
for it, and all of her smiles gone. 'Why, for *Robina*,' *says
Annie*, all (it seemed) in amazement, 'I didn't know you had
friends here already,' *she then says to me.* 'Give it to me –' *says
Mlle Weiss*, and the packet is ripped open in an instant, with
Mlle Weiss's nail, which was as thick and yellow as Horn.
'Prince P—' *says Mlle Weiss* in tones that were the first Cold
ones I had heard from her. 'He shall answer for this.' And
sure enough, as if it was destined to fall out just to satisfy the
gasps of the Girls, a great stone, about the size of a Pigeon's
Egg and set as a Ring, tumbled on to the table and into the
pages of *Manon Lescaut.* 'Did you know anything of this?'
Mlle Weiss says to me very severely. 'What is the meaning of
this?' and so on, until I was half in Tears, but determined still
not to say that I was Engaged to be Married, though I heartily
wished that I was not. 'Prince P— is a Rogue,' *says Mlle
Weiss.* 'You shall not reply to this, *Robina*; I shall deal with it
myself.'

If I was grateful for this, still I hadn't the courage to say
that Prince P— in person was coming for me on Saturday
morning; and remembering that I'd told *Annie* the night
before of my Plans I felt afraid even more that she would give
me away to *Mlle Weiss*. But this, to my face at least, *Annie* did
not do. 'I shall give this to the Maid to take round to his
College as soon as she is back from her Errands,' *says Mlle
Weiss*, and, dropping the Ring back in the packet, went out of
the room. As she was away some time it can be imagined
how the giggling and the Talk started up. 'Never mind,' *says
Annie*, 'it is only Paste.' And the others, all taking out bottles
of Nail Polish which they had hidden before, started to paint
their nails and talk of the Plans for Saturday. But I dared say
nothing.

Our French lesson being over for the day (for *Mlle Weiss*, it appeared, had met old *Mr Clarke* in the hall and they had decided to take a walk together, it being very fine and sunny) we were told by the Maid coming up that we might go and walk in *Christchurch Meadow*, which some of us did, though others, and I was counted among them, walked up *The High* and sat in a Shop and had Coffee. For all my confusion, *Annie* was at that time so kind and helpful that I felt only pleasure at being in this strange and beautiful City with her. Nor did I know, even when *Annie* and *Susan*, who were my companions, ducked to the back of the Shop and disappeared completely, that to sit and have Coffee was Strictly Forbidden; that the Shop was Out of Bounds; and that it was the sight of *Mlle Weiss* coming along the pavement arm-in-arm with old *Mr Clarke* that had caused my new Friends to run away so quickly.

Mlle Weiss's face was, if possible, even more severe when she saw me in the Shop Window and she came in with the same force as she had shown when she thrust the Ring back into its packet. 'I'll Pay,' *says she*, seeing the waitress come up. And to me, 'You'll pay me back from your allowance –' then, on taking the Bill, 'so who are the other two coffee-drinkers, pray?' (for *Mlle Weiss* had a most old-fashioned way of talking, as if she had come over from France and learnt to speak English from an old book). *Mr Clarke* stood quite silent through all this, and I wondered if *Mlle Weiss* knew of his showing me his Pictures in the night; but these were only the wild thoughts of a Prisoner, for I thought *Mlle Weiss* would be bound to lock me up as soon as we returned; and now I had had a taste of the Pleasures of *Oxford* I had no desire to be confined, or to Study, even. 'The Girls just went a moment ago,' *say I*, for I was as ignorant then of loyalty as any Girl who has never been to that other Prison, Boarding School. 'They are *Annie* and *Susan*,' *I say* like a Goose; and I honestly do think that the Misfortunes which befell me from that time onward stemmed from that Folly on my part, to Tell on Another Girl to the Teacher; and that I sincerely deserved every one of them. 'Thank-you,' *says Mlle Weiss,* taking my arm quite roughly. 'This is the second time you have been due to be Gated since you came here.' And she marched me down *The High* with poor old *Mr Clarke* trying to keep up, and me with Tears falling again, for I was destined at *Oxford* (and then very often in the rest of my Life) to be either happy or miserable in the extreme. It was when the dismal thought of being Locked in the stuffy flat in *The High* and the horrible Old Man coming in with his pernicious pictures was bringing me close to Falling in the Street that *Mlle Weiss* began to speak to me in a low voice and at speed. 'You shall be an Example here, *Robina,' says she.* Then, before I could think her quite Mad, *Mlle Weiss* cried out that she had great hopes for me. I must not fall under the influence of others. 'Don't think anything of that Idiot who calls himself Prince P—,' *says she,* clasping my hand warmly with hers by now, and taking my arm and dropping it again as if she tried to mould me to the shape that would most have pleased her. 'He is a fake just as much as his Jewels, my dear, and I have forbidden him Entrance to the house.'

All this astonished me greatly, as may be imagined. 'Prince P— said he was a great Favourite with you,' *say I* before I can reflect what a Fool I am. 'He said you would be bound to ask him to Dinner. But he has asked me out on Saturday first,' for I saw that this might be the time, while *Mlle Weiss* was still soft with me, to prepare her for my Plans. 'Go out with him?' *says Mlle Weiss.* 'Certainly not. But I'll have a word with him, you can Count on That!'

By this time, we were at the end of *The High* and I was about to cross over, thinking my spell of Imprisonment must be about to begin, when *Mlle Weiss* pulled at my arm once more and guided me along M— Street to her house. 'We shall have a *Croque-Monsieur* together in my room' *says she,* and seeing that I didn't know what this could be, she laughed merrily. 'Come up with me,' she says, 'and we'll forget all about it.' And this was the first of many times that *Mlle Weiss said one thing and meant another,* as I was to find out, for when

I was Banished and sent North again, the Letter that came after me held also the bill for the Coffee Shop that day. I don't think *Mlle Weiss* could forget anything; and certainly, after we had talked and laughed and she had asked me about my Uncle and Aunt and had sighed over the Great Family where she had been Governess before Love for old *Mr Clarke* had driven her out, she grew grave again and drew me to her, placing her hands very firmly about my waist. '*Robina,*' *says she*, 'you will tell me when you are about to be *Sixteen*. I think it is soon.' And on my saying the date was indeed soon, *Mlle Weiss* nodded her head as if she had spent a long time puzzling it out and had now at last reached a Decision. 'We shall give a Birthday Party for you, *ma chère,*' *says she*. 'And you shall ask anyone you please to it.' By this I thought she must mean Prince P—, as a special indulgence; but however hard I tried to fathom the workings of *Mlle Weiss's* mind, I was never able to understand her.

The next day was the day before Saturday, so the talk of Plans going on as soon as *Mlle Weiss* went out of the room was very intense. I couldn't say what of French History of Art we were supposed to study, though I do think there was a picture in a book of a Raft and a great-many half-dead and half-alive Men and Women on it and that we were set to read books by *Sainte-Beuve* and *Delacroix* and to study this Dismal Picture, which was a relief at least in that it did not resemble old *Mr Clarke's* Collection of Eastern Art. It seems often to me, that if I had followed more of good *Mlle Weiss's* Advice and applied myself to my Learning I would have prepared myself for a Busy Life and a Suitable Marriage, which was the Aim of the Establishment for Young Ladies. But, as I have said, it may be that the Foundations of this School being so peculiar, viz. Set Up by an Adulterous Pair, that the Very Air we breathed was conducive to Idle Thoughts and Dreams of Love.

There is no sillier thing in the world than a Young Girl with her first Admirer and I may as well say now that I spent half the day trying to recapture the appearance of Prince P—, which I found myself quite unable to conjure to my mind; and that I considered myself at the same time wholly in-Love with him and extremely grieved at the Ring being snatched from me and Sent Back. *Annie*, who was also to be Confined at Home on Saturday for her Japes on the night I came to M— Street, was as grieved as I; and it was not-long before she had made a Wicked Plan to set free the two of us, thus teaching me more of Deceit and Cunning in one day than I was likely to learn of French History of Art.

'Tell me,' *says Annie*, when *Mlle Weiss* had gone from the room to see to old *Mr Clarke*, who was brought coffee and tea two or three times in the morning by her, 'don't you want to see Prince P— more than anything you've wanted? Be honest with me . . .' etc. etc., while the other Girls broke out giggling, for they were very probably jealous, as I see now, of my being so rapidly sent a Ring. 'I do,' *say I*, 'but how can it be done?' And I went on with my sighing – and, as I remember more clearly than the words of the great French Historians, digging the nib of my Pen into *Mlle Weiss*'s pine table. 'If you tell us about the Nights in *The High*,' *says Annie* (for I had passed two nights there by then, the second one perfectly quiet except for the Sounds next door of the Old Man's Panting and Snoring).

'You've seen the Collection,' *says Annie*, speaking as solemn as if we were talking with *Mlle Weiss* about the Men and Women in the Picture of the Raft. 'Oh yes, I have,' *say I*, upon which all the Girls fall silent and *Susan* the Bishop's daughter in particular leans forward. 'You know what the people in his pictures are doing?' *says Annie*, still very straight-faced. 'Why yes,' *say I*, though becoming annoyed by then for I was not entirely sure of it. 'That is what he wants to do with you,' *says Annie*; and even I couldn't hold back a smile, for old *Mr Clarke* could never have got himself into such Positions. 'He asked you to do that with him,' *says Annie*, seemingly very indignant by now, 'he is a Dirty Old Man.' And she walked out of the Room, pulling the door shut behind her, at which all the Girls looked at me pityingly at last, as if they would forget the Great Fortune which was supposed to be Mine; and the Engagement to the *Russian Prince*, for the Sake that I was forced into these dreadful Poses in *The High*. Then *Mlle Weiss* came in, before I could ask what all this had to do with my seeing Prince P— on Saturday; but I was to find out soon enough, for at the end of the Lesson *Mlle Weiss* said I was to stay Behind and the others went off downstairs, to start on the frugal meal that was known as *Déjeuner*.

'Robina,' *says Mlle Weiss*, 'I think I have been too hard on you. This is a beautiful and ancient City and you must see it in the Company of Friends.' And she went on, much to my astonishment, to say that Prince P— had called round early that morning and had apologized handsomely for sending the Ring; that he had in mind to take me to a Luncheon Club in *The Turl* on Saturday; and that the President of the Club was Lord E— (and here *Mlle Weiss's* eyes were smiling, which I was always pleased to see). 'He is a great Catch, is Lord E—,' *says Mlle Weiss*, 'and I have told your Aunt that you will meet Suitable Friends while you are in M— Street; and Prince P— has given me his Word of Honour that he will Behave Himself.' 'So I can go?' *say I* with my voice choking with Happiness, and *Mlle Weiss* takes me in her arms and says I don't mean to be a Naughty Girl and I must be in by eight a clock. 'And *Annie?*' *say I*, to which *Mlle Weiss* replies that *Annie* is free to go out too, though she has not been invited to the Luncheon Club in *The Turl*. *Mlle Weiss's* voice was much Colder this time, so if I had not been dwelling on my happy reunion with Prince P— and the Romantic Love we bore each other I would most certainly have smelt a Rat. 'Also,' *says* this kind woman, 'I have been thinking that you are not Comfortable enough in *The High*, my dear, and that it is not the Right Place for you.' And she said a Camp Bed had been Put Up for me in M— Street so that we could all be one Happy Family together, and I was to bring my Things over now and Settle In.

I would have been more overjoyed at this, perhaps, if I had not dreaded where the Camp Bed would be placed, and, sure enough, on my asking *Mlle Weiss* while thanking her with as much Sincerity as I could Muster for her Kindness to me, she told me that I would go-in with *Susan* and *Annie* and that I must bear in mind that there was to be no Talking after Lights Out. We then went down to the Dining-Room, with *Mlle Weiss*'s arm linked in mine, and she led me in in that way; but I could see, from *Annie*'s high colour and triumphant air that she had spoken to *Mlle Weiss* of old *Clarky* and me – and had threatened no-doubt to Expose our Supposed Indecency to the NEWS OF THE WORLD – and so it was that this was my first knowledge of BLACKMAIL.

If I slept little, with *Susan*'s eyes open, or so it seemed, half the night and staring at me from the next bed, it showed little in the morning, when *Mlle Weiss* called me down the stairs and said how Fresh and Pretty I was; and it's true that in a Life of too much Dissipation, which I sincerely regret, I have kept always a clear Complexion and grey eyes very bright and undimmed by any Excesses.

Prince P— was in the Hall and I was at first too confused to look directly at him, but his laughing and Jovial Ways were charming *Mlle Weiss* too, as it was plain to see. 'Now, *Weissy*,' *says he*, 'you know I'll take good care of her!' And he turns to me and holds out a hand and then comes forward to give me the Polite Kiss on the Cheek that would allay *Mlle Weiss*'s Suspicions, or so he must have hoped. (For in all Truth Prince P— was the Roughest of all my Admirers; he came at you as if you were a Mare that must be captured on the Steppes and bridled and Held Close; and had I known what a Fight was to take place later in that day I might have elected to stay back at-home with *Mlle Weiss*, to study French and French History of Art.)

'*Robina* is not Sixteen yet,' *says Mlle Weiss*. 'And when she has her Birthday Party you may come to it.' And her eyes sparkling, *she says*: 'You may invite Lord E— today if you wish,' and she named a date. 'You'll all see the Number of Candles on the Birthday Cake and that she's too Young,' she says, though it was hard for me to see why I am too Young for Prince P— but not for Lord E—, in whom I became interested all-over again, despite Prince P—'s handsome, laughing ways.

'And she will be in by eight a clock,' *says Mlle Weiss.* 'When I will smell her Breath to see if she has been Drinking,' she added, but absently, for she heard *Clarky* call in a feeble Voice from the Study by the Dining-room. 'Bless you,' *says Mlle Weiss* and she went at pace to the Old-Man, which made me think that Young Love, such as Prince P— and I were at that moment feeling, could turn into such old, wizened Creatures making a Farce of Love. Or so I thought, though there wasn't much Time for it, for as-soon as *Mlle Weiss* had gone Prince P— swept me into his arms and kissed me a long-time in the Mouth. All the while he pulled me down the Steps into M— Street, so that it was Frightening and Danger-ous in the Extreme to Kiss Passionately when at the same time running down Stairs, but Prince P— loved any Rashness of this kind and I think he hoped that by setting-up great Sensations of Fear he could catch a Girl Unawares.

'We'll go straight up to *The Turl*,' *says* Prince P—, and he held his nose and laughed loudly. 'Have you got Used to the Smell of Cabbage at *Weiss*'s yet?' *says he* – and other such Jokes – and we walked up *The High* arm-in-arm as if we'd come straight out of Church; and sure enough, the incorrigible Prince P— pulled the Ring out of his pocket and slipped it on my finger as soon as we had turned the corner and M— Street was out of sight.

I was too young still to understand that of all the Deadly Sins, Envy is the most dangerous; and when Prince P— and I passed *Annie* on our walk up *The High*, we thought nothing more of it; yet there she was again when we stood outside the *Bodleian*, which Prince P— said was a famous Library and there again in *The Broad*, where we stopped at a Bar and where he made me go in even though I was Under-Age. 'Why *Annie*,' *say I* seeing her standing there and looking at us with a small Smile on her lips, 'aren't you going out with your friends today?' (For there had been talk for days of the

26

rich *Lords* and visiting *Americans* who would escort her to a party in the *Randolph Hotel*.) 'They didn't turn up,' says she with an even smaller smile. 'Come with us,' *say I*, and all this while she was walking into the Bar with me and smiling suddenly with great liveliness at Prince P—, so that I liked *Annie* a good deal less then than had been the case since I came to *Oxford*. 'If only it were possible to invite you,' *says* Prince P—, 'but there are places round the table and everyone of them filled up.' And he looked long and hard at *Annie*, whom of course he knew very well and got all his information from – for she had been already one year with *Mlle Weiss*, having nowhere else to be; but I knew none of this. 'Never mind,' *says Annie*, and out she goes from the Bar, leaving her Drink untouched. 'Well, well,' *cries* the reckless Prince P—, 'all the more for me,' and he quaffs it right down. 'No, *Robina*,' *he says* as if there is very serious business to discuss (and in fact Prince P— was like that: if there was bad Trouble he laughed and fooled about, and if there was an important matter in hand, he drew faces on the table cloth; but if there was some joke going on he would make a very lengthy face), 'you'll find that everyone at this Club is mad for you. You will hear of their great Fortunes and their Country Estates and you will kindly remember that you are Engaged to be Married to me.'

How small are the measures of self-confidence in a young Girl who has been brought up strictly by her Aunt and then plunged into this dissolute Society! – For I promised Prince P— faithfully that I would look at no one else, however magnificent he might seem; and there I was, not yet sixteen years old! Especially Lord E—, as Prince P— told me over and over again. 'I am in my Third Year,' *says he*, 'and I have known a few Girls at *Mlle Weiss*'s as you will not mind, my darling *Robina*, for I was waiting for you' (all this before I could protest at it) 'and as I told you on the Train, there were a good-many Sent Down as a consequence of Lord E— and others who went to *Switzerland*.' With which words and before I could ask further, Prince P— said it was late, and he ran out of the Bar and I after him, down *The Broad* to *The Turl*.

The luncheon Clubs in *Oxford* at that time were all Goblets, Coats of Arms and Boasting of Names and Titles, and I was soon to find that my own name had been well broadcast before I got there, for several Young Blades rose to their feet from the most unimaginable positions of Sloth in heavy chairs and with feet up on the Club Fender and came towards us with Bottles of Champagne and Declarations that I was just as pretty as Prince P— had promised I would be. If I was asked once about my Uncle's Elder Brother I must have been asked a hundred times, but all this was done with such Laughter and Good Spirits that I could hardly take offence, and nor did anyone seem to mind at all that I had no News of my Family, for the Name seemed to be quite enough. I daresay I should have guessed then that *Annie* had supplied Prince P— with the most daft information, viz. that I was the possessor of Twenty-five thousand Pounds a Year, and that this had turned a light-hearted Episode on a Train to Determination, for Prince P— when we had all sat down and ate a quantity of Plovers' Eggs and Scotch Salmon, told me quite loudly – and so that none of the other Blades could fail to hear: 'I have spoken to my Father and Stepmother, and they are very delighted at our Engagement.' A cheer went up at this and Prince P— says: 'We are to go to *London* next Saturday to meet them.' And he grips me in the Bear Hug again, of which by this time I was tiring quite rapidly. 'You'll need some new clothes,' says Prince P— with his jovial Laugh, 'for you must look lovely to meet my Stepmother, and I shall take you to her Dressmaker as soon as we're there.'

If it's thought that I was too Slow to know my Mind in Affairs of the Heart, the Reader will kindly remember that I had never been to *London* in my life; that I was ashamed of the *Circular Skirt* and *Black Top* which I was wearing, as I had nothing else, for the Luncheon Club; and that the idea of these new Dresses and the meeting with Prince P—'s Relatives was a great-deal more intriguing than the study of French or French History of Art. 'Shame,' cried some of the young

Nobles at Prince P—, as at the same time a great Crown of Lamb was brought in by a Footman in Livery – 'No, no, the Flesh is Fine,' cried one of the wittiest, to the startled servant, 'it's Prince P— here who objects to the Dressing.' And in all the Laughter that followed, while I was red as a Beet and had nowhere to look but down at the floor, there was only one who was quiet, and when I looked up again it was to gaze, quite without knowing it, straight into his Eyes.

Lord E— I had seen when I came into the narrow room on the first floor of this old house in *The Turl*, where portraits of young men with Curls and long Noses hung on the walls above the likenesses of their Descendants; and it's true to say that I had at first thought him a little like a Sheep. The second Time, however, when all Eyes were on me and my humble Outfit (that was made by my Aunt and declared unsuitable by Prince P— for meeting his Stepmother), I found him very fine indeed. A Stag, he seemed all-at-once to resemble; and soon I saw him in the Highlands, in the heather and with a great Castle behind him; and I smiled at him gently, to thank him for his Concern at all the Teasing.

*

Prince P— wasn't slow to see all this, and before long we were out of *The Turl* and hurrying at Prince P—'s dreadful pace down *The Broad* again. 'I've told you how admired you'd be,' *says he* as we ran along, still arm-in-arm like skaters, 'and most of those at the Lunch today shall be invited to our Wedding.' He then went on to say our Wedding would be a very Grand Affair and would be held in the Russian Church in London; that Kings would come to it, no less than a dozen or so; and he said their Names: 'the *King of Italy*, the *King of Greece*, the *King of Albania*', etc. etc., *says he*; and I could have wished I'd had a better education than the Village School my poor Aunt sent me to, for I had no knowledge that these Kings had long been Deposed and lived in Hotels; for Prince P— certainly wouldn't have it so. 'There is a great-deal of Incense at these Orthodox Weddings', *says* Prince P—, 'for someone brought up in the Church of Scotland. But you will get used to it, my Sweet, and we'll drive away in a Sleigh.'

With all this talk I had hardly time to reflect that there might be no Snow in time for this Great Event, so how would the Sleigh pull? Nor did I see, other than Prince P— assuring me that we were passing the *Ashmolean*, a famous museum, before we had mounted stone steps and were pushing in a Swing Door. 'My family donated some of the Paintings in the Museum,' *says* Prince P— (and all the while we were twirling round in the Door, which was Prince P—'s idea of Amusement). 'We had to Smuggle them out of Russia at Dead of Night,' *says he*. 'They were graciously presented to the City of *Oxford* to commemorate my First Year at the University.'

Young Girls will listen to all-sorts of Lies and I believed this, but we were so breathless by then that when the Swing Door finally gave us up into a big Room, very warm and Carpeted, my Senses were completely Confused, and this was no doubt how the Mischievous Prince P— wanted it, for he now told me we were in his College and he was taking me up to his Rooms, when, as I was soon to discover, we had in fact come to the *Randolph Hotel*. We went up the Stairs at a great Rate, however, and along a murky Corridor, and Prince P— flashed some keys from his Pocket and we were soon in a Great Room, with all the Shutters closed and the lights of a Chandelier on a Bottle of Champagne standing next to a bunch of Red Roses, both pushed into a Silver Bucket.

Here I must testify that *Annie*, for all the Terrible Things for which she can be held Responsible, was on this occasion my Saviour. Yet, had she not been in the Hotel, searching no doubt for those friends who had Let her Down on her day away from *Mlle Weiss*, and had she not come to my Rescue, I would very likely not have continued to Confide in her and Trust her as I did. For her Tricks were becoming clear to me. Anyway, Fate threw her in my Path that day, and I was thankful for it.

Prince P— locked the door of the Room and came forward

to open the Champagne, which went off with a great Noise. My nerves were already tired; seeing this, Prince P— took me over to sit on the edge of the bed and brought a glass of Champagne over with him. 'How d'you like my Room?' *says he* with a laugh. 'No, no' (for I was beginning to look alarmed), 'don't worry, my pet, you won't find Students here to Bother you, for although this is the Best Place in *Oxford*, it isn't a college and I can't have Lord E— ogling you again in that way.' Saying this, Prince P— held the glass to my lips and I was forced to drink; while his other Hand went where it had been before (when we were on the Train) but this time a great-deal Higher and penetrated my Knickers altogether. 'You are Safe with me,' *says* Prince P— and he took the glass and set it down on the Floor, which then freed his other Hand so that it could go down my *Black Top*, which it did without meeting any Obstacle. I tried to cry for help, but as I cried, Prince P—'s Mouth came down over mine and I was silent except for my Thrashing and Wriggling.

Prince P— soon had my *Knickers* halfway Down and had pushed me back on the Bed, while I pulled so hard at his Hair that his face was purple with Pain, when there was a great Knocking at the Door, and Prince P— had to stop a moment, which gave me the chance to jump off the bed and pull down the *Circular Skirt*, which had been up round my Neck like a Ruff. 'Stop! Thief!' *shouts* Prince P—, who would at that moment have as gladly seen me go to Prison, I'm sure, as fail to Yield myself up to him, 'Who is it?' as the knocking went on and always more Menacing in tone. 'It is the Manager,' *says* a gruff voice; and by this time Prince P—, who had loosened his Trousers, has done them up again and is standing to Attention, with a very sickly smile on his Face.

With what a sense of relief I opened the door need hardly be said: to see a Young-Man not much older than Prince P— and *Annie* standing there and trying to hide their laughter was as wonderful a Sight to me as it was galling for my Seducer. 'Why *Robina*,' *says* Annie, 'I was downstairs when you came in, and I thought you must be giving a Party

31

without asking me.' And although her eyes were very Spiteful, I was too full of Gratitude to see. *Annie* then introduced her friend, whom she had just met in the Lobby and had persuaded to come upstairs to play a joke; and as people of that age need very little persuading, in *Oxford*, at least, when it comes to Horseplay, he had come upstairs with her gladly. 'You know what time it is,' *says Annie* next .'It is nearly eight a clock.' And I felt myself in a Dream once more, for we had sat a long time at the Club no doubt, and we had walked and talked and gone through the Scene just related; and yet I had no Idea how the time could have flown by so fast. This was the first I knew, you could say, of DALLIANCE; and it was an attempt to stop this on the part of *Mlle Weiss* which caused her to set out a Timetable (to which the Girls, and regrettably She, did not always stick).

We all went down the stairs and left the Hotel perfectly Friendly, as if an Act of Violence had not been acted out by Prince P— and as if his Desires were not still unquenched. 'I will see both of you Girls to *Mlle Weiss*'s,' *says he;* and he took us an arm each, like an old Grandfather, though staggering and joking all the way down *The High.* 'And next Saturday I will come for you,' *he says to me,* 'and we go to *London* to meet my Family.' 'But how can I do that?' *say I.* 'You'll tell *Mlle Weiss* your Aunt is coming to *London* to see her Friends,' *says* Prince P—, 'and that you will be away the night and back on Sunday.' And so we came to M— Street and *Mlle Weiss* ran out suspicious as a Dog, to sniff our Breath (but luckily she detected Nothing). Prince P— said good-night to us and we turned in; and already, which I am truly sorry to say, I looked forward heartily to my first visit to *London.*

*

If I had still a great-deal to learn about Life in these early days, the next week at *Mlle Weiss*'s went a long way to teaching me at least something of the meaning of Lies, Misplaced Hopes, Secret Ambitions etc., of which I had been only too ignorant before. I can't pretend, either, that the study of French or French History of Art made much of the Reality of Life any the clearer; except perhaps that *Manon* was a pleasant book to read aloud (though we were frequently interrupted by the snoring and panting of the old Poodle *Ras* under the table, or the petulant calling of *Clarky* for his Mistress). Yet without French History of Art our Education would not have been complete, for it was *Renoir*, whose paintings we were looking at in a big Art Book, who set off the following Scene with *Susan* and *Annie*. In my innocence, reared on a farm by my Aunt and having only the most simple friendships with the Farmers' Bairns, I knew nothing of the Feelings one Girl can bear toward another.

It started with *Annie*, as these things invariably did. In the classroom, and when *Mlle Weiss* was downstairs, the subject of the Birthday Party came up, as it was bound to, and the eyes of all the Girls were on us as *Annie* asked her Taunting Questions. 'You'll be Sixteen, *Robina*,' *says she*, 'so will your Family be sending you a Car? Or will you get an apartment in New York?' And so on, until the loud and unfriendly Laughter was near to drowning out her words. 'Or will there be yet another Knock on the Door and a Messenger with a Chest containing the most Fabulous Pearls?' the Minx asks. (All this talk of the Knock at the Door got more unfriendly Laughs too, for it must be said that since my visit to the Luncheon Club there had been a Stream of Cards, embossed and many with Coats of Arms, inviting me to a Ball here or a Supper there, or to go out in a Punt while there was still fine weather and the leaves were still on the trees.) All of these cards and letters I had shown to *Mlle Weiss* and she had thanked me for doing so; but *Annie* had stolen them out of her Drawer and shown them around and I had felt the Brunt of my Unpopularity for some days. Let me say only that there was no Card from Lord E— and I was sad to have felt the Lack of it. 'The Birthday Party,' says *Annie*, '*Weiss* has asked Prince P— because in the end, you know, she always does.' 'So what's that to me?' *say I*, and made a show of being angrier than I was, for I feared that something Bad was coming. 'Prince P— has been Engaged to be Married to eight girls, and all from *Mlle Weiss's*, since he has been Up,' *says Annie*; and gleeful laughter all round duly followed. 'The candles can stand for his number of Brides as well as for your Birthday, my dear!' 'Brides?' *say I* without pausing to think, as I should have done, leaving *Annie* alone with her Enjoyment. 'He's not Bluebeard,' *says Annie*, and this time a howl of Mirth went up, 'but he can't seem to hold a Girl for long; he's always the first one they meet, and then they meet Another and it's the one they take a Fancy to. He's harmless, you might say, and in fact *Mlle Weiss* is quite fond of him; but you mustn't break the Rules of course, with any-one, even Prince P—.'

Not for the first time since I came to *Oxford* I wished myself safely out of it and at-home in the North again. The guilty Feelings occasioned by *Annie's* speech (for was I not already in-Love with Lord E—?) and the Sense, at the same time, of being so easily Seduced by Prince P— and his proposal of Marriage, made me go a fine red in the cheeks; and I suppose I must suddenly have looked very Pretty, for *Susan*, who was *Annie's* staunchest ally and friend, rose to her feet and a pile of *Cahiers*, as *Mlle Weiss* would have us call them, fell to the floor from the table-top. '*Robina* has had enough,' *says Susan*, and I could see now that her eyes, which were a very bright deep blue, were exceedingly fine under a fringe of curly black hair, 'hasn't she just come here when some of us have been here one Term already? And yet others of us' – and *Susan* turned to *Annie* with her eyes quite wide in indignation – 'have been here a whole Year or more!' The class fell silent at this, and it became instantly clear that this Fact was not widely known. 'Eighteen years old *Annie*,' *says Susan*, 'and should know better than to tease someone so much younger!' A silence fell, after this, and some of the Girls went back to polishing their Nails, which was their Favourite Occupation. 'You Bitch!' *says Annie* to *Susan* very low, but with a sound like Spitting. 'I'll get you for this!' And she comes at her hard, with a copy of *Manon Lescaut*, which,

34

if it had fallen on *Susan*, would have harmed her horribly.
'Come,' *Susan says to me*, as *Annie* in her fury descends on
both of us; books fall everywhere; the other Girls scream,
with the Nail Varnish going on the floor and making sticky
Red Puddles; 'Come quick!' And before I know what is
happening, *Susan* has pulled me into the bedroom next door
and pulled shut and locked the door behind us.

I'd spent some nights already in my miserable Camp bed
in this room, while *Susan* and *Annie* talked and Confided
long after Lights Out, and I may say I was surprised at
Susan's being all-at-once my Friend. But this she was, and
left me in no Doubts about it, for she led me to sit beside her
on her bed and then sat some time staring long and hard into
my eyes, as if she hoped to find some Answer there. '*Annie* is
a Liar,' *says Susan* after she had been quiet some time, her
only movement being the continual wetting of her finger in
her mouth, with which she then proceeded to trace the
Contours of my Face. 'She is here because she is the daughter
of an old pupil of *Mlle Weiss*; and this old Pupil ran off with
another man so *Annie* was thrown out of her home too and
Mlle Weiss in her kindness took her here.' 'But her allowance
of two thousand pounds a year,' *say I*, and then blushed at
this being my first question, for which I blamed my Family,
who must have implanted in me without knowing a far too
great Interest in Money. 'She *had* that,' *says Susan*, and now
she starts to gather up my hair and twist it into a Bun, which
Tweaked it badly, with me too shy all-at-once to make
Objection. 'She has nothing now: she is here all the Holidays
too!' 'Poor *Annie*,' *say I*, for I could hardly help but feel sorry
for the Girl; and wondering too how many times *Annie* had
had to read *Manon Lescaut*. 'Your hair is true Gold,' *says
Susan*, as if bored now with the other Talk; and she brushes
her face, which has a cool, floury feel, up against mine.
'Scottish gold,' *says Susan* with a sigh; and before I can lean
back, she has wetted her Finger again and drawn round my
face feverishly. 'This is what I like to do,' *says Susan*, and
being a Big Girl she falls heavy against me so I have no

choice but to lie back on the bed, while she soon covers me as thoroughly as a Quilt, her Finger still writhing about on my Cheeks. As for me, I was cold with Fear, that *Mlle Weiss* would come in with a Master Key and see us there; or, even worse, that *Annie* would find some way of climbing in the window and discovering us, for I was sure she and *Susan* must have practised some of these strange things before I was put in with them. 'I love you,' *says Susan* in a whisper: and this low voice is succeeded by a very Loud Shout from the passage, for which I was truly thankful. *Mlle Weiss* was ordering the Girls back into Class.

*

In the next days, *Annie* was always with *Susan* and jealously guarding her; and I was glad to be left alone, to work on French and French History of Art, although it must be said that I was also exercised on the subject of my Trip to *London*, and how I could bring myself to lie to *Mlle Weiss* when she was Goodness itself to me, even down to the Baking and Icing of my Birthday Cake. As we shall see, the matter was taken soon enough out of my hands.

The day of the Birthday Party being fine, *Mlle Weiss* told the Girls to take a walk in Christchurch Meadows, and we did this and then went into *Magdalen* College and listened to the Choir, which was so lovely that my eyes were filled with Tears, and would have filled more if I had known this was to be the last I would see of my beloved *Oxford*. For *Annie*, the Evil Genius of my Life, had prepared a Surprise for my return; and when we walked into M— Street, and looked back at the Spires and the black Shadows that fell on the Stones, I had the first sudden knowing then of the new Phase of my Life that was about to begin.

Mlle Weiss hugged me and kissed me before a crowd of Young-Men who had been invited for the Occasion, and Prince P— in particular was told to blow out the Candles and to make sure he counted them, which caused laughter and Ribald Jokes. '*Robina* is still young, and working happily

here,' *says Mlle Weiss* to the Young Nobles and Rich Merchants'
Sons, all of whom had seen me, either at the Luncheon Club
or walking down *The High* on a visit to the Ashmolean
Museum to continue my Researches into History of Art.
(And every one of these Young-Men had sent me Cards or,
one at least, a Bunch of Red Roses, which annoyed the other
Girls exceedingly.) 'It's only sad her Family can't be here,'
says Annie when the candles are out and Prince P— had put
on a paper hat, to my Eternal Shame. 'As *Robina*'s Aunt is
coming down to *London* on Saturday and hopes to see her,
we must wish *Robina* a happy time in London too!'

The looks that went between *Annie* and Prince P— were
this time seen by me; but not by *Mlle Weiss*, it seemed, for
she starts at once to press me to ask my Aunt to come and see
her here in Oxford, and how she could stay in old *Mr Clarke*'s
flat in *The High*, which made me tremble to think of, if my
Aunt should come across the Collection of Eastern Works of
Art. 'She won't be able to have the time,' *say I*, and curse
Annie heartily for making me tell a Lie, for my Aunt of course
had no Plan to come South at all. 'Well then you must go to
London,' *says Mlle Weiss*, 'if you are back Sunday by tea-time,'
and so on. Prince P— was darting the most Adoring Looks at
me while all this charade went on and the kind old woman
was deceived; and I was glad when *Annie* took the subject
away from my Trip to *London*, even though it was only to
joke over my Clothes. 'It's to be hoped that *Robina*'s Aunt
will buy her a pretty dress,' *says she*, and another Laugh went
up for I was as usual in my *Circular Skirt* and *Off-the-Shoulder
Black Top*, which were much laughed at, but fondly, for it
was said that I was prettier wearing a piece of material cut
from a Billiard Table than all the other Girls in their fine Party
Dresses. 'She is a Pupil,' *says Mlle Weiss*, but I honestly
believe that no one heard her, for one of the Girls had put on
a Record in the next room and we all went next door to
Dance. I danced as little as I could with Prince P—, for he
clasped me so maddeningly and muttered dangerously in my
Ear that he would see me on the two-thirty to London on

Saturday, that I was sure *Mlle Weiss* would hear him; and the less I wanted the Plan the more trapped I was in it, for *Mlle Weiss* came over to me several times as I stood resting or drinking Orangeade between Dances, and told me how many messages I must give to my dear Aunt; and talked of other members of the Family, of whom I had never heard. *Annie* I saw most often standing by the Wall, for it seemed that many of the Young-Men had seen her too often in the course of a Year and no longer had any desire to Partner her; whereas I, who was new, was in demand by all of them. I can't say, however, that the fiendish plans made by *Annie* for my downfall came from Envy at my looks and Popular Ways, for I came to learn that the driving force of the wicked Girl was always Money. Yet the foolish thing about the whole Party was that I wanted to dance with only one Young-Man and he hadn't come, although Invited; and this, it goes without saying, was Lord E—.

*

It seems that *Annie* and Prince P— had long planned this Abduction, for such it was, of an Heiress, which I had the misfortune to be considered. It's true I went to the Station with a heavy Heart, and even *Mlle Weiss*, who was usually so cheerful, kissed me a hundred times as if I was leaving for good. Then the old poodle *Ras* started up its barking and old *Mr Clarke* called out for his morning Chocolate and I went away down the street, knowing very well that *Susan*, who was quite sick with Love for me by then, was standing at the window and staring out. And further, as if I knew that nothing could be done to forestall disaster, I saw nothing strange in *Annie* being on the very same Platform as mine, and talking to Prince P— in a Low Voice before either of them turned and saw me.

'Ah,' *says Annie*, as if it's the most ordinary thing in the world for her to watch the *London* Train pull in and then go out again without her stepping on it, 'have a lovely time in *London*, *Robina*, with your Aunt.' And she and Prince P—

burst out laughing so that several Students turned round to stare at us and I felt the Mortification in which these cruel people so often plunged me. (Yet Prince P— was a Boor, only, I believe; and did honestly think he loved me and I him; and that I would restore his Family Fortunes for when we came to *London* and went to the Apartment of which he had boasted, there was no Furniture, there were no Pictures and I was to learn that Prince P—'s stepmother, the *Astor*, had in fact left his father some months before and they were now destitute.) I knew nothing of this, though, at the time and could sense only some kind of Plot between *Annie* and Prince P— and indeed there was one, as I was shortly to see.

London, with its great streets and the bustle of a Saturday, quite took up my thoughts until we came to Prince P—'s Family Flat and I had no choice but to see the sad truth of their circumstances. 'We are moving to a great house in the Country,' *says* Prince P—, but in so gloomy a voice that I can see there is no truth in it. 'Look, there is just one sofa left,' the Scoundrel goes on, and tries to draw me to a shape well-covered in a white sheet which was indeed the last remaining piece of furniture in the room. '*Robina*, I love you —' and so on, while trying all the harder to pull me down on the dust-sheet and complete what had been so precipitately begun in *Oxford* at the *Randolph Hotel*. 'But where are your father and stepmother?' *say I*, and silently cursing the Trap into which Prince P— has led me, where there was no Porter who could hear me cry, for we were high up in the Building, and no Servant either, for these had no doubt been dismissed at the time of Prince P—'s father's desertion by the *Astor*. 'They're coming soon to find us Married,' says Prince P—, breathing with such Heat in my Ear that I can hear nothing but the sound of his Hot Breath like the sea. And he pulls me down with him. The dust sheet fell to the floor and soon Prince P— had me flat on the sofa, where my screams and kickings were quite unknown to any-one.

Ill Fortune has followed me often in my Life, but so too has Good, for Prince P—, being right on the edge of taking me or so I thought must be the case (for with the *Green Baize Skirt* around my neck I couldn't see what he might produce below) there was a sudden stampede of feet on the Parquet floor and for the second time Prince P— must loosen his grip to discover who came to disturb us there. As for me, I was as confounded as my Seducer to be caught in this terrible Position, and swore at the day my Curiosity to see this magnificent Apartment and enjoy the Delicacies and Gifts promised by Prince P— had overcome my good sense. 'Good evening, Miss,' says a tall woman, Red-Indian in the face, and immensely thin in the body, which was swathed like her head in cloths of intricate wrapping and Design. And to Prince P— she says she is amazed to see him here, she has brought with her several Men to remove the rest of her Belongings and she would like us to leave Immediately. 'Of course, of course,' *says* poor Prince P—, for it is clear the *Astor* has no love for him, 'but we are just Engaged –' and he says the name of my Family at great speed, as if this would mollify her, which, her being as already stated an *Astor*, it did not. 'We'll leave now,' *says* Prince P—, very red in the face. And so we were bundled out like so much dirty linen, which was in all probability how we were seen by this woman with the hard jaw like a *Tomahawk*.

Prince P— then in the street earned my greater Loathing by holding me tight in every doorway and hugging me so that I had no breath in my body to cry out or even to let in air; and the fact I had no money except for two pounds from my kind Uncle's Leaving Present filled me with even more Disquiet, for I saw we might end in the streets and then in Gaol.

How I was to break away from the embrace of Prince P— I can't tell, but I did find myself free all of a sudden and running back to the Building where we had been, for it was the only place of shelter I knew in *London*. Prince P— was too full of consternation to come after me, and this time the tall Woman was more considerate, asking me to sit down while she called *Mlle Weiss*, which was the right and proper thing to do, or so I thought in all my innocence.

Alas! *Mlle Weiss* spoke some time to the Tall Woman, who then turned to me with a grave look on her face. 'You were seen on the London Train with a Young-Man, which is against the Rules,' *says she*. ('Seen' by *Annie*, I think, and could truly have killed the girl then.) 'And you are Sent Down.' And now she begins to look Impatient and to give orders to her Men for packing up a case of *Objets de Vertu*, which she says must go in the finest Tissue Paper. 'This has happened often enough,' *says she*, and I recall too that Prince P— has had many Engagements, ending in all probability in this way. 'Here is fifteen pounds, which *Mlle Weiss* will refund to me,' *says she*, as if indeed this is a familiar scene. 'You are to go to *St Pancras* Station and take a train back to your Uncle and Aunt in *Carlisle*. A Cab will be at the door shortly.' And so she kept me there in silence some quarter of an hour as her crystal and enamel Boxes were packed up, showing me at one time a Russian egg of diamond and Glass with a miniature coach and horses within. She asked me too of news of my Uncle's Elder Brother, but as always I had no news to give on this score, and so I went off with a heart even heavier than early in the day to the Station and the anger of my poor Aunt in the North.

*

Of all the places that are gloomiest to the spirit when Trouble comes about, the platforms of *St Pancras* Station at night must be counted high. There was only one diversion known to me, which was to read the list of Names stuck to each Sleeper Carriage window on the Train, proclaiming the names of the Passengers and their Destinations. My own coach, where I would sit all night through to *Carlisle*, was just behind them. And to pass the time and calm my agitation I walked the length of these distinguished Lists, looking and not-seeing the illustrious names of *Politicians, Peers, Bishops* and the like, while pondering on *Annie*'s meaning in her Betrayal of me (for certainly it must have been she who had

41

told *Mlle Weiss* she had seen me break the Rules by boarding a Train for *London* with Prince P—). So it was some time before my eye alighted on a Name I knew, and one, moreover, which brought a fine blush to my cheeks.

No sooner had I seen this name, which was to me as fine a Name as any I had ever read, than a hand came down on my Shoulder and I heard the voice of its owner, Lord E—. 'Why, *Robina*,' *says he*, 'I didn't know you were going up to Scotland. Is the Term over already then?' Hearing some laughter in Lord E—'s voice, I was careful not to look at him too long, for Lord E— I could see, was with a group of Northern men; and, while he was by far and away the best to look at among them, there was some interest in who I was, etc. starting up on the Platform, and Flasks produced, which made me fear I would be molested all through the journey. 'You've been Sent Down,' *says* Lord E—, highly amused at first. 'This will be nothing new for Prince P—, I can assure you.' I felt mortified at this, and was not sure in what way I could explain my Dislike for Prince P— which had now become immense. I thought too of how on the Train South he had told me to beware of Lord E—, who was, according to Prince P—, responsible for a great-many Sendings-Down, whereas it now appeared that Lord E— was Innocent, and Prince P— a Scoundrel. 'I'm very unhappy,' *said I*; and was surprised myself to find a tear falling, which it did most shamefully on Lord E—'s hand. Then I told Lord E— in all Confidence that I loathed and detested Prince P—, that he and *Annie* had played a Trick on me, by telling *Mlle Weiss* my Aunt was in *London*, which she was not, so *Mlle Weiss* insisted I go; and that I had been reported as seen at *Oxford* Station with Prince P—. 'I'll tell you,' *says* Lord E—, who was looking quite grim now, understanding my Plight, 'that *Annie* and Prince P— are Old Friends and *Annie* let it be known that you were an Heiress and therefore she would encourage Prince P— to take you to *London* so that you could visit your rich Uncle. Prince P— and *Annie* hoped to get as much out of him as they could, or that is how it sounds to me.' 'But that is foolish,' *say I*, and explain how I don't know my Uncle, but, as I was so often to discover, Lord E— seemed not to hear this at all, and pulled me roughly into the Train, saying we were Moving and did I want us both to fall on the Rails? 'No, no,' *says he*, as the kilted Men came with Flasks into the Train too and we were all packed together in the Corridor. 'We have no need of your Company tonight, thank-you,' and the Men laughed and hooted in so unpleasant a way that Lord E— without further ado pushed me into his Sleeper and closed the door and locked it, so we were subjected to the Hooting for a while and then they went away. 'This is most unfortunate for you,' *says* Lord E—. 'You have no Sleeper, I suppose?' I said I hadn't, and he went on that I should have this one and he would sit up all Night, and where were my Bags? To which I replied that I had none, for this was quite true: owning only the *Circular Baize Skirt* and *Black Top* I had travelled to *London* without a Bag; but luckily, which would at least assuage the anger of my Aunt a little, I had with me the *Fur Coat*. 'You have been abominably treated by *Annie* and Prince P—,' *says* Lord E—, 'and I'm sure it was *Annie*'s wicked Jealousy at the last moment that made her tell *Mlle Weiss* you were on a Train with Prince P—, though she had at first thought she would profit from it.' And here Lord E—, seeing perhaps that I was yet again on a Train in this compromising Situation, but that there were no Rules to break because I had been Sent Down, fell silent; as did I, after the Speech of my near Abduction by Prince P—, when it was in fact true that I had looked forward eagerly to my Trip to *London*, without the slightest fear of the Consequences. So it was that we stood there deep in Thought, each deceiving the other and becoming every minute more ready to sit down together on the Berth, which we did after the Train had got going and a decent interval had elapsed.

Lord E— soon took out a Flask of his own, of a Whisky which was very pale but which he said came from the Highlands and was Harmless; and when we had drunk this he put out the light and we lay together on the Berth, while the Lights that went round in front of my eyes I was foolish enough to think must come from the passing Stations beyond the Blind.

I must have slept soundly, for when I woke Daylight was coming in and I was able to see that we were very Rumpled and that Lord E— slept still. I could thus look at the admirable features of this Northern man with some attention; and I must say I never saw anything so pretty, gentle and charming in repose, which was all the more agreeable for knowing that when he was awake Lord E— had the air, as I have said, of a noble Stag which no one would dare to wish to put at Bay. In all the time I had with Lord E— I received nothing but kindness and generosity to the point where I must refuse his kindness sometimes; but I daresay I learnt to receive without asking, in this way, and also the extreme Success of this, for all of which I blamed neither Lord E— nor myself, but attribute to a happy mixture of my youth and his sweetness of character, although it was my youth, alas, that was to prove my disadvantage with him.

If I felt satisfaction at gazing at Lord E—'s head on the pillow, this soon vanished when I turned to look out the window at the landscape as it went by. The train had slowed and we were among hills, with here and there a pine or silver birch tree: but try as I might I couldn't see this as Border Country – the hills were too high and too wild, even the heather seemed darker. And a terrible Suspicion took hold of me that we were indeed in the Highlands and that I had Overshot the Mark altogether. By this time Lord E— had awoken and was looking at me fondly, for I was now in distress that was quite Hysterical and was almost ready to pull the Emergency Chain above my head, although it was of course too late for that to be of any help. 'Dear *Robina,' says* Lord E—, 'we are coming into *Inverness.*' And I knew this to be true, for the Station had shown that the Train we were on went *via Carlisle* to *Inverness.* 'You'll come and stay with me,' *says he,* 'at the Castle,' and he says the name of a Castle very famous in Scotland where it was said that the old Scottish king was murdered and where the wicked Lady Macbeth is still seen to walk in her Sleep. 'We are passing through the Blasted Heath now,' *says* Lord E——, laughing, for he was quick to see my Interest when it comes to Historical Characters or Picturesque Scenery. 'But what am I to wear?' *say I*, for I was all-at-once taken shy at the thought of Lord E——'s mother the *Countess* and saw her in my mind as a Cold and very Beautiful Woman, which indeed she turned out to be. 'Never mind,' *says* Lord E——, showing for the first and certainly not the last time his Affection and Kindness to me. 'We'll stop at *Inverness* and you shall buy all the Clothes you need.' And he pulls from his pocket a bundle of pound Notes, very familiar to look at because they were *Scotch* Notes, for which I shall always hold a peculiar fondness (these being the first Money given to me and rightfully mine, though doled out in small quantities by my Uncle and Aunt). 'There are fine Cashmere dresses and scarves,' *says* Lord E——, 'at *Inverness*,' and he tells me we will go to his Clan shop too and he will fit me out in his Tartan, which made me think in my foolish happiness that we were as good as Married. The train then got slower and came in to stop at *Inverness*. And so began my stay at Castle G——, and all thought of my Aunt, I am sorry to say, quite gone from my Mind.

*

I shall have to pass quickly over my stay at Castle G——, for the memory of it brings me sadness still; and I can truthfully say, that despite the Manner of the *Countess* (who became kinder halfway through my visit, as shall be told) it was the only time in my life I had been completely happy; and even today I think this happiness could never be repeated, because it had all the freshness of Youth on its side.

Lord E—— took every chance to make me at ease in the Castle, which was cold and grim enough, it was true. His father *the Thane* addressed hardly a word to me, the old Servants looked at me askance in the dining-room, and yet I felt I had never been so smiled on in my life. Lord E—— took

45

me in the Oak Woods round the Castle and was soon talking of marriage, as I had thought he would. 'My father may make some difficulties,' *says* he. 'But I'm ready to leave *Oxford*: why should I stay on there if I'm married?' And so on. He kissed me very sweetly and said we should sit up tonight in the small sitting-room when *the Thane* and his *Countess* had gone to bed. 'They don't mean badly,' *says he.* And he went on to say that his father had problems with the Estate which were almost insurmountable, that the Castle in its battlements had had Dry Rot discovered a year earlier and that there was a question of them moving out altogether to a smaller house. 'Never mind that,' *says he* when my face clouded, for I was thinking sure enough of my life as the Châtelaine of this grand Castle, with people coming up and calling me Ladyship. 'We'll live in it, we'll make the place splendid again, as you shall see.'

Alas for a happiness that is built on dreams of the future, on ancient masonry and historic Names! And, most of all, on a Lover who knows only half of what he says, as turned out to be the case with Lord E—. That day, waiting for the evening, as I supposed, he was very quiet, and we walked in silence together over the moors, putting up here and there a red-legged bird that had more to chatter about than we did. It was nearly winter now, in those Northern hills, and Lord E— pointed me out a Hare, too, as it went slowly along the side of the Scree. 'It will turn white when the snow comes,' *says he.* 'It will change according to its needs, as we all must.' And he sighed, but I had no way of knowing what he meant; though later, when we were in the Great Hall in the gloomy Presence of *the Thane*, I began to wonder if Lord E— was talking of himself and saw his coming Change as more needed than desired.

That evening Lord E— formally told his father that we were to be married, and in doing so said my Name, which had not been said in the days I had been there, *the Thane* and *Countess* paying as much attention to me as *Robina* as if I had been a Village Child brought in for the amusement of Lord

E—. On hearing this Name, *the Thane* rose from his Sofa, which was heavy and strewn with cushions in Tapestry, and came to me to stare hard into my face. 'This is very Great News,' *says he*. And he went on that he was overjoyed, that there was no one better suited to his son, etc., which was all the stranger in the circumstances, for only the night before the *Countess* had been pressing Lord E— to attend the Highland Ball where a *Lady Malvina* would be looking forward eagerly to meeting him, and no mention of asking me to go along too. 'My dear,' *says the Countess* coming forward, for it had taken her a little time to lay aside the tapestry she was making on her seat, 'I am so delighted,' *says she*. And she put her cheek against mine, a cold Cheek if ever I did feel one. 'All the better to leave *Oxford* and settle down into a Serious Life,' *says the Thane*, who the night before at Supper had spoken his usual few words, these concerning the importance of the continuing of Lord E—'s career as a Student. 'You may do up the Dower House first.' And he went over very briskly to a Desk and drew out some papers, which he said were an Estimate for the costs of rebuilding and decorating the Dower House, which would be necessary, it seemed, before the house could be seen to be fit to live in. 'When you have children,' *says the Thane*, 'you will live here in the Castle.' But these words unaccountably filling him with gloom again he turned from us and went over to the Fire. 'You must excuse my poor husband,' *says the Countess* in the sweetest tones, although I never trusted her any the more for it, 'he has had too many Emotions come at once.' And she went on to explain that *the Thane* had heard only that morning that the Battlements were in Danger of collapsing entirely any day now and that we might all be buried in the rubble – apart, of course, from the very great Shame of Letting Go a Famous Castle from which the early Vikings and Picts had fired their arrows so busily. 'And now this happiness,' *says the Countess*, and looks skywards and then at me, as if I am somehow to repair the battlements without further ado. Then *the Countess* asked me News of my Uncle's Elder Brother, and when on

47

being told that I knew nothing of him she laughed as I had come to expect and made little of it. 'Now we must go up to Bed, we are quite late in all our Excitement,' *says she* and gave Lord E— a meaningful Look, which shamed us both. 'You shall have a fire in the small sitting-room if you wish . . .' and so they went up to bed, Lord E— bidding his father Good-Night, and I at the last saying Good-Night as well. 'If we're spared,' *says he*, and so the happy couple went up the stairs.

I can't say that Lord E— knew what he did; but that night I lay very quiet in his arms on a Rug before the sparking Log Fire, to which we had looked forward gladly all day. If we thought, both of us, that *the Thane* had made it too plain that he considered me a Great Heiress, neither of us said so. A hundred times Lord E— asked me why I wasn't happier, and were we not Engaged now? 'There's the G— Family Pearls,' *says he*. 'You shall have them straight-away for my Mother never wears them.' And he said we would go South and buy other Jewels too, in particular an Engagement Ring, which would be a Sapphire to match my eyes, etc. Yet I couldn't find any Joy in it; and in the end I said I was tired after all the walking we had done that day and Lord E— went with me down as far as my Room and kissed me good-night at the door.

*

I must say that our spirits were all recovered the next day, and that only one question remained for me, now I could look forward to a life of happiness with the Northern Lord in just the way I had hoped and prayed for. And this was that Lord E— showed little insistence on going-all-the-way with me, which I could not be sure was the usual thing to do and thus a sign of respect for my Youth and the fact that we were not yet Married; or whether Prince P— had been unusual in his Clasping and Perseverance. I feared, as will surely be understood, that Lord E— did not in his Heart of Hearts Want me; yet, as I have since discovered (in my life at least), most often when my Blood is up and I think longingly of a man, there is nothing Up with him; and it's as if the Cruel Fates had arranged this purely for their own Enjoyment. However, I was proved to be not so far from the mark, in the end, and my instinct and prying ways were to lead to my downfall, as we shall see.

All went very briskly on the day after the Announcement and Lord E— took great Pleasure in showing me round the Castle, into Rooms and Wings I had not been into before, some of the Rooms being Priests' Holes and others having holes in them by the door, which the removal of a Boulder would open up to a dizzy fall to the Cobbles below. 'We have been a war-faring family and very Vicious always,' *says* Lord E— and it was clear he was proud of it, which made me sad, for I can hardly see a fish killed and could live easily only if there was no Violence in the world. 'We have been a Catholic family always', *says he*, and smiling all the time (so sweet-natured to me that day that he began to press on me jewels and antique shawls and cashmere from the moment I woke, as if my Engagement was to be celebrated constantly with gifts from the Family). 'Your Uncle will no doubt make Objections to your marrying a Catholic?' he went on, in a teasing kind of voice; yet he had Concern, it was clear, and it seemed that his Father had asked him to discover from me as quickly as he could whether this would be an Impediment between us: perhaps that there was so little time before the Battlements would come down and my Trust must be put to upholding them; or that at least is what I believe now, with some knowledge gathered from my time in the World and particularly with the Nobility. I can't say, to this day, that I believe Lord E— pretended his Love as a part of the Plan to rebuild the older Parts of the Castle; indeed, his Love for me was Real enough I am sure, but not Strong enough, and this Sad Truth I had to meet for the first time in my few Years quite innocently and without Experience of any sort.

I replied to Lord E— that my Uncle had no Religion at all, but my Aunt was a very devout Woman and always in the

Kirk, at which Lord E— was quite downcast. 'But she'll make no Objection,' *say I*, for I knew my Aunt would be very pleased to have me Off her Hands and would have cared little if I had married a Mohammedan. 'My mother is very Religious too,' *says* Lord E—, and he goes on to say there is one Tower he has not taken me to visit and that this Tower contains *the Countess*'s Oratory, where she spent most of the day in Prayer. 'I don't dare go up there,' *says he* with a laugh; but leaving me uncertain, which I am to this day, if he meant that the danger of falling Masonry was so great as to be foolhardy to risk the journey, especially for the heir to the Castle and his Betrothed, or that he hardly dared disturb his Mother at her Prayers.

However it was, we soon found ourselves in a room no bigger than a low grave, under the steps of the old Castle, which had been a Dungeon and also a Hiding Place in a Time of Raids, or so said Lord E—, and here he began at last to show some of the Heat which had been lacking in him up to that day. 'It's dark,' *says he*, and pulled me down into the rubble, which was fourteenth-century rubble, he assured me, but none the less uncomfortable for that. 'No one will see us here.' And he pulled from a niche in the wall an ancient black slipper, such as might fit a young child. 'This was the shoe of a *Countess* who was walled up here when the *Campbells* were coming,' *says he*, 'and she died here.' All of which made my spine Tingle, as it was doubtless intended to. '*Robina*,' *says he*, pressing his mouth to mine so that I could answer him no way at all. 'Let's see if the slipper fits.' And he dived down between my legs in a pretence of finding my foot, which was quite lost to sight in the Darkness. 'Ah, I have it here,' and so on, while pushing the slipper between my Knickers and My A—s so that I went as hot as a Beet all-over. 'It fits,' *cries he*, and I was indeed on the point of feeling a hard object which I could not tell if it was the toe or the heel of this ancient Slipper coming right into me, when a Loud Noise went off and Lord E— fell back a moment so we lay in silence with our hearts Beating out of Rhythm. 'What is it?

say I, beginning to cry, which spoilt the mood and sent Lord E— to pull open the Dungeon door, thus letting-in a great stream of light. 'It's only my Mother,' *says he*, but sulky this time as if he no longer cared for me; which I think from that moment was very likely True. 'Your Mother?' *say I* in some alarm, and particularly alarmed too to see no sign of the Slipper, although my Skirt was very disarranged and my Knickers right down at the Back so that I was sitting on the crumbling Rock quite Bare and Uncovered. 'My Mother fires off her Gun at Strangers if they walk up the Drive,' *says he*, in order to explain to me. 'She can see them from the Oriel window of her Oratory.' 'Oh, is that all?' *say I*, but it was too late and Lord E— had strode out of the Dungeon before I could pull myself up and follow him looking calm enough for his Father to see, if *the Thane* happened to be passing.

When I caught up with Lord E— he had arrived in the Great Hall and was demanding Tea and Whisky of the old Servant, who looked at me, or so I thought, with greater Suspicion than usual. Yet I was to wish, later that day, that there had been more Grounds for these Suspicions: to learn that to Refuse a Man may provoke some to greater Ardour, but for others will cause them to Cool-off completely; and to experience for the first time in my life the Pangs of a most fearful Jealousy.

*

It turned out that that night was the night of the Highland Ball, for which I had such a longing to go; and now I was Engaged to be Married I was of course Invited. 'But,' *says the Countess* as we are standing over the Tea Things, 'you have nothing to wear, my dear *Robina*, and you shall come upstairs with me and choose a dress.' I said I could just as well go to the Ball in the *Circular Baize Skirt* (which had become a jest with Lord E— and, insofar as *the Thane* ever laughed at all, with him too), but *the Countess* would hear none of it and soon I was in a long and gloomy corridor lined with dark wooden cupboards, each one bulging with dresses in sequins and velvet and crêpe-de-Chine and every manner of material; although it was a dress of Shot Silk I chose, whether in my Heart to please my future mother-in-law because it was clear she was fond of Shooting and I thought in my ignorance that she had somehow shot this dress (which was indeed Limp) or because I liked the colour, a sea Green which I thought became me at that time, I cannot rightly say. At least, when it was chosen, the *Countess* took me into her Boudoir and took me then to stand under the Oriel Window so that we could examine the dress to see if there were any Marks on it. 'It is lovely,' *say I* to Lord E—'s Mother, but didn't have the Courage to reach up and kiss her; and in fact I am glad now I didn't, for once I was out of Favour with Lord E— she wrote to my Aunt to ask for the dress back, which was not Noble. 'You look very pretty,' *says the Countess* when she has made me try on the Dress and is thus able to see the wretchedly torn state of my Knickers, from lying on the Mediaeval Rubble. She goes on, 'You won't mind there being a Girl Over tonight –' and she says she can't find such a thing as an Extra Man anywhere. 'We'll find you as many Partners as you like when we arrive at the Ball,' *says the Countess*, 'it's only the Dinner.' And I had no will to ask why I should not be expected to dance all the evening with Lord E— now I was Engaged to be Married, except that I could guess the answer lay in the *Countess*'s still having Preferences for someone else to succeed her as the Châtelaine of the Castle. Indeed, I was to be proved right; for the *Lady Malvina* of whom I had heard the day before came to the Castle in a Pink Dress that looked like Spun Sugar, and with a Great Sash of her own Tartan across the Bosom. Lord E—, while holding on to my hand whenever he was not employed in fetching Refreshments for the Guests, was clearly much taken with her; and at the Ball, which seemed to take an Age to arrive at, travelling over the Blasted Heath and with Lord E— steering and *Lady Malvina* in front to spare her Dress, or so she said, I felt as wretched and humble as a Peasant in the back seat, the dress of Shot Silk hanging round me.

After this great Length of Time, which from the Glances they exchanged in the front seats made them close to being Engaged to be Married, in my Mind at least, we arrived at another great Castle and there went in, where I was to pass the most miserable evening of my Life. Let no one say that Highland Dress is splendid; or that the Scots have a single Heart between them that can beat true; Vicious, Cruel and Cunning they are without exception, and dancing about with bare Legs and Daggers makes them all the more Alarming to see.

Lord E—, who was more and more like a Stag (and I regret to say at his most Handsome and Winning that night), danced all the evening with *Lady Malvina*; and whether this was to Punish me for the disappointment in the Dungeon I will never know, for I fled soon to a distant Bathroom and lay sobbing on the floor, while more Antlers looked down on me, and a stuffed Salmon in a Glass Box. I would gladly have ended my Life on that night: my dreams of Marriage with Lord E— were dashed; my life in the Castle and wandering in Winter in the Oakwoods quite destroyed; I had only my Disgrace with my Aunt to look forward to; and would at least have saved myself the final Ignominy if I had not had a surge of Fighting Spirit after some minutes of lying there Prostrate and gone off in search of the fickle Lord E—, which, as I have said, was a part of my prying and foolish nature and likely to bring about my Downfall.

The corridors of this Castle, laid down with Tartan as was Castle G— (but a different plaid, naturally), were long and Bending and I had not gone down on my Toes for long before I heard Laughter from behind a door. Nor was this door completely closed, and soon I could look round it, to see the Pink Dress like an Upside Down Cake on the bed and two Legs sticking out, an a—se on a Pillow and Lord E— screwing away as if he had no idea to open his eyes and see if he was being observed. Yet I was out of luck, as has been my Lot so often in my life: my Shock caused the door to make a Noise behind me and the Couple to roll sideways off the Bed in

Consternation. Lord E— saw me certainly, even if *Lady Malvina* was more encumbered by the confections of her Dress; and I fled, too frightened to cry, down the corridors and out into the cold, dark air of the surroundings of the Castle. For I was still Intact, remember, and swore then that I would never indulge in an Activity like the one I had just seen: indeed, it was some time before I could be persuaded to share my Body with any man, as shall be told. But for the Time Being, my thoughts were more with my route of Escape, as may well be imagined. As I ran, I heard by the sound of wheels that I was being pursued; fortunately, though, by a Young Couple who had taken Pity on my Appearance and offered to take me home. '*Inverness* Station,' *say I*, as if they were no more than a Common Cab; and off we go. But I give this information only to show that in times when all is darkest, Human Kindness may suddenly put in an appearance; I must also say that this charming Couple were English, and simply visiting the Highlands for the Sport.

*

My feelings in the Train on the Dark journey down to *Carlisle* need little describing. Let it alone be added that I was penniless and must write out for the Guard a Warranty that my Guardian would pay the Fare when the Bill was presented to him; and my Family's Name being very well known in Scotland this caused some Laughter in the Carriage, all of which went towards making me a great-deal more unhappy than before, particularly as I was a Sight to See in the Shot Silk Dress lent me by *the Countess*. For all that, I was thankful for my Aunt's *Fur Coat*, which I had taken to the Ball, as the Highland Nights were cold, yet every mile that drew me away from Lord E— and my lost Joy in the mountains at Castle G— the more wretched I became; and even to think of the cold evenings and Lord E—'s arms round me (for even the sight of a *Fur Coat* would produce this kind of Morbid Reasoning) made me all in all more wretched than I had ever been in my Life.

My Aunt was no more pleased to see me, I must confess, than I was to see her, and even less pleased than I no doubt, for the Cab from *Carlisle* had to be paid on my Arrival; although this outlay must have come from Money that was rightfully mine and withheld by my Aunt and Uncle in Trust until I should reach the age of twenty-one. 'Speak of the Devil,' cried my Aunt, who had gone quite pale when she saw me, and, holding out a letter in Green Ink, she says that this is from *Mlle Weiss* and has only just arrived today; that I am Sent Down from M— Street as I must doubtless know; but that I am also an ungrateful *Fool*, a *Tart* and a Host of other Things which I had no way of knowing whether they were from the Tongue of *Mlle Weiss* or my Aunt. 'After all the expense that has been Laid out,' *says she*; and this I know must come from my Aunt, and not *Mlle Weiss*, who is the Recipient of this Expense. 'Prince P— I gather abducted you on a Train,' *says she next*, before I had time to say that the Fees paid to the Establishment for Young Ladies must come from my Trust and thus from the Money that was rightfully mine; although I had remarked on this *à propos* the Cab from *Carlisle* and my Aunt had given me a Cuff on the Cheek for it. 'It was a Lie, as I was never coming to *London*,' *says* my Aunt, who had gone very Red in the face after her Pallor. And it came clear to me that, as *Mlle Weiss*'s Letter had only arrived today, my Aunt knew nothing of my Visit to Scotland or the feelings I entertained so strongly still for Lord E—, and that to compound my Misery I should have to bear with teasing on being in-Love with Prince P— from my Uncle and others, when Prince P— seemed as far away from me as the Man in the Moon. 'Go to your Room,' *says* my Aunt, who thought it impudent probably that I didn't deign to answer her. 'And your Uncle and I will fix on you going to St A—'s instantly.' (St A—'s was a Boarding School of the greatest Strictness, and my Aunt had long recommended it, being deterred only by the momentous size of the Fees. Now, however, after all the Scraping and Saving, a year there, which would take me up to my Seventeenth Birthday would not stretch her at all, for my Trust could indisputably provide it.) 'Not St A—'s,' I cried, and then my Uncle came in, and all the Teasing started, which I had come to expect, driving my Aunt out of the Room at least, for she disapproved of my Uncle's taking such matters as the loss of my Virginity (as she supposed) so lightly. 'Prince P—,' *says* my Uncle, laying down his Guns (for he never went about without a brace of them on his arm), 'surely you don't want to marry a Foreigner, *Robina*, do you?' And so on. I replied that I had no plan to marry Prince P— at all; that I disliked him extremely and that I prayed only not to be sent to St A—'s for the simple Sin of having wanted to see *London* for myself and thus taking advantage of Prince P—'s offer to Escort me there. 'I see,' *says* my Uncle, when he learnt that this was indeed my Aunt's threat; and he frowned, for he was a genial man, as I have said; and sitting on the Brass Fender, for we were in the Nursery now, by a low fire, he drew me on his knee and stroked my hair thoughtfully. 'You liked your work at *Weiss*'s,' *says he* after a while. 'Oh yes,' *say I* and in a much happier tone, for I was taken back by my Uncle's affectionate gesture to those days when I was very small in this same Nursery and he would draw me on his knee and say it was a terrible pity I had lost my father and mother and that they should have Run-Out on me in that way, and that he would take me down to *Cumberland* some time, to the *Solway Firth* and the house by the ruins of *Castle Carlaverack*, where my father had apparently lived before his Bride bolted away from him. And, calmed by my Uncle's kindness, I began to sob bitterly, for I felt a true Orphan now if I was to be sent off to St A—'s and said as much between Sobs. 'You shan't,' *says* my Uncle and shifts uncomfortably under me, so I felt for a moment as if I were in the ancient dungeons of Castle G— once more and encountering some hard and blunt Object. 'I'll talk to your Aunt,' *says he*, and starts to kiss my Face very fully, so I leapt from his Knee to the Floor, at which my Aunt came in and looked hard at my Uncle, who, jumping up, says he will finish off his Rough Shooting and bring home a Rabbit or Two for the Pot. But he was first restrained by my Aunt, who says in no Uncertain Terms that I am off to St A—'s in the morning. 'No, no,' *says* my kind Uncle and goes to the door and shoots straight through it at a Crow that happened to be passing so that it fell dead (for in Scotland there is no garden in front of a house; the gardens are walled away at the side and the door of my Uncle's house opened straight on to rough Field and Woodland). 'Stop it,' *cries* my Aunt, who was driven mad I think by my Uncle's continual shooting, but not so much for the Cruelty to Animals as for the Headache she said the Noise would often visit on her. 'No, I won't,' *says* my Uncle, amiable as always. 'I see some Woodies coming over' – and he aims his Gun, handing me the other so I ran obediently behind him, for since my earliest days I had been used to be his Loader. 'No!' *cries* my poor Aunt again as my Uncle fires off and I load for him and ä whole flock of wood pigeons came down, which later his black bitch Moll went off and fetched for him. 'Well, *Robina* shall go on with her Studies of French History and History of Art,' *says* my Uncle over the din; and it was in this way that my Uncle gained his point and would only desist in firing off when he had gained it; so by the time a Score of Rounds of Cartridges had been spent, it was settled that I should go to *Paris* to continue my education, despite the Prohibitive Cost.

*

My Aunt was kind enough to take me to *Paris*, to Settle me In; and after a few days (for we went down to *London* and visited *Oxford Street*, where there were Stores, my Aunt said, that sold Clothes very Reasonably, as she would on no account pay out for a dress in *Paris*, which was a Sink of Iniquity when it came to Charging) we arrived, after a Channel crossing and a very cold Train, at the *Gare du Nord*.

Had I known on that sad journey, when my heart was low for thinking of Lord E— and all that I had lost, that I would also suffer extreme Deprivation at this next Phase of my Life, I do believe I would have leapt into the grey waters under the

Ferry that carried us across (and indeed this would not have proved hard for my Aunt had bought the cheapest tickets and we were ensconced right down by the Waves, and surrounded on all sides by people being Sick). Or, more certainly, I would have taken the offer of Dinner that was made me by a rosy, bearded man almost as soon as we had set foot in the Train, travelling very modestly as usual and this time, to compound the Discomfort, on Wooden Seats. It was when I went down the Corridor that the Frenchman, for such it was, bowed and asked for my Pleasure at Dinner; and Indeed I was Starving, but my Aunt had packed two apples and slices of white bread with thin Cheese and was all the while unpacking these, while the aroma of the *Table d'Hôte*, the first specimen of French *Cuisine* that I was to savour, was blowing to us strongly down the length of the Train. '*Bon Soir, Mademoiselle,*' *says* the Stranger as I, looking shy at hearing the Tongue which poor *Mlle Weiss* had tried so unsuccessfully to teach me, was also constrained to stop myself from laughing. And he went on, still in French, to say that he would keep a table for me by the door of the *Wagon-Restaurant*; all of which I was glad enough to understand. However, my Aunt, who had crept up behind me during this Exchange, said instantly that I was engaged to eat with her in her Carriage and, taking me by the arm, led me back there; and this was the last I was to see of the kind Stranger or the Dinner which had just previously declared itself with such Enthusiasm. 'You will remember when you are in *Paris* that it is entirely Incorrect to speak to a Stranger,' *says* my Aunt when we are sitting and eating the Bread and Cheese. And she went on to say that Men in *Paris* were known for their Wicked Intentions, some even going so far as to take a Girl into the White Slave Trade, by luring her first into a *boutique*, where a trap door in the Changing Room will prove to be the first step to Captivity in South America. 'The *Comtesse de B—* has undertaken to Keep a Close Eye on you,' *says she*. 'They are of a very respectable family and there can be no Scandal such as there has recently been in *Oxford*,' *she tells me*, adding that I am to keep to the Rules laid down by the *Comte* and *Comtesse*; that my Aunt will come out to Paris with my Uncle to see how I am getting on in a month or so; and that I have been enrolled in the *École du Louvre* to study French History of Art. 'There are a few other girls at the *de B*—'s,' *says* my Aunt next, which made my heart sink even lower than before, for I now expected to repeat the terrible Shocks and Disappointments that had been my lot with *Annie*. 'They are at the Sorbonne,' *says* my Aunt, 'and if you don't attend the *Louvre* as you should, you will go with them.' And all this said as if some form of Punishment lay ahead for me, whatever the choice; though I was hardly to know that the Punishment lay already in my Stomach and would consist most importantly of going Hungry. 'You are not to be asked to any Parties,' *says* my Aunt, as the Train now comes through groups of low Houses and I see that we are almost in *Paris*, my Heart lifting slightly, despite all my sorrow over Lord E—. 'Is this clear?' *says* my Aunt, and she says I am to be very careful with her *Fur Coat*, as her mother gave it to her before she died, etc. and my Aunt is very fond of it, but it will be cold in *Paris* and I will most certainly need it. 'It is raining and will be hard to find a Cab,' *says she*, when the Train does finally come into the Station; but the new Sights and Smells were already affecting me deeply; and for all the Cruelty I was to undergo in *Paris*, and all the unhappiness I was to know there, I was to love this City and flee *London* often for its Beauty.

My Aunt stayed one night at the house of the *Comte* and *Comtesse de B*—, which as she had said was indeed very cold. It was late when we arrived: a Tall Room with grey Panelling and no Fire at all was our cordial meeting-place with the French Family; and after a wad of Notes had been handed over by my Aunt to the *Comtesse* we were shown to our Rooms and pointed out a door, thin and High, which was, according to the *Comtesse*, 'Le Watter', which in turn my Aunt said to me was a Lavatory and known as a *Water Closet* in this country. Being too tired to keep my eyes open one minute longer, I went to lie on my bed and was soon asleep;

being grateful at least that there were no other Girls to share the Room with, though I was less grateful for this after a short time, as we shall see.

In the morning my Aunt left without saying good-bye, as she wished to take an Economy Trip that was On Offer and involved an Early Start; and I was woken by a Girl coming in and telling me I should rise and be in the *Salle à Manger* downstairs within five minutes for the *café au lait*; and this was said with an almost wolfish expression, which as I was soon to discover was because my added presence in the Household would diminish rather than increase the miserable supply of *brioches* and *baguettes* made ready for the Girls twice a day. 'The *Salle de Bain* is down at the end of the Passage,' *says* the Girl and then goes out; and I was late downstairs, as I knew I must be, for the house was Gloomy, the Doors all tall and grey and alike so it was some time before one did open and show a Bath, standing alone on a cold Tile floor and a Small Man in it, almost completely covered with Hair. '*Pardon*,' *say I* and pulled the door to without leaving hold of the knob, and so ran from the *Salle de Bain* and arrived in the *Salle à Manger* quite dishevelled, which *Mme de B*—, a hawk-eyed and Parsimonious Woman, was not slow to see. Here, in a silence that was interrupted only by the arrival of the *Comte* (at which none of the other Girls, of whom there were three, dared even to lift their eyes, murmuring only a *Bonjour* which went unheeded) we consumed our *café au lait* (in bowls, which I found most uncomfortable, and the coffee all milky, for the *Comtesse* with her system of saving could make my Aunt appear a Profligate Spender); and we were told to serve ourselves with Bread thin to Transparency from a Basket, though there was no Butter and just a little Jelly, which was Quince. Here, *Mme de B*— told me the way I must take to find the *Louvre* which she said was down near the river; and that we were now in *Passy*, which was the most Exclusive part of Paris and was therefore hard to Reach so we must walk quite a way before we could arrive there. 'You will return by five thirty,' *says the*

Comtesse to me, while her Husband sits quite Satisfied behind his *Paris-Matin*, and I have to wonder if *the Comtesse* knows of his Strange Habit of leaving unlocked the door of the *Salle de Bain*. All of which, it goes without saying, made me forget to listen with attention to the kind instructions of *Mme de B—* and to find myself lost on my first day in Paris, with unpleasant consequences.

*

For a young person as I was then, *Paris* on the first morning it Presents itself must be an Unforgettable Time; and certainly it was for me, for I lost all sense of the passing Hours, in my wandering in the *Louvre* and by the River outside, which was very Bright that day, with Young-Men selling pictures and old Books and smiling at me too, for I was much admired and invited often to take a *Verre*, which I was always careful to refuse and to recall the kind warnings of my Aunt. In the great Galleries I was at least thirty minutes before the *Raft of the Méduse*, the picture I had contemplated in my Studies with *Mlle Weiss*; and although the sight of it brought back fond Memories of *Oxford* and sad thoughts of Lord E—, I resolved to Dedicate the rest of my Life to study of such magnificent Works of Art as this; and after passing a long while before the *Mona Lisa* I went off to the Basement, as I had been directed by *Mme de B—*, to enrol in the Course of French History of Art.

In the great Vaults of the Louvre were Parties of Young Girls, and I had to think myself very Fortunate to be so Independent; also, wherever I walked, Heads Turned; and I was in fact as Pretty that day as I had ever been; for I had tied up my Red Hair in a piece of *Chiffon* which I think became it extremely, and I had painted my lips and cheeks, so that I was a gayer sight than many of the gloomy Old Masters; and soon I was stopped, as may be surmised, by an Old-Man in a *Beret* as I walked through the Rubens Room and asked if I would stay a while and pose for him. 'I must go down to the School,' *say I*, though all this Flattery had made me very happy, as alas it was always wont to do. The Old Man asked me then if I was Flemish, with such gold hair and Skin, and I replied I was *Écossaise*, which was soon heard by a Group of Students in the next room, who were gathered in a Weighty Examination of the fat Ladies of the great Artist *Rubens*.

On coming through and seeing me, Smiles and Compliments came out on all sides, and many Cards were pressed on me, with the name of *Atelier* and Student, and I said in the end that I would reach them all one day, when I had studied French History of Art, which I was expecting to do in the Basement. On which, as again needs little wondering at, on a Spring Morning in Paris, and on the part of a score of Young Men who had passed the last weeks in Contemplation of the Creases and Folds of the Juicy Mistresses of the Flemish School, I was Followed briskly down to the *École du Louvre* and joined in the underground auditorium by a *posse* of ardent admirers, despite the fact that I had enrolled for a course on French History of Art and not Flemish. Then the great Patriotic Battle Scenes of *David* came on the Slides, while the Students, with Torch in Hand, were instructed to make Notes on the Pronouncements of the Professor as he spoke from the darkness by the Screen.

I could only wish later that I had taken some of the Students at their word and eaten and drunk with them: and here I must add too that Ignorance in a Foreign City is a dangerous thing, as I was to discover when I came out into the sunlight from my First Lecture on French History of Art and went to change my Money, searching as if I were in *Carlisle* for the Familiar outline of a Bank. But every building was closed, and no one would say when it might reopen, if ever; and the *Crédit Lyonnais*, to which I was at last directed, looked once at the Scotch five-pound Note my Uncle had been kind enough to give to me and refused outright to have anything to do with it. Here I was indeed in Trouble! I was Penniless, and had certainly not gleaned a happy enough opinion of the *Comtesse de B—* to expect her to pay a Cab Driver if I should arrive back in *Passy* in such a Conveyance.

Also, my Head was spinning now from the long hours of Immersion in Art, to which I was most unused, and I had lost all Sense of Direction, forgetting entirely the way back to the house of my Protectors, the *Comte* and *Comtesse* (although, as it was to be proved, it was I who needed Protection from the very home in which I had been placed, rather than from Dangerous Strangers of whom my Aunt had warned me). I was Thirsty, and Hungry, and had of course no Money to buy a Map. However, on an island with the great cathedral of *Notre Dame* standing directly over me, I stopped at a *Tabac* and asked if I might consult a *Carte*, but here I was treated with great Rudeness and Contempt by the lady within this Round Edifice, which was a way I was to find very often in *Paris*: that the women were Angry and the men Polite in the extreme. 'Mademoiselle,' *says* a voice at my shoulder; and when I turned, there stood the *Comte* himself, which was certainly very extraordinary, or it seemed so at the time. 'You are lost,' *says the Comte*, and on my Bursting into Tears, which I am ashamed to have to say was the case, *M. de B—* put his arms round me and says he will take me to a restaurant on this very island, which is one of the best restaurants in Paris, for the reason that it moves along the water. To my Astonishment (for I thought the *Comte* must have taken leave of his senses) he said I could come with him straightaway and I would see what he was talking about; and true enough we had crossed a wooden gangplank a few minutes later and were sitting on deck in a *Bateau Ivre*, as the *Comte* said these Craft were named; and sitting very prettily too, in the Spring Sunlight, and in front of a table laid with a damask cloth the colour of strawberries.

Greed I may have learnt then, at the hands of the *Comte*: for in many ways it seemed as if the Devil Himself had sent him, to provide this fine Meal just at the time that I was most Hungry and Lost. And he was very kind to me too: 'I'll change that Foolish Note of Yours,' *says he*, and laughed a great-deal over the Scotch five-pound Note and then over the stories of my Uncle's Ways, which I am sorry to say I told him, being much encouraged by the Wine and the Excitement of moving through *Paris* on the *Seine*, on a beautiful morning that was all Innocent Joy. 'You shall learn *La Civilisation Française*,' *says the Comte*; and for all this I couldn't help but see his Hands which were very much covered with Hair like the rest of him (as I had seen in the Bath) creep over towards mine; and on my drawing back they dallied awhile among the butter-pats and the Napiery, like Animals I thought, and very Disgusting. 'You have left the Land of the Barbarians . . .' etc. (for I had told of my Uncle's way of Shooting out of the window, and indeed of the Predilection on the part of the Scottish people to fire a Gun at all times, even extending to a Northern *Countess*, Wife of *the Thane*.) 'In France we live for Love,' *says the Comte*, and he said all manner of other things as well, as a Gâteau arrived that was a perfect egg-shape but in reality a confection of Ice Cream and Caramel such as I had never dreamed Possible in my Life. These were the first signs of my weakness for Pleasure, and for fine Food and Wine; but it must be said that the *Comte* had easy prey, in me, for I was soon as near starved to Death as any Martyr, as shall be laid out for all to see.

First, on being told I must make my own way back to *Passy*, I soon saw the *Comte* had lied when he told me it was an accident (a Miracle even as he had said on the Boat) that he had come across me on the *Ile St-Louis*. From his manner, which was *chétif*, as I had learnt the word at *Mlle Weiss*'s Establishment for Young Ladies, I could gauge that he had followed me there Express with the purpose of Feasting me and later for Seduction; and I returned with a Heavy Heart to the house of *Mme de B——*. Now I had the evening to dread, and the one after, and indeed the whole of my stay in *Paris*, to which I had so much looked forward, in the promise of studying French History of Art. I did indeed feel like a Wreck, a Member of the Raft of Méduse, as I left the Public Transport and walked up the quiet hill to the gardens of *Passy*. My Aunt would certainly listen to no Complaint on my part, after handing over the Exorbitant Sum which is demanded by these French *Comtesses* to keep an Ignorant English Girl in their house, while my Uncle, concerned with care of his Sheep and his Pheasants, would hardly come out to *Paris* to rescue me, particularly as he spoke not one word of French. Alas! Even here my hopes were to be raised and then dashed again, for a Letter did shortly come from him, saying there was a Beef Fair in *Rouen* and he would come down and visit me if he went to it, for he wanted to buy a fine *Charolais*; but by then it was too late, at least in all ways but One.

Sure enough, as soon as I was back at the House, the *Comtesse de B*— came to my Room and asked me where I had been, and on my saying I had been at the Louvre she asked me a long time what pictures I had seen and what Lecture I had attended, until, satisfied at last, she went away, saying Supper was at seven-thirty and the Girls should study afterwards. So I stayed in my Room, hearing, I thought, the sound of the *Comte*'s return and the Shuffle of Feet outside my Door, until it was time to go out in that long gloomy Passage of grey doors and down the stairs to the *Salle à Manger* (for the Girls were never invited into the *Salon*, to sit with *Monsieur* and *Madame de B*—).

The other Girls were Mousy Creatures, though one, *Miranda*, did try to help me in my Plight; without Success alas, but she had a good Heart. Her face was frightened and small like the others, however, and her teeth stuck out from her Upper Lip, while her eyes were Vague and Protuberant; and neither of the other Girls was better-favoured, as I saw with a Sinking Heart when we sat down at Table: I was the Beauty there and no doubt about it; and while at other times I have felt Pleasure to be Singled Out for my Looks and Charms, I was then very alarmed and Despondent, particularly when the *Comte* and *Comtesse* came in to join us at the simple Repast.

The Stomach, Betrayer of every Need and Hope, at once showed me to have eaten my Fill that day; for the other Girls fell on the Thin Soup and Transparent Bread and Gobbled it Up, while I was still Sated, having Eaten and Drunk Late on the *Bateau*; and when a Choucroute came in I was quite unable to Consume it, overtaken as I was with a sense of Nausea at the smell (and reminded too of my Happy Days with *Mlle Weiss*, for she often served this, as all women must who have many Students to feed and the Strict Need to make a Profit). 'Why don't you eat, *Robina*?' *says Mme de B*—. '*Tu es malade*?' And so on, but without a trace of the kindness that would be in the Tone of *Mlle Weiss*. Indeed, at that moment I was so overcome by homesickness for *Oxford* and for the first love of my Life, Lord E—, that I was soon Blinded with Tears; and it may have been this that saved me, that night at least, for the *Comtesse* told me sharply to go to my Room and the *Comte* kept his Eyes down on the Tablecloth, where as usual his small, Hairy Hands darted about amongst the Cutlery.

*

To suffer as a Pleasure of the Chase was now to be my lot in *Paris*; and with the weather turning every day to rain I was forced indoors too much, either in the great Halls of the *Louvre*, or in the *Jeu de Paume*, where the paintings of *Boucher* hung in profusion, or in the *Grand Palais*, where they showed the statues from Antiquity, usually half-clothed or with only a Towel thrown across the back, leaving the Breast exposed. Then, wherever I went, and this I had come to dread after our first meeting by *Notre Dame*, M. de B— was surely there, and following me with all the eagerness my Aunt had told me I might expect in a FRENCHMAN: but I could not complain to her, as it goes without saying, because she had paid the *De B*— Family a substantial sum for the Purpose of Providing a home while I followed my Education. When I reflected, which I was bound to do, that the money paid out to keep the *Comte* in his sport was rightfully mine, the indignity and the injustice became almost too much to bear; and as I have said, if I had not had the company of *Miranda* on some of these excursions to the centres of French History of Art, I do believe I would have fallen sooner, from pure Despair. As it was, *Miranda* accompanied me solely out of Pity, for she was studying *La Civilisation Française* at the Sorbonne and might well have suffered serious reprimands from the Professors if she had been found to be Missing. Yet she too had a Sadness which she liked to speak of; and which for her was a fear of the Future, whereas my sorrow belonged to the Past, to having lost Lord E— and my feelings of unassuageable Grief. *'Robina,' says she* as we are standing by a great rosy canvas of Naked Nymphs sporting themselves in green fields, deep in the Heart of the *Louvre* and yet far from safe from the *Comte*, whom I thought I had seen already lurking by the *Venus de Milo* as *Miranda* and I climbed the stairs, 'I have decided to Run Away.' And she asked me very piteously if I would come with her to *Brussels*, where we could both hide from the fate that Future had in store for us. 'The *Comte* will snare you in the end,' *says* the poor Creature, who seemed as terrified for me, I must say, as for herself. 'And I shall have to go home to London, where my stepfather has said I must have a Ball.' And here the poor Girl burst out crying, so that a Guard of the Paintings came by and looked curiously at us, in wonder that we should be so moved by these Nude Women, unless it was the Case that we were *Lesbians*. 'A Ball?' *say I*, for I knew nothing then of these things and had been brought up very quiet and proper by my Aunt, as I have told. 'I shall be forced to Come Out,' *says she* and begins to weep again in a most heart-rending way. *'Come Out?' say I*, still in Astonishment, and wondering too why coming out of something should be bad, particularly if it were Prison, when Going In would be a good-deal Worse. 'I am too Shy,' *says she*, and she then says we must all Curtsy in Full View to her Majesty; that we must then face at our own Balls at least four hundred people, all of them Strangers, and that we are expected to go to the Races too, and be seen by the Multitude as we go to and fro. 'I'd rather die,' *says she*, and she goes on to say that she has a little money of her own, for her mother, who married her stepfather a strict City Man, is generous (and I am sorry to say here that my spirits rose when I heard this, for my five pounds had all but gone, and it only came to me slowly to conjecture that the *Comte*, in changing my Scotch Note, had

Short-Changed me, and all in order to get me hungry the quicker, which was certainly the case). 'What would we do in *Brussels*?' *say I*. 'There's a Cousin of mine attached to the Embassy there,' *says she*, and looked up at me with her great eyes; and as we had moved into another gallery by now and were standing by the paintings of *Greuze*, I couldn't help but see how like a Girl by Greuze my friend *Miranda* was, which is to say very touching and gentle, but unfortunately not tempting to such members of the Gallic Race as the *Comte*, who now appeared from behind a Pillar and echoed my very thoughts, by complimenting Miranda on her likeness to one of the portraits on the wall. 'Not like *Robina*,' *says he*, and I do not speak too rudely of him when I say that he smacked his lips as he spoke. 'I have seen you at the *Bouchers*,' *says he* and he laughs in a meaning way. 'And in the *Salle de Bain*,' he adds without batting an eyelid, while my friend and I found our colour going up and our knees weak at the Idea of the Depravity of M. de B— looking through the keyhole at his Wife's Charges in the Bath. 'You will kindly leave us,' *say I* very cold, but the *Comte* only liked this the more, as I since discovered Sportsmen do, and seized my arm, entreating *Les Demoiselles* to join him at a fine restaurant; and although I was famished and my mouth watered so that anyone could see it, I was determined to refuse; knowing by now, it was true, that *Miranda* had some francs and that we might at least eat that day. For I can say no more on the subject of the food at the *Comtesse de B—'s* in Passy but that the Portions diminished daily, as if *Mme de B—*, on resolving to Save, would do so in no half-hearted manner. Our slices of Bread, ragged as they were, had shrunk to one in the morning and one at night; the soup was watered so that the shred of carrot or potato it had once contained was no longer palpable at all; and we saw neither meat nor fish except on Fridays when there was a small piece of Hake boiled and served without Sauce. We were supposed, no doubt, to receive a large Allowance from Home to supplement these Rations; but I for one could hardly approach my Aunt and Uncle for Funds, which reticence hardly needs explaining. So it was no doubt that the *Comte* found his Victims suppliant, for Hunger will remove all traces of Dignity; yet, relying on the kindness of *Miranda*, I refused the wretched *Voyeur* and we went off together to the *Champs Elysées* to eat cheaply in a *Snack Bar* which also happened to be near a Picture House where we aimed to amuse ourselves for the rest of the Afternoon.

*

Trouble has often come to me without my knowing the Reason; yet I do believe that if I had been permitted by my kind Hosts to study French History of Art, this being the Cause of my Stay in Paris, I would have gone through Life in a less troublesome way: Qualified for Serious Work (for it was always in my Nature that I loved to go deep in some Subject, and learn its Mysteries) rather than a Prey both to Men's Emotions and my Own, and continually searching for Love (although it does also seem to me that this Path might have been chosen for me at Birth, whether I studied or not). However that may be, I was soon to find myself in very great Trouble indeed, and this was because *Miranda*, saying to *Mme de B—* that she was going for a few days to visit her Cousins at the Embassy at *Brussels*, decamped altogether, and there was no longer a friend in the world for me, to frighten away the *Comte* when he was standing outside my Bedroom Door or to lend me Francs so that I could eat.

Paris was very cold, too, at that time, and the *Comtesse* remarked often that Spring would never come, which I must say I thought she did from pure Viciousness, for as she made these remarks she cut down severely also on the food and even the Hot Water, so that it was no longer possible to have a Bath, a fact which I bemoaned less than I would have done before I knew that *M. de B—* had a secret Spyhole on to our Naked Bodies. The soup, as I say, became now pure water and the Bread vanished altogether, to be replaced by *tartines* which were as small as postage stamps, and many nights I cried myself to sleep, wishing I had gone with *Miranda* to her

Cousins and had not been so much afraid of my Aunt and Uncle that I dared not, for fear they would put some punishment even more Awful on me, which they had every right to do, as Trustees. At last came the day when Hunger kept me at home, for I was too cold and weak to attend the course on French History of Art at the *École du Louvre*, and there need be no doubt in any mind that *M. de B—* would take full advantage of this State of Affairs to let himself into my room with his Skeleton Key when the *Comtesse* was out at her Bargain-buying, and sit on the end of my bed with a Bag of Buns and Éclairs in his hand. '*Robina*,' *says he* (in French, which alas I could understand only too well by then), 'I have bought you some charming little *pâtisseries*,' etc.; and I can truly say that in all the years when I have known the Real Love of men and received their gifts of jewels with pleasure and delight, I have never in my Life desired anything so much as those *Petits Pains*. 'You shall have them for a Kiss,' *says the Comte* and laid the Bag on my Bedside Table, where the edge of the Icing of a Coffee Éclair peeped out at me. Had it occurred to me then that the *Comte* and *Comtesse* planned this sort of charade together, so that the Victim, falling into the Clutches of the *Comte* from sheer Hunger, was in some way bringing Happiness to the Ménage, I should have been more acquainted with the Ways of the World than I was; and yet I will never know for certain if this was the Case, only that I know now that the Vices and Depravity of the Gallic Members of the Nobility are without number. 'I will show you a French Kiss,' *says the Comte* now in English, which would have brought on Laughter if I had not been ill, famished and in Danger, as I well knew. The *Comte* then thrust his tongue in my Mouth, all of which I am ashamed to relate, except as a warning to Young Girls if they should find themselves in Paris, in a Family. It being impossible to cry out, my Teeth were forced to resort to Biting; and the *Comte* withdrew his Tongue hastily. 'You are too hungry for this,' *says he* and he pulls me down on the bed, but at the same time pulling the bag towards me so that the éclair was in my hand and before I knew how it could have happened, in my mouth as well, where the the fresh, light Pastry and sweet coffee cream were met with feelings of great Ecstasy. 'And you will find a *Pain au Chocolat*,' says M. De B—, who was now sitting on the bed with his hand on my knee. And if I can be understood only by one who has suffered the extreme Deprivation of Hunger in the Capital of Fine Fare, that is how it will be, for I must say that I lay quite contented on the bed eating the *pâtisseries* and only when the Last Crumb had gone did I come to my Senses and see that the *Comte* had moved down the bed and was licking my feet, which was all he appeared to want in return and had no intention of stopping.

*

All this went on for several days, and it is true if regrettable to say that the more I dreaded the visits of the *Comte* and his Hairy Hands holding a bag of the latest *tarte aux pommes* or *mille feuilles*, the more insensate with greed I became; so it seemed an Act of Providence indeed when one morning a Letter arrived from my Uncle and Aunt, announcing their imminent arrival in *Paris* to visit me. Although I knew I could never confide in my Aunt on the Habits of the *Comte* I thought I could beg my Uncle, on the pretext I was ill with Unhappiness, to take me home again; for he had a kind Heart. Also, A Traveller's Cheque for twenty pounds accompanied the Letter; and I will swear to this day that in my great agitation to get away from my Gaoler, *M. de B—*, and his terrible Bribes, I could not have read the purport of the Letter, which was that this Cheque was to be kept carefully by me until the arrival of my Aunt and Uncle in a Hotel near the *Madeleine* and that the reason I was to guard it so carefully was that Currency Regulations were strict and my kind Guardians would not have enough to Pay the Bill without it.

Whatever the Blindness that seized me over all this, I had no Choice, as it seemed then, other than to spend the twenty

71

pounds on feeding myself and thus on being able to repulse the Advances of the *Comte*, which I did; to his Anger and Surprise, it must be said, for he thought, no doubt, that he had me secure in his Grasp. The *Comtesse*, on hearing of the proposed Visit, went out and bought Veal for the dinner my Aunt and Uncle would attend, which made me smile too, for I was beginning only then to learn the Hypocrisy of the Nobility; yet, as it happened, there was no Dinner Party in the end, and *Mme de B*— and her husband and the other miserable Girls lodging there must have eaten quite unexpectedly that night. For my Uncle, when I arrived at the Hotel where they were staying, on asking me for the Traveller's Cheque and being told it was Spent, flew into a Towering Rage. 'This is intolerable,' *cried he*, 'we will return to London instantly.' '*Robina*,' *cried* my poor Aunt, who had just a moment before said that she looked forward greatly to visiting the *Bon Marché*, 'how could you do this?' And so on, while my Uncle, who, far from understanding my Unhappiness, had lifted his Fist, which was Purple and Large above his Head, and rushed from the Room, only to find that he had run into le W.C. and must come straight out again. 'We are sunk,' *says* my Uncle when he was calmer; and he told me to go home and pack and he would pick me up on the way to the *Gare du Nord*, which he did. 'You will be in London earlier than was thought,' *says* my Aunt, 'but you can get ready there, *Robina*, for your Coming Out.'

*

If the flat to which I was taken by my Aunt and Uncle was any different from the house of M. and Mme de B— in *Paris*, it was only in size and shape; for while corridors were lower and rooms smaller, and there were *sofas* and chintz once more, the same Smell, as I have mentioned before, of a *Gratin* that made up to be as much as a Meal, and of Parsimony and Ill-Working Water Heaters, made themselves apparent immediately; and so Low were my Spirits on finding myself in this manner in *London*, of which I had so often dreamed, that I swore then that I would find a Way Out: and it was this Desire for Beauty and Comfort, I do believe, that led me in the end into Trouble. The woman who would be my chaperone for the Season, a Lady S— of B—, was as threadbare as her Flat: 'She will make up the Lists for you,' *says* my Aunt, and on my asking what these might be, my Aunt says that I am on a List and I shall have a List of my own, for my Ball, which will be at the H— P— Hotel, on account of Lady S— of B— having so poor a Flat, where it would be hard, on account of the Lack of Amenities, for her even to give a Dinner First. 'We shall give it for you,' *says* my Aunt, while Lady S— of B— sat with her hands folded in her lap, and not before putting away in her Bag another Large Bundle of Notes given by my Aunt and intended no doubt for my Keep. My sense of Injustice, which I will say grew at the same rate as my Love of Beauty and Happiness, was affronted by this, but I was still powerless, for my Trust, as always, lay in the governance of my Uncle and Aunt. When I heard of this Ball and all the Expense it would incur I begged my Aunt in the presence of Lady S— of B— to let me study History of Art instead; but it was as if I hadn't been heard; and soon two miserable Girls came in, as Dull to me as the Girls in *Paris* had been; and to make Matters Worse I was then informed I must share a Room with both of them, because of the extreme Shortage of Space in the Flat. 'Lady S— of B— is a practised Bringer-Out,' *says* my Aunt when the Poor Woman had gone to greet the other Parents, and certainly to Fleece them too. 'We live too far away to make a List for you,' etc. etc. until I had to come to understand that Lady S— of B—, for all her Greasy Clothes and Hair on the Upper Lip, had Connections and would present me at Court, which she, my Aunt, couldn't do as she had not been Presented herself, though this last was said with a certain Pride, for my Aunt was pleased to belong to the Church of Scotland, which shows no obeisance to the Queen. 'I know a Little Woman a few Streets from here who Runs Up dresses,' *says* my Aunt, and all the while she looked at me so pleadingly that I came to see that all her Scheme of the World, which she shared with my Uncle and with all who knew her, would go awry if I didn't do as she said: viz. invest my own Money in the Catching of a Rich Husband, for this was the aim of the Season. None of this was so much as Said but I knew it more and more and with a further Lowering of the Spirits, and I saw then too that the extreme Discomfort of the Flat would drive a Girl into the arms of any Husband who had a reasonable income and could provide Privacy and Hot Water at least. All this I saw while agreeing with my Aunt to visit the Little Woman with her without delay; and the more I saw of it, the more I determined to break out of it, even if I should go on the Streets (of which I had no idea, as may be imagined) or lead a Life of Crime instead. 'I'm off to my Club,' *says* my Uncle, who had been present at our first meeting with the Titled Lady who would steer me through the Season. And he came up and pinched my cheeks and said I would be the Belle of the Ball and many other foolish jokes, for my Uncle had forgiven me my Spending in *Paris* and I honestly think had no Ambitions for me to be a Duchess at the end of the Season, or some such thing, but wished me only to Enjoy Myself, for which I was exceedingly grateful. Lady S— of B— then came in and said there would be a Cold Meat Salad for lunch, and my Uncle fled; but not before pressing some of his Scotch Notes in my hand and saying I and my Aunt should go and eat in a Restaurant, to make up for the tiring Fittings, and so on; then we were left to make our own way out.

Never was a Harder Time had than that between me and my Aunt when it came to Clothes, and I wished then that I had run off down the street and never gone into the Little Woman's Flat, for I was on the one hand fainting with Hunger and on the other hand quite Opposed to all my Aunt's ideas of Dresses, which, coming close after the *Circular Skirt* and *Off-the-Shoulder Top*, appeared all the more Unacceptable to me. 'You'll need two Ball Dresses,' *says she* and the Little Woman agreed with this, although her mouth was full with Pins and she was incapable of replying. Indeed, there was no Replying to my Aunt's strictures, which were that my first Ball Dress should be of white Net (and this was fastened on me soon by the Little Woman) and should have a row of Artificial Roses on the bosom and another Row on the Behind, so that I would look like some kind of walking Hedge (and my Aunt had not considered that these Borders of Roses would hinder any Dancing Partner from clasping me, nor that I would be unable to Sit Down, for fear of crushing the posterior Arrangement, and would thus spend long hours standing at the Bar; but it may be that my Aunt did things without knowing why she did them, which I have since learnt is common with the *Scotch Calvinists*, that their Real Thoughts and Desires have been forced down in them and come out only in surprising ways). However that may be, I was soon pinned fore and Rear with these accursed Roses, and the Little Woman then brought forward the Plan for my other Dress (for it was coming clear my Aunt worked all this out in advance with her and had decided beyond any question of Doubt how best to spend the money that was rightfully mine). This second dress was of silk tartan, which was our Clan Tartan, *says* my Aunt, even though we are Lowlanders and she considers it to be Common, particularly as my Elder Uncle has draped it all over his house, or so she has heard. 'Please tell me about this Uncle,' *say I*, for it may well be understood that as this was the first time my Aunt had spoken of him I was excited to hear more and imagined she had Brought Up his Name in order to tell me. I went on to say that everyone I met was extremely intrigued by him and he was very Rich, so I'd heard, at which my Aunt frowned frightfully, darting looks of Great Meaning at the Little Woman, as if to say she now expected the Bill for the Dresses to go up by one hundred per cent. 'Where is his house?' *say I* and so on, but to no avail, and soon I was quiet again, but had resolved to find this Uncle, and all the while pretending to help with the pinning of a bunch of Parma Violets on the shoulderstrap of the Dress's Bodice. 'He sent the silk tartan,' *says* my Aunt, for she wished to show, evidently, that she

75

had not Laid Out herself for silk and that Net was as far as she would go. But this indiscretion of my Aunt's was to cost her far more Dear than if she had kept silent, for I knew now that my Elder Uncle was interested in my Progress through Life; that I was conceivably within a hair's breadth of an Exciting Life (for all the Girls at *Mlle Weiss*'s said that my Uncle's Elder Brother was often at *Court*, or going to Balls in *Venice* and was known at the *Casino* in *Monte Carlo*, and that my Family in comparison must be Dim, which I now saw they were). So for the first time I learned to DISSEMBLE and I told my Aunt that I was very happy with the Dresses, and also with a Coat and Skirt that was too Dreadful for description, in order to pursue my Plan. And I hoped too that when I had found this Paragon of Excitement I would be bound to hear more of my own Father and Mother from him: – as I have said, my Aunt and Uncle were Obstinate in the extreme and would never tell me a word of them, or whether they might even be Dead or Alive. So I lasted out the Fitting in great Impatience, of which I gave no sign whatever; and, as was to occur so often in my Life, under the Illusion that I would find Happiness myself, and bring it to Others too (in this case my Parents) if they could be discovered. But, as we shall see, the finding of my Elder Uncle in the first place was far from Easy.

*

I shall say no more of the beginning of the Season, than that Lady S— of B— informed us we should prepare ourselves for QUEEN CHARLOTTE's Ball, where we must wear White and do our Obeisance to a Cake, which would be carried in; and that this ceremony opened the Season; and we would then be Out; and that we couldn't on any account take separate Cabs home as this would cut into the Expenses paid out by our Guardians or Parents: indeed that we should at all times contrive to go-home together, for there was a List among the many Lists presented to us by Lady S— of B— which had the name NSIT and was of those Young-Men who were known to be Not Safe in Taxis; though whether the chance of these

Young-Men paying the Fare would soften the Chaperone's Heart was never clear. Of the other Lists, as may be imagined, there was no trace of Lord E— for whose name I scanned in hope that some Ball or other would bring us together again; and this was because his Engagement was already announced to *Lady Malvina*, as one of the Girls at the Flat told me (for I had great difficulty in forbearing to say his name, Love being then as it has since remained, a Chief Preoccupation with me). 'He was struck off the List weeks ago,' *says* the Girl, whose name was *Stella*, and very bold and brash she turned out to be, while the other Girl was Mousy. 'Lady S— of B— is most annoyed when a *Viscount* or young *Marquess* thinks to announce his Engagement before the start of the Season, and all the Dinners have to be replanned.' Then *Stella* goes on without seeing my Blushes, that there is a Tradition at the Ball we are all to attend tomorrow and I must do what she says, which I am sorry to say I did, but only for lack of Support in this great City where I had neither family nor friends, nor any-one to give me kindness and Cheer. 'Here is a mouse,' *says Stella* and the wretched Girl took a white mouse from a box with a ringing Laugh that would have brought in Lady S— of B— had she not been Resting after the midday *Gratin*. 'O *Robina* – come, come!' – when I jumped on a chair and let out a Scream, for the mouse was running between the beds quite bewildered – 'we'll let it out at the Ball,' *says Stella*, 'for it's done every year and this year I was chosen.' 'But by whom?' *say I*, for it seemed Lady S— of B— would have little to gain from releasing a mouse in the skirts of her *protégées*, the fleeing and hubbub that followed very likely causing Repairs to be needed, and all these taken from the Allowances made by our Protectors and Kin. 'By some of the Girls who are In the Know,' *says Stella* and then says no more, so I have to hear my Instructions without Complaint; and, as hardly needs describing, to hear myself the One who must let out the Mouse, while *Stella* distracts the gaze of the Crowd elsewhere.

How many times in the next Night and Day I prayed

myself back in *Oxford* where all my Happiness in Learning
and my Love of French *History of Art* first came to Light, need
not be told. I cursed the wickedness of *Annie* and Prince P—;
I wept at the thought of my poor Aunt Laying Out so much
for my Dresses and for a Ball I had no Longing for; and yet I
could think of no other way than to obey *Stella*, for I could
hardly go to Lady S— of B— with the Tale, when I had *Stella*
as my Room Mate all summer and right up to the time of
Henley Regatta. My despair brought on this Sadness again,
that I could be in the Northern Castle, had not things been
wrong for me on account of my Youth (for the fact I wasn't
yet Out had weighed heavily against me with the *Countess*, I
was aware) and that I was instead a Prey to a Mouse, which
snuffled all night long in the Shoebox by our beds and must
be tucked away when the other Girl came in, for although
she was known as Mousy (or was thus summed-up by my
Uncle on his Visit to the Flat) she would have found little
affinity with the animal and might go to Lady S— of B—. It
was with such trivial and Desperate thoughts that I passed
the hours, and it may truthfully be said that when it came to
be time to go-to the Ball my Eyelids were dropping from Lack
of Sleep. I dreamed only of Escape, yet 'Hurry along *Robina*,'
says Lady S— of B— as we set off for the Dinner First that
was to be at the Flat of another impoverished Member of the
Nobility forced to Take In Girls; and I must run with the Box
under my Aunt's *Fur Coat* (for it was a Spring Evening and
still Chilly). How I suffered the Dinner, knowing the Mouse
to be in the Hostess's Bedroom in a Pile of Coats, hardly
needs telling; yet it may be that to be Distracted was good
Fortune indeed, for the Dinner was very poor to Taste and
was the first time I was served a Ball of Fish in a white Sauce
that was called *Sole Dugléré*; this Dish then appearing on
every Card at Balls and Dinners in the Season, whether
because it was Cod and a way had been learned to tie it up to
look like Sole or for whatever other Reason of Economy
cannot be known. The Conversation, at any rate, was very
Slow, and, once having turned on the subject of my Elder

Uncle and away again at my saying I had no Knowledge of him, faltered and died down altogether. Yet even the Name of my Elder Uncle failed to arouse me to search for him by the time the Night was out, on account of the Mouse; and I was hardly to know that I would lose the one and find the other before the Night was out, Luck as I have often observed in my Life having the Property of taking away with one Hand at the same time as the other is busy Providing.

*

We were Two Hours At Least at the Dinner, with all of my Thoughts on the Damage that might be done in the Hostess's Bedroom, and with the Host himself exceedingly absent-minded: 'Tell me, my dear,' *says he* to me, 'have you dusted the pictures today?' and on me telling him I hadn't, for the reason I didn't live there, etc. the poor old *General*, for such he was, became very confused; yet I was uneasy, for I knew the ways of Old Gentlemen after my stay in *Oxford* in *The High* and suspected him, quite rightly as it was to prove. 'You'll stand on the sideboard to dust that particularly lovely picture,' *says* the Old-Man, showing with his hand a Dull picture of Cows in a field and as I knew from my Studies in History of Art, very likely *Dutch*. 'I can see the dust on the picture from here,' *says he*, his voice shaking now and all the other Young People from Society beginning to laugh; while Lady S— of B— looked extremely displeased. 'Stand on the sideboard,' *says the General* now with great feeling, so I almost felt sorry for him; and had not my thoughts been on the Mouse, which I thought must by now have eaten through the Shoebox I would have gone and climbed on the sideboard, to break the Boredom of the Dinner, if nothing more. 'He wants to look up your skirt,' *says Stella* in a Loud Whisper, for we were of course divided by a Young-Man, who was Chinless and thus easy to talk Across. 'He thinks you're the maid; we've all heard of his tricks,' and when I whispered back, but with great discomfiture as all the other Guests and the Hostess herself were listening to us, that I wondered how

79

Stella knew this: 'The Girls in the Know,' *says she* as before and I was none the wiser for it. By now, however, the *General*'s foot was pressing against mine painfully, and on seeing my face the wicked *Stella* burst out laughing and says she has bribed Lady S— of B— to give me this seat; while all the others *hum* and *haw* and make a great show of getting down the *Sole Dugléré*, which was difficult indeed. If *Stella* had stayed in my Life as long, even as *Annie* did (alas I wasn't to know then that I hadn't seen the last of that Fiend) I would most certainly have gone North to my Uncle and prayed for Peace; but Fortune was to rescue me from her Teasing Ways, as we shall see.

If Dinner was long in the Passing, then my Discovery of the Mouse, as may be imagined, was as short as the poor Animal's Life, for when we went to the Bedroom for our Capes it was found to be Dead, having died from the Exertions, as must be presumed, of biting through the Shoebox and into the sleeve of my Aunt's *Fur Coat*, where a round Hole now was. To describe the suffering of the Animal would be to provoke Anger in those who, rightly, love Animals; to describe my own Suffering over its disposal and the annoyance of *Stella* at its going at so unfortunate a moment, would appear heartless. It remains only for me to say that the Ball was as dull as the Dinner had been; that I saw no Man or Girl with whom I could have exchanged a Word and that there was no-one Lively, as there had been at *Oxford*: in short, I was glad to go-home, and felt as much of a Fool for having curtseyed to a Cake as if I had found myself on a Desert Island and become a Cannibal. But even in my Desire to share a Cab with Lady S— of B— and seize some sleep before my tormentor *Stella* should return with more Recriminations over the Rodent, I was to be Thwarted, for the Line for Capes was long and the venerable Lady disappeared, having looked for me in vain I suppose, and I was bound to use some of the exceedingly small Allowance with which I had been entrusted for the Season, in paying a Cab to take me home alone. The dejected Sight I made needs no describing; for the Roses on my Bust and Behind had drooped in the course of the miserable Ball and I stood like a Hedge when it has Rained and quite ignored by the Doorman, who showed no Kindness to me in the matter of getting home.

That this may all have been a part of Fortune's strange Wheelings I will now conjoin; at the time I felt only utter Hopelessness, and a Half of me thinking I would take the Cab to *St Pancras* and go North, except at the idea of seeing my poor Aunt's face. But, for all of the Disappointments of the Dress I must have seemed, to some at least, a Worldly Girl and a Pretty one, too, for a Car stopped by the Steps and a voice called that I should get in and I would be given a Lift; and on my squeezing in the Back Seat I saw I was with a party of Young Blades, who were roaring Drunk and in High Spirits and who told me with a great deal of laughing that we were off to the *Bag O' Nails*, the very Saying of which Convulsed them all the more, except for myself, who knew nothing of the place and kept Silent. For I must own I didn't have the Courage to demand the Lift Home which had at first been Offered; and there lies in me too a constant Desire for Adventure, which these roistering Young-Men may have seen, despite the Roses that hung so forlornly round me.

*

I must Confess to an Agreeable Surprise when going-in to the *Bag O' Nails* for here all was Dark and lit with Dim Red Lights (whereas the Marquees of these wretched Balls were always white and brightly lit) and also I must confess that here I was seen as Pretty, with all Heads turning as I went in, etc. while at the Ball no one had thought to ask me to dance: this I came to see was a peculiarity of Lady S— of B—, that she took Money to Bring out Girls but then saw fit to Introduce them to no one; and as the Pretty, Ambitious ones such as *Stella* made all-out for the LORDS and the Heiresses were courted for their Fortunes with little Attention to their looks, I was as it were between two Stools: being neither Ambitious for a Husband (for I still mourned the loss of Lord

81

E—) nor known for my Name which Lady S— of B— neglected to give out, so I must then find myself in an Awkward Position, where I had rather be Chased for my imagined Fortune than not Chased at-all. Here in the *Bag O' Nails* however, a Loud Talking started up as soon as I had Sat Down with my Party at a Table by the Wall; and I was soon gratified to be asked to Dance by a Young-Man, very tall and with a head as thin as a Bird but not bad-looking for all that, and with a very amiable Smile. '*Robina,' says* the Leader of the Young-Men with whom I had come-in (for I had told them this Name and no Other) 'if you go and dance away from us we shall have to ask over the Girls' – and so saying and laughing without stopping, they waved to Girls who sat alone together at a Table in the Back and who I at first thought to be *Wallflowers*. But I was to find, in this world of the *Bag O' Nails* that the real World was as in a Mirror to it; for all that was thought to be Good in the World was held to be Bad here; and *vice versa*. These Girls, as I soon saw when they Came Over, wanted only Instant Money from the Young-Men rather than the Meal Ticket for Life expected by the débutantes at the Ball; and though they would give their Services to the Customers they were to give also a great-deal of their Wages to the *Manager*, for I saw this Gentleman speak to them before they came and then again when they were sitting with us, asking in a sharp way if another Bottle of Champagne had been ordered, and Charging £3 for a Tea-Cup full of Whisky, which complied with some strange Law of which only he knew; but was certainly a great-deal of Money in those days. 'I am *Fiona,' says* one of the Girls; and the other says she is *Jean*, at which the Roisterers laughed again like Fools, which they certainly were, for they were too Drunk to see the Manager and the Hostesses, as they were called, were Fleecing them. As I have said, it Puzzled me at-first to hear these Women (for such Close Up they proved to be) called *Hostesses*; but as I was to learn the World was Upside-Down here, and as Lady S— of B— was no more of a *Hostess* than they, despite the engraved card which proclaimed her *At Home* at the H— P— Hotel for her *protégées*, I determined to put the whole Matter out of my mind and enjoy the Dancing.

Whether it was because I looked back with such grief and fondness to my Native Land or because the Tall Young Man was a fine Dancer, I don't know; but soon we had the Floor to ourselves and a Cheering went up as we danced a *Scottische* very Fast and with elegance. I must say I have always liked the Admiring eyes of Others on me, and as all that impeded a Dance of a very High Degree of Excellence was my Dress, I soon had a knife from one of the Tables and had slashed the skirts off up to the Knee, to great Laughter and Applause. I daresay the row of Roses Behind looked all the more Absurd now, yet I heard Approval in the Cheering and not Ridicule and on we went, faster and faster, until we were so Out of Breath that we must fall on a Bench, most of the Customers by now standing to Applaud, and particularly strongly at the Back, where a new Party had come in and there was a great Bustle of Waiters and Napkins and Silver Buckets and Tea Cups of Whisky and the Like. 'We'll dance round the World,' *says* my Partner, when he can get out a Word; and seizing my Hand he told me we were Made for Each Other and should go to *Paris* at-once to show our skills, 'where they like Dancing,' *he says*; and then goes on to give the name of the House he is from, which is L—, one of the Great Houses in the Country, and he is C—, or rather Lord C— M—, as he is the younger son of the old *Marquess*, whose Seat this is. 'You shall come down for the Birthday Celebrations,' *says* Lord C—, and he says we shall Dance there, for it is his brother's *twenty-firster* and we shall all go on until Dawn, etc. Here I must say I was glad to be called back by my first Escorts to their Table, for Lord C—, although sweet by Nature and as fine as an Eagle to look at, had also the Brain of a Bird: in short, he was almost Idiotic; and I feared that he would think himself about to Marry me when I had given him no Promises of any kind. 'This is *Amanda*,' *say* my Drunken Companions of a Third Woman who has Come-over to them; 'she is

Mandy,' they go on with much Laughing and Slamming of their Fists on the TableCloth, until a very Loud Voice came out at us and Prayed Silence for the *Cabaret*, which was nothing more than a Comedian making Coarse Jokes, which were however greeted with Gales of Laughter; and in this time Lord C— M— had crept up to our Table and joined us, so that Fisticuffs broke out between him and the Young-Men, as I had feared they would. 'Hush,' *say Fiona* and *Jean* and *Mandy* very agitated at the Skirmishing; 'Take Care!' *says* Mandy, 'The *Prince* is here!'

It is hard for me to describe the effect this information had on my New Friends (for I was without friends, remember, since leaving *Oxford* and would take any-one as a Friend who was Kind to me) for it had no effect at all, whereas I, who had never seen a Member of the *Royal Family* in the Flesh, must Peer over the Heads of Others to see the Table at the Back, where it seemed this Personage was Sitting. As I recalled the Flurry of that Party coming in while I was dancing, my Blood was up that I had been seen by a Royal Prince at my most *Wild* and *Capricious*; yet I thought I could come to no Harm for it; and indeed this was to prove True, but in Another Way to the Way I then supposed. 'We don't give a Fig for the Monarchy,' *says* Lord C—; and he says they are HANOVERIANS and very *Common*, and of recent Descent Compared with his own Family, all of which I daresay was true but appeared to me to be Cheeky and to be yet another example of the Foolishness of Lord C—, for more People would Turn Out to Cheer the *Sovereign* than would Stand on a Chair for the old *Marquess*, and that was for Sure.

*

If I leave out some of the Rest of that Night it is for Reasons of Discretion, which I hope has always been mine when Trouble was near and could in any way be Circumvented. Let it only be said that my Companions were bent on going up to a Suite of Rooms above the *Bag O' Nails*; that they prevailed on me to go-up with them; and then were followed by the

Hostesses, who were, as it soon appeared, At-Home up there if nowhere else, for they had their Dresses Off and were standing in their Knickers before the Door was shut; and still more People trying to put their Heads round it.

I soon saw my Situation was perilous indeed. *Fiona* and *Mandy* Clasped the Necks of two of the Young Blades, and called to me to take a Third; there was Loud Merriment; and to make Matters Worse the Lights went out, as I had known once before at *Mlle Weiss*'s and with no Happy Results. I wished for Lord C— M—, who was at least a Gentleman; and forgave my poor Aunt all her Economies if she would Rescue me from the Grasp that had already now gone round my Waist; while the Roses were pulled in no uncertain Fashion from my Behind and at-least Four Hands went up after them: 'Are there Thorns there?' *cries* one voice, very Merry, which Voice I hadn't heard before and yet I thought I knew, which made the Darkness and the Assault all the more Eerie. Soon my Knickers were pulled off; and this time I'm sorry to say with the Aid of the Hostesses, who, finding No Doubt that I was the most interesting Prey of the Evening, were willing to earn their Salary without too much Effort, for it was less Tiring to disrobe an Innocent Girl like myself than to Succumb to the embraces of these young-men, Badly Bred as I could now (but Too Late) perceive they were.

Discretion, as I have said, must keep me back from telling of the Fingers that then Probed and Pinched me; and Certainly, in the Darkness, a Hard Object, such as I had felt at G— Castle, came Close to Rupturing me; but, 'She's a Virgin, my God!' *cried* this same Voice I thought I had heard before in my Life; and there was a Pulling-back: then, 'I never knew they took in Maidens in the Bag, eh?' and Coarse Laughter, but I was at-least Left Alone now and on the Floor, with the White Net of my Dress up above my Shoulders and the Roses on the Bosom quite Trampled as if a Herd of Cows had walked over them, all of which brought me the Remorse that I have too often, alas, suffered at the Last Moment so there was Nothing to Do when it came to making Repairs, which were clearly impossible. For I had thought, even when I cut the Dress up to the Knee, that I would do the Hem and it would do-well as a Short Dress; yet now it was Ruined, and I couldn't Restrain myself from Weeping: at the Bad Company where I found myself (for the Drunken Young-Men, having lost their Sport with me were now Plunged into the *Hostesses*) and groaning and Moaning came from all round that made my Shame all the greater, that I had not found Lady S— of B— to go-home as I should, and so had missed the Dangers of NSIT.

My weeping, however, brought a Kind Voice, as I was to find so often in My Life, that Rage will be mistaken in a Woman for Remorse and Tears much Applauded: 'My poor Girl,' *says* the Voice, 'we must Look After you.' And then, as I have said, I shall Keep Silence, for the Lights went on and we were all in Disarray, with the Manager saying it was time to-go; and with no Respect in him that I could hear for the Royal Personage, for such it was, who had tried (and successfully) to Save my Virginity, and whose Voice I had heard addressing the Nation. I will only say that Lord C— M— who had searched in vain for the Room we were all in (having mistaken the Back Stairs for the Main Entrance and been wandering about a good Half-Hour on Landings) then came in and stood staring at us; and I begged him to take me Home for I knew I could come to no Harm with him; yet he, thinking he had missed all the Fun, and seeing the Revellers buttoning themselves up, opened his Fly with a Whoop of Joy, at which we all fell Giggling, for it appeared there was Nothing There, or at-least that Lord C— M— had misplaced it, for he Fumbled like a Conjuror who has lost his Rabbit: 'Damn it,' *says he* and as we were all restored to Good Humour and laughing we went down to the Dance Floor again, where all was Closed for the Night, and if it had not been for Lord C— M—'s Futile Search, which I was sad to see, the Royal Party would not have gone before I had time to catch another Glimpse of my Saviour.

Yet Fortune, who had held back from me a long time now,

showed her Face once more that Night; for as I left with Lord
C— M— and we saw Dawn was breaking and one cab in
Regent Street coming our Way, I heard the Head Waiter
behind me remark on the Royal Party and in particular on the
Host that evening, who had my Name so that I started and
the Blood came up in my face; for I knew now that my Elder
Uncle had been one of the Party, and had indeed Paid for it.

The Reader need not try to think of my Emotions at this
News: viz. that Lord C— M—'s Missing Member was the
Cause of my Losing the Subject of my Quest, when I had
been so near to Catching him (and there was no doubt of my
Uncle's Generosity for: 'He tips better than Royalty,' *says* a
young Waiter to the Head Waiter as we all go out into the
street and Lord C— M— Flags down the Cab, for which I had
none the less to Pay, for Lord C— M— was as Broke, as I was
to discover, as if he suffered from a congenital Disease
despite, as he said, the Estate at L— being Worth Fourteen
Million Pounds Sterling, but this I was often to find with the
Nobility). My Pique was all the greater, that I could have
been Twice Saved in the course of that Evening and counted
Myself Lucky, first to have made the Acquaintance of a *Royal
Prince* and second, to be Rescued from my Poverty and
Unhappiness by my Elder Uncle, who would be Kind to me
indeed, I now knew, after his Reputation as a Tipper. My
Resolve, also, needs little describing, for an early Escape from
my Present Circumstances; and in particular when I say that
when I returned to Lady S— of B—'s and went into the Room
I must share with two Other Girls, the hard-hearted *Stella*
had put a Toy Mouse on my Pillow, so that I must scream,
thinking she had found the corpse of the Mouse I had earlier
disposed of; and she woke, as did the Mousy Girl, while
Stella upbraided me: 'You ruined the Ball,' *says she*, 'and I
have told everyone it's your Fault,' and other Cruel Remarks,
so that I wept again at the outcome of my First Evening; and
must then Console myself with the Thought that I was glad
indeed to have Caught Sight of my Elder Uncle (although I
wasn't sure which of the Royal Party he had been); that it

was better that the real Mouse was Lost than if it had been Running About, as it had last night; and that my Kind Relative was surely about to be Found by me.

*

If I stop only a short time at my season at Lady S— of B—'s, it is because the time was Unfortunate for me; and I have known much kindness and Happiness in my Life, so that the Days when I was Sorely in Need are best Forgotten; unless an Account is to serve as a Warning to the Parents and Guardians who give over their Daughters into such Uncertain Hands. For it was soon clear that Lady S— of B— was without a Home in many Ways: she was not *At Home* at the H— P— Hotel, it was True; nor was she *At Home* in the Flat, which was clear to us-all on the Occasion of the Bailiffs visiting and saying they would Eject her if the Rent wasn't paid At Once; and all this, as *Stella* told me, was caused by Drink: 'I've seen her at it,' *says she,* 'and it is GIN', etc., which I hadn't seen except for wondering at the Quantity of Green Bottles that Lady S— of B— had piled up in the Passageway. Now we were in Hard Times indeed; for Lady S— of B— soon took the Curtains and even the Blankets to pay her Rent and her Drink Bills and we were cold, too, so that I was grateful as I hadn't thought I would ever be, for my Aunt's *Fur Coat* (although I must suffer Remorse at the sight of the Hole made by the Mouse and feel in my Heart for the poor Animal as it struggled to be Free) while I was at the same time afraid for my Aunt's coming Remarks on the Hole. Our situation was not improved by Lord C— M— who was always Coming Round; and I must say I used him cruelly for my own Ends, which were to get-out of the Flat before we were thrown in the Street; for now I had seen the women who were indeed as near to being on the Street as it was possible to be, viz. the *Hostesses*, my Resolve grew each day to find my Elder Uncle, and to Dance my way to him if there was no other Path open to me.

Lord C— M— had no Idea, as it goes without saying, of

my Plan, and was delighted to take me High and Low to seek
for my Uncle, so that we danced in Houses of Low Repute
and at Balls, I am sorry to say, without seeing the Difference
between them; and became so well-known as Partners that
we were invited to *Hotels* and to *Banquets*, where we danced
some of the old Dances of the American South, and most
often our Scottish Reels, in particular *The Wee Drops of
Brandy*. Yet we saw my Elder Uncle only once, when he was
on his Way Out from a Party; and the Prince, or the *Royal
Duke*, for such he was, I didn't see at all; and then when I did
it was in strange circumstances, as shall be told. The worst of
it was that we had to eat: '*Robina*,' *says* Lord C— M— when
we were in the Bar in *Jermyn Street* where we were used to
Eat, 'my Credit is run out here, or so they tell me.' And the
poor Fellow broke down in Tears, for I truly believe he loved
me, and could think of no other way that we could go-out
together, for he had no way to Earn a Living any more than I
had, with my sudden Ending of my Education in French and
French History of Art. 'We'll go down to L—,' *says he*; 'my
father will let us work there in the kitchens or something of
the kind;' and he sobbed again so that I must say I would go
down to L— too, which I had no wish to do, to work as a
Servant, when my Elder Uncle was so near to Found; and
also I feared the Long Hours of Drudgery and Very Small Pay
at the end of them, for the Nobility thinks it is put in the
World to be served. My Kind Heart has often persuaded me
in this Way, so that I must run at the Last Minute, rather than
do what I have been pleaded with to do; yet here I tired of
Lord C— M— and I must confess it, and in particular his
saying the worth of the L— Estate being £14 million, and
then saying they are all too Poor to live, all of which I knew I
had Heard Before. 'We'll live on the Tips,' *say I* (for when we
Danced there were Coins thrown, and sometimes a Note,
screwed up), but I saw here, as I have often seen with the
younger Scions of these Great Families, that there was no
Backbone: Lord C— M— said we would Starve at that rate;
while I, for all my Love of Comfort and Beauty, would

happily have lived on the Embankment and spent my Tips on Cheese and Bread at the Stalls, so-long as I wasn't in Truth on the Streets and had a Protector to Stand Over me. It can hardly be surprising, then, that I had no Love for Lord C— M— and Prayed only for my Escape. Indeed, although I didn't know it, I was near Release from my Predicament when I spoke of the Embankment, whence I now persuaded Lord C— M— to accompany me: 'Our Credit's gone,' *say I*, 'and Credit you don't need with the Tramps;' and I kept my Spirits high, although they were each minute Lower, with the Prospect of Starvation or a Visit to L— as I had Promised, for Lord C— M—'s Brother's, Viscount P—'s Ball. For it was clear to me that the old *Marquess* would take me as a Slave, just as my poor Aunt had warned, when we came to *Paris*; but that in this case I was Kidnapped already by Lord C— M—, who had been despatched to *London* by his father to seek Cheap Labour. Yet I do believe that only Hunger gave me such Thoughts; for soon, when we were by the River on a Sunny Day and drinking Soup, my Spirits Recovered, as they so often do; and particularly on seeing a Fine Gentleman (whom I recognized from the Royal Party at the *Bag O' Nails*) come out of a Great House, that stood in an alley way near the *River Thames*.

*

If there is one kind of Person that should be Shunned it is a Fool; and alas! poor Lord C— M— was as big a Fool as it would be possible to find: 'Hey!' *says he* at the Top of His Voice seeing the Fine Gentleman stand awhile on the side of the road next to his Car, which was very Large and Fine; 'we'll dance for the Millionaires, *Robina*;' and Laughing (and showing his Scorn, for Lord C— M— considered himself to be higher than the *Sovereign*, as has been told), he danced Crazily in the Street, so that the Traffic was brought to a standstill and other Cars were Diverted; and I was soon swept into the Road by Lord C— M— and we performed a Fine Reel, as I was too afraid to leave him, for fear of his being run-over and so danced at my most Sprightly, which brought a Hoot of Applause from the Cars, and a Smile from the Fine Gentleman. This latter was joined now by a Dark Woman, very lively in Expression, who was handing him a Rug and talking loudly while gesturing, in *Italian* (which I knew she must be from my study of History of Art and from the Picture of *St Anne*, by *Leonardo da Vinci*); and certainly she was as beautiful as that Saint, which gave me a Pang of Jealousy, I must confess, at her Happy Life with the Fine Gentleman and my Precarious Existence with a Fool. By this time, however, Lord C— M— was at his Wildest, and I had to Pull him on to the Embankment, in Fear of his Life, for the Traffic was growing Impatient; and I had the Irritation of seeing the Fine Gentleman drive away, without being able to discover his Name; and thus it is that a Fool will bring to Ruin the best-laid Plan as well as the Plan of the Spur of the Moment, for I had thought of dancing up to the Fine Gentleman, something telling me that I had found my Elder Uncle at-last, and asking him point-blank who he might be, in consideration of his kind Reception of my Dancing. Yet now, all was once more Lost: the *Italian* woman had gone back into the Great House and closed the door and would never open to me, I could well surmise, thinking we were Tramps and Down-and-Outs, of whom there were many on the Embankment, as I have said, and who crowded round Lord C— M— and myself now, under the impression no doubt that we were rich and Eccentric Aristocrats who would give them Alms. How bitter it was to me to have to run down the length of the Embankment and hide in a Bush by Chelsea Bridge while the Forces of Security (who had been called out by the maddened Residents) Combed the Area for Vagrants and Gypsies, and made Arrests on all they could find! And how much greater was my Resolve to get-away from my present State of Life and find my own Security, which was so sadly Lacking.

It was with such Low Thoughts that I made my way, as Torn and Dishevelled as an Hour under a Bush can procure, to the Flat; and crying sorely all-the-way, for I reflected I might as well have let myself be Locked Up, being as Homeless as those wretched people who had been taken into Custody for no Better Reason than that they lacked a Roof over their Heads. Lord C— M— had gone off on Foot to L—, saying he would get a Lift; though he was himself so Wild in Appearance by then that I thought he would very likely have to Wear his Shoes out and walk all the way to W—Shire without help. And I had little Idea, even, if I would find the Flat still inhabited by Lady S— of B—: yet she was there, and saw nothing amiss in my Looks when I came in, all of which sums her up as Chaperone without *pareil*, for I do think if one of her Charges had given birth to a Baby under her Eye, she wouldn't have seen a thing. 'Ah, *Robina*,' *says she* when I came in, 'this has Come in the Post for you,' and so saying she held up a Large Parcel. 'It is your Dress for Presentation at Court,' *says she*; and she goes on to say that she hoped I hadn't forgotten, the Presentation is today at three o'clock; 'your Hat is in the Parcel too,' *says she*; and she tells me my Aunt had Ordered the Outfit for me when she was in *London* and it's only just now Ready. 'And perhaps you should take a Bath,' *says* Lady S— of B—, for at-last I think she did see the state I was in; but as she had a Bottle of GIN on a Tray by her, I was surprised at it, and all the more surprised to hear I was shortly to make my Curtsey before *Her Majesty* that day, for I don't believe anyone had told me of it, despite the fact that *Stella* came in now in Long White Gloves and very Pleased with Herself at that.

*

Whatever the Vanity and Indulgences that may have been the Property of Lady S— of B—, I must say here that the Poor Woman did me no Harm; and that I may have thought she did at the time was due only to my Inexperience; for since I have come to know what it is to Suffer and Steal for the Lack of Money, and to see the Hard Face of the Law. She was Human, like the Rest, and if she should have Brought Out

Young Ladies and instead brought out the Bottle, there were Reasons no doubt which we in our Youth and Arrogance would Ignore. Besides, as I was to Discover in the Cab to the Palace (and *Stella* and the Mousy Girl and myself all near to Stifled by the Fumes of her Breath) Lady S— of B— was a great Reader, for, 'My Dears,' *says she*; and in a tone we hadn't heard for it was *Valedictory*, as we were soon to Learn, 'You'll find me reading in the Lobby.' And she brought out from her Bag, instead of GIN, a Volume of *Autolycus*: 'I find the time is long at these Presentations,' she said to us, and she said she liked to Get On with her Reading, which, as we were astonished to see, was in LATIN. 'I'll make my Bow,' *says* Lady S— of B—, but all in an Absent Way, as if she had forgotten her Gender even; and then we were at the Gates of the Palace and all of us too Excited to ask where the Lobby might be in so Great a Mansion; and in particular I was excited, I am sorry to say, by the Crowds; and I do think I would have been Happy to go-to my Own Hanging as long as a good Turn-out could be arranged for it. So, despite my fear of my Life going down in this Nonsense, and that I might never study History of Art or Earn my Living in the World, I knew myself very Pretty; and all this drew Gasps from the Crowd; and all this again, I must say, in Spite of my Dress, which I had taken from my Aunt's Parcel with a Sinking Heart. *Stella* being the first to remark kindly that my dress was like a Wilting Cabbage Leaf (and indeed it was, of a Fine Silk that had wilted away altogether on the journey down from *Carlisle*) she now took the Opportunity, for it was clear the Crowd was cheering me (although my Red Hair was half-hidden under a Hat that was also a Leaf, of Boiled Spinach in Colour and down over my face as if it had just Slipped from the Pan) that I would be eaten up at the Palace before I could rise off the Floor. 'They'll eat you up for a Salad,' *says she* and laughs a great-deal, while Lady S— of B— sat with her Nose in her Book, for she Had Had Enough of these Occasions; and had I taken Notice of her more eagerly instead of exclaiming at the Crowd's Love of me, I would have made better provision for myself in the End. Yet my Thoughts were always important to me; and I went where Fate told me, so there is no Way of Knowing where greater Prudence might have led me. I did think then that the Crowd was foolish, to enjoy the Spectacle of Young Girls Dressed Up to Look Silly, and with too much Money to Burn (or so the Crowd must imagine) and I resolved to lead a Different Life, as soon as this Farce was over: of how soon this would be I was fortunately Ignorant.

A great Mass of Young Girls and Chaperones waiting for admittance to the Side Door of the Palace allowed me to look in the Cabs and Fine Cars, one of which so exactly resembled the Car of the Fine Gentleman by the *Thames* that I wanted only to Jump Out and accost it; yet on looking further inside there was only a Woman with a disagreeable Face, like a Pug; and with her was *Miranda*, my friend from *Paris*, who did indeed show all the marks of Terror, as she had prophesied. I saw Girls from *Mlle Weiss's*, who, I Regret to say, turned their Heads from me when we disembarked and went all together up the Wide Steps of the Palace, which were Laid with a Red Carpet: yet in my Pleasure and Relief that *Annie* was not among them (for she was too Poor I suppose and her Mother having Run Off had no one to pay Lady S— of B— for which I thanked God) I forgave my old Companions; and seeing a Diamond Engagement Ring on one Finger and a Sapphire on Another was gracious with my Compliments, even if these went Unheard. In having no Longing for an Engagement in the Season I believe I was quite alone; My Desire for Liberty from Lady S— of B—, which was at-hand and I too Foolish to know it, was too strong for me to wish to Settle Down with any Man.

If I lack in Love from other Women, it may be that I am too quickly flattered by the Attentions Paid to me by Men: at any rate, out of the great Assembly in the Room with the Throne, it was I who brought one of the Royal Personages on the dais to Lean Forward, as if he had just Spotted a Prize Animal at a Show, and to tap his Programme; and it was I who laughed back at him, mischievously, I am sorry to say, for he was the *Prince* who had been in the *Bag O' Nails*, and I saw from his Glance that he had Missed me and thought of me with Longing ever since the Occasion there when he had been in my Uncle's Party, supposing no doubt that I was a *Tart* and going back again and again to find me, in Vain, as was indeed the Case, or so he later told me. I heard the Gasps, and this time of annoyance, from the Presenters and their *Protégées*, at my being Singled Out; and I made a deep Obeisance, to make up for my Embarrassment (at my Saucy Laughter, which I instantly Regretted) and to the Surprise of the *Sovereign*, who did not at that time wear Spectacles and looked about her in some Confusion. For a Pandemonium started up and there was then a Rush, to get me Out of the Way, so that I was nearly trampled again, the same Fate attaching itself to all my Dresses, whether Rose Borders or Cabbage Fields that I was wearing at the time. I confess that it was with Difficulty that I held down a Desire to leap on the Dais and speak to the *Prince*; but not, as these Ambitious Mothers must think, to Get him for Myself; rather to ask if my Uncle lived in Chelsea, by the River *Thames*, for I couldn't go-back there until I knew for Sure. I was Stopped, however, by *Stella*, who had already done her Curtsey and who now made her way to me in the Agitated Throng: 'She has disappeared,' *says she*; '*Robina*, what shall we do?'; and then goes on to say that she has been in the Tea Room and out in the Lobby and everywhere she could go in the Palace and there was no Trace of Lady S— of B—; and all this as the Mousy Girl performed her act of Reverence to the QUEEN, so that, hearing this, she Swooned and more Panic Broke out in the Throne Room. 'I know she's skipped it,' *says Stella*; 'But I'm glad of it: we're Out now, after all and I shall go back to my Father's Stud'; and she goes on to say she has always liked Horses better than Men and she might at a Pinch, in all the rest of the Season, go-to the Derby. 'We must go to the Flat,' *say I*, for we were in the Lobby and half-holding the Mousy Girl, while another Mother held Smelling Salts under her Nose; all of which gave me Time to see that Lady S— of B— was indeed Absent. 'We'll take a Cab,' *says Stella*; and the Minx at the end of the Journey then said her Allowance had run-out and I must pay for it, which I did with a heavy Heart, for this was the last of the Tips I had had, dancing with Lord C— M—.

The Flat now being Completely Empty, as I had come to expect, and *Stella* making a Great Din over the Disappearance of her Pearl Necklace (whereas I hadn't been Robbed, for my Uncle and Aunt had never bought me Jewellery from the Money which was rightfully mine), I saw that Lady S— of B— had left my Silk Tartan Dress, I daresay because she was Too Fat to fit into it; and with the Kindness of Heart for which I am happy to be known, and in particular towards those Less Fortunate than Myself, directed my Pity on the Mousy Girl, who appeared half-dead now from the Shock of Coming Out and finding Herself Abandoned all in one day. 'Her Ring is gone,' *says Stella* and with some Pleasure which I didn't like, for I have never Enjoyed the Misery of others. 'But it's insured,' *says* the Mousy Girl; and she goes on to tell us that it was her Engagement Ring; that only Last Night she had accepted the Proposal of an IRISHMAN who was the *MacGuddle of the Gurks* and she would go and live in IRELAND now before the Season was done, and her Ring would be replaced by the *Insurance*. All of which led me to Reflect, as hardly needs the saying, that I was yet-again the One without Happiness or Security; that even the Mousy Girl had Seen It Coming and had the Presence of Mind to get Engaged on the night before the Presentation, at some Ball, no doubt; and that while she went off to her *Matrimonial Bliss* and *Stella* to the Stud, I must Make my Way to L— in the County of W—Shire, where I could have no Idea as to how I would be Welcomed.

*

As I had with me only one Small Bag, Cars stopped for me on the Way; and as my Aunt said I should be Modest I won't add that there was Whistling, at my Red Hair no doubt, which slipped from its Scarf as I went; and that I was taken in the End as far as *Salisbury Plain* by a Convoy of Soldiers, who were liberal with their praise and with Bars of Chocolate, so there was no danger I would go Hungry. Yet I confess I felt Lonely and Afraid when they left me there, on the Great Plain which had seen so many Crimes and Tragedies, and not the least of them concerning a Young Girl like myself, namely TESS. It was hard to go-past the Stones without a Shudder; and in particular it was growing Dark, so I had no idea if the Owls that Hooted were Young Rustics, set on Teasing a Town Girl in this Desolate Spot, or the Birds themselves, making their Ghostly Calls. The Reader must only imagine my Ignorance of the Scene, my Fear of the Future (for I couldn't go back to *Carlisle* with the Season scarcely Begun and my Uncle and Aunt's Rage too Terrible to Contemplate, when they heard of Money Down the Drain and Lady S— of B— Decamping with it). I must walk on, with my Head down and it so dark that my Hair was very likely the last Beacon, and with my Heart thumping, till: 'Why, my dear Young Lady,' *says a voice* and a Car slows: 'You must be a guest for the Ball at L—,' *says the Old-Man* in the Car and says to me then that I should Hop In, and gave my Knee a good Squeeze as I did so.

If Lord C— M— was an Eagle to look at, as I have said, the old *Marquess* his father was a Vulture, for his Pate was Bald, his Nose long and Wicked and his Face as narrow as every member of his Family's, as I was soon to see, so that I must come to the Conclusion that there was not Room enough in so confined a space for a Human Brain. 'We'll see more of you when there's Light,' *says* the old Bird of Prey as we went down a Steep Incline to the Great Pile, which was lit in a hundred windows very prettily with Candles; 'You'll find your way about after Dinner without a Torch, eh?' *says he*; and I had no wish to reply to him, for I thought there must be another Curfew here, and I wasn't fond of them, knowing all the Danger and the Groping that must follow a sudden

97

Lights Out. 'Poor *Mouse* is cold!' says the old *Marquess* next, while I gazed around and saw the fine Park and the Trees and a white Staircase far off, which turned out to be Water, trained to go down in Wide Stairs from a Hill. 'Poor *Mouse,*' *says he* again; I confess I feared then for my Sanity, for I thought the Mouse of QUEEN CHARLOTTE'S Ball was some-how come here, dead or alive; but then he had my hand held tight in his and pulled it into his trousers which were like an old pair of Breeches a Stable Hand might wear and were now unfortunately Open. Whether I have had luck at these Times it is not for me to say (or whether, in the case of this Family, there has been, in all the long years they have bred together, a shrinkage in Certain Parts of the Anatomy I will never know) but for all the Old-Man's Protestations of Cold, my Fingers touched Nothing, this I can certainly Swear, that neither Mouse nor Man lurked there. 'Later,' *says* the *Marquess,* for a Woman was coming out of the door of the Mansion now and walked towards us; and there was Lord C— M— too, who was as harassed as I had feared I might find him, and in the stained shirt of a *Scullion.* '*Robina,' says he*; and the poor Fellow's Features Lit Up, but only to fall despondent again when the *Marquess* directed him to return to the Kitchens; and the Woman being his Mother and doing nothing to countermand the Instructions, he said I would find him down there and there was a great-deal to do before the Banquet. I thought my heart would burst for poor Lord C— M—, but as I was to Discover, the Nobility have no Care for their younger Sons or their Daughters and will treat them Lower than Servants or throw them out altogether to Starve: that the great House of L— where I was now taken in by the old *Marchioness* was as filled with costly Treasures as Aladdin's Cave and many Retainers went about, but there wasn't so much as a Penny a Day for the young scions; and little indeed for the Eldest Son too, as I was to see.

The corridors of L— being non-existent, for the House had been put up before the Idea of Privacy was Current, I was shown to a small ante-room with Doors leading off to other

Rooms on both sides; and my Spirits sank indeed, to see the Doors had no Keys and to recall the Threat of a Curfew as I had heard earlier, and then no doubt more visits from poor *Mouse-a-cold*, etc. The old *Marchioness* had perfect dignity and composure, however, and told me there was no Bathroom in this part of the House, which was very old, and I should use a *Pot*, which she indicated to me as being in a Commode by the side of the Bed. She then directed me to get-ready for Dinner and went away; and if I say here that I wept, and took out my Silk Tartan dress from its Bag with a great Sadness, it was because I saw no Hope now of Peace, Happiness or Security; I was far from home and in an Estate where the word of the *Marquess* was Law: and who could tell what rash or foolish word the old *Condor* might say. It doesn't go-too-far to say I was as dejected as a Girl captured and put in a Harem in *Turkey*; and I would have lain on the Bed and given myself over to my Grief, I believe, if the door hadn't opened and a Young-Man come in, and stood staring at me some time, though he was the stranger to look at, as shall soon be told.

Viscount P—, for this he was, was very Fine in appearance and like a *Falcon*; and his Hair, which was in Long Braids, was plaited with Ribbon and hung down his Back, which was clothed in a Brown Velvet Jacket, very Handsome, with *Frogging*. Yet the air of Excitement that Viscount P— had about him, and his Burning Eyes, could hardly be attributed Solely to his Twenty-First Birthday and the Ball that was to Follow, and my Grief was replaced by Fear, for it was clear to me now that the whole Family of L— was Mad; and that Lord C— M— had but a Feeble variant of their Mania. 'I'm glad you came,' *says* Viscount P—, 'and I'll show you Round: how would you like that?' (and indeed I was to hear that L— and its Halls and Fields were all that the young Heir could Get Round, for he had been a long time confined to the Estate, it being considered Unsafe for him to go-out into the world). On my replying that I must Change for Dinner, Viscount P— said I could do so straight-away, and as there was no Getting

Rid of him, I must dress in the least Comfortable way Possible, that is to say without a Mirror or Bathroom and in Front of a Stranger; but Viscount P— who was perhaps a GENTLEMAN unlike his Father (or perhaps an even Greater Sufferer from the Congenital Complaint, and thus not roused as his Relatives were, with what little they Had), Paced about the room as I put-on my Dress and showed as little Interest in me as if I had been one of the Sheep in his Park, though I knew myself, even without a Mirror, to be suited by this Dress and Exceedingly Pretty. 'We'll go-to the State Rooms first,' *says* Viscount P—, his Excitement rising each minute; 'they've made a Fine Display for my Ball: You'll See.'

I have told of the great Riches of the Nobility, as I was to come to know them, and of their pleading Poverty at every Turn, but I must say that the State Rooms at L— were the Finest I ever saw: 'This room is by *William Kent*,' *says* the young *Viscount*; 'and this room is *Chippendale* and the carpet *Aubusson*', etc. etc.; but most Noteworthy were the Treasures the old *Marquess* had seen Fit to put round the Rooms, to Celebrate the Coming of Age of his Son, viz. an *Eagle* (with a strong Family Resemblance, so that I must wonder if I hadn't indeed entered the Kingdom of the Birds, and might be Carried off to an Eyrie at any time, which was in a certain Sense to Happen, as we shall see). This *Eagle* was fashioned of one Great Amethyst and had Diamonds for Eyes; *Gold Bowls* chased with gods and Nymphs, *Silver Candelabra*, *Pendants* in Cases and as big as Pigeons' Eggs if they were Rubies, or Green leaves in Emeralds, dazzled me altogether; Cartoons by *Raphael* and *Leonardo da Vinci* and Paintings by *Poussin* and *Caravaggio*, and a fine Canvas, mounted on Red Velvet, by *Stubbs*, of the Park at L— where Lions Prowled, all caused me to pray that one day I could go-back to my Studies in History of Art, for it was clear that Viscount P— had no Idea of the Meaning of these Fine Possessions, but was only Proud of them because they had been at L— since the *Third Marquess* had been on the *Grand Tour*, etc; and that a Lack of Education is the most Terrible of all Lacks, and more Terrible even, I daresay, than the Lack of a Prick, which I was beginning to believe must Run in the Family (for I'd caught sight of My Face in a Pier Glass in the Drawing-Room and saw that any man would turn to a Satyr who could see me that Night). For, as must often be Plain to Women and Young Girls, extreme Misfortune brings in its Wake a Greater Beauty, and it is for this that a Woman will Suffer, knowing her Sufferings to bring a Compensation in Looks. Whatever the Reason, I saw that my Oval Face had eyes now as dark as the wings of the Amethyst Eagle and that my hair, in Auburn Ringlets, burned like the Rubies so carelessly displayed by the old *Marquess*; and the Fact is that I thought to myself that I should have all this if I wanted it; and so I turned to Viscount P— with a Smile on my Lips; and I confess this was the first-time I knew of another Crime added to my List and this was CUPIDITY. Viscount P— saw Nothing, however, and was in Haste to show me the State Dining-Room, where the Banquet would shortly be Served: 'These are my Favourites,' *says he*, pointing to the Pictures on the Walls; 'they are by *Wootton*': but the Pictures were as encrusted with Dirt as a Horse after a Long Hack home from Hunting, and this was indeed the Subject of these Equestrian Masterpieces, which were however buried under Grime. 'I'll show you my *Stallion* tomorrow,' *says* Viscount P— in his usual Excitement; but then the Company came in and Lord C— M— behind them, with a Mighty Swan on a Platter, and we were shown to our Places, under a Chandelier of *Waterford Glass* and at a Mahogany Table that was opened out to Seat over a Hundred Guests.

If I dwell briefly on the Dinner, it is because I was soon Flattered by the Gaze of all the Men Present, and strongly felt the Dislike of the Ladies, though the old *Marchioness* was quite uninterested, and the Shame I felt then when they Stared at me so Openly may be the Reason for my going-out with the old *Marquess* when he took hold of me; though I fear the Shame may have more to do with the fine Presents he laid down before me and which I was Unable to Refuse. I was brought up very Simply, remember, and had no Money and no Way Out; and when Lord C— M—, who was too Red in the Face with Work even to see me, began to Cut the Swan, and a Gasp went up, as was Intended, for a Capon was inside, and inside that a Pheasant and then an Ortolan, as in the old Feasts, my head was Swimming with the Grandeur of it all, and in particular as a Swan is the Rightful Property of the QUEEN and cannot be Killed, and the Old *Marquess* cared Nothing for that, for he had his own Fiefdom here that had been Strong before the GEORGES came to the THRONE. 'Come, my pretty Puss,' *says* the Old Rogue, for he had pulled me to his Side and there was now a Hubbub, with poor Lord C— M— Leaning Over to cut the Swan with his Sword, and Women coming in to take their Places, each one of them in a Strapless Dress held up by Whalebone, 'this is for you': and he hands me a *Gold Bee*, exquisitely Fashioned, with Sapphires for Eyes and Spun Gold on the Wings. May all those who are too Virtuous to Read on, desist from Doing So; but when the LORD and MASTER of this Great Pile then pulled from his Pocket another Insect, this time in Jade and Gold, which was a *Dragonfly*, and took me by the Hand to lead me from the Room, I confess I went without a Struggle; and besides I knew that the Possessor of this aforesaid Pile did not Boast a neighbouring Excrescence and went-out with him quite Happily to the Hall and then to the Minstrels' Gallery, where an *Orchestra* was Tuning Up. 'This way,' *says* the Old Lecher; and we must Push Past the Young *Musicians* with their Instruments to Reach a Small Staircase, quite Hidden, which led, or so the *Marquess* told me, to a *Priest's hole*.

Let no Accusations be made that I speak Too Late of my Alarm at finding myself in a Chamber no Bigger than a Bed, which was, indeed, all it contained, and with a Low Ceiling and No Windows, so the Place was very Likely a Hideaway at the time of the Burning of the Abbeys (for the L— Family was Catholic at that time and had not Gone Over to King Henry the Eighth). Whether they did this out of a Wish to take Six Wives, like the King, I can't tell; but certainly the old *Marquess* seemed Ready to Make up for his earlier *Fiasco* and pulled a small Whip from his pocket with as great an Alacrity as he had produced the jewels. 'I'll pin these on you, my Pretty,' *says he*, and swoops forward; but while he held my Bodice still so that he could pin on the *Bee*, he had the Whip lodged between his Legs and sticking into me where the Flesh is softest, so that the Hairs there tore and I cried out at the Pain of it: 'Hush my dear,' *says he*, 'for no one can hear you'; and it was True that just then the *Minstrels* struck up with *Greensleeves*, so that I saw the Foolish Old-Man thought himself a *Plantagenet* and in his Fancy deflowering a Maiden: 'Poor Mouse,' murmured he next, and then asked if I would Lift my Dress so that he could see me: 'If the Hair's as Red at the Bush,' *says he*, 'you shall have a Gold Sovereign, my pretty young Thing!' All this being the most insufferable Agony to me, I did scream and fight, as my poor Aunt had always said I should if I were Set On by one of the Farm Hands or some such, and the *Marquess*, quite incensed at this (for he considered me a Subject, no doubt, and therefore Receiving an Honour at his Hands) dug in ever deeper with the Whip, so that I must in the end bring up my Knee, which certainly my Aunt had never Taught me, and deliver a Blow in the *Groin*, although I had no Way of Knowing if any Harm could be Delivered there.

That something at-least hung in the old LORD's Breeches was clear, however, for he let-out a Shout of Pain in Turn, and Clawed at me with his Talons, so that the side of my Face was Scratched and Bled; and I cried out in Terror that I had lost my Beauty; and, bringing up my Knee again, Brought him to his Own Knees, where he stayed, with the Jewels beside him on the bed, and also the *Parma Violets* which had been sewn on the Bodice of my Dress; but I was in too great a Haste to get-away, to try to Regain them, and I ran down to the Gallery and through the astonished *Minstrels* and down once more and out of the Great Hall and into the *Park*, for I had no Desire to be seen in such a State of Disarray.

If Innocence can only too easily be Led to Corruption, as we have seen, it can also Save Lives, by Virtue of its very Lack of Complicity in a Dangerous Situation; and this I was to find when I was Alone in the Park, where the Full Terror of my Future opened up to me: not the Night, only, where the Old *Seigneur* would most Certainly exact his Droit; but the Months ahead, where I now saw I might be shut in the Kitchens, a Serf like Lord C— M— and with no Prospect of Escape, other than work in a Similar Household, for I hadn't even, remember, Shorthand Typing. Besides all these Gloomy Thoughts, the Rustling in the Park, on a Night without wind, which this was, made me take Fright: but, as I have said, it was my upbringing in *Scotland* that Saved me, for, Ignorance having gone Hand-in-Hand with Innocence, I had seen the Lions in the painting by *Stubbs* and imagined they roamed Freely in the South of England and were Harmless, whereas in Scotland I had known only *Bullocks*; and was therefore less Afraid to see a Companion, in the shape of a Great Cat, than I would have been to have stayed Alone a moment longer. (Nor did I know of the Lions of L—, which, it seemed, People came from Far and Wide to see, but were always careful to keep inside their Conveyances.)

The Lions, as I have said, cared little for me because I wasn't afraid of them; and one, even, came up and Prowled round me and then lay a few Feet off on its Haunches, in the most Friendly Way possible, while another, a great Male, came up and Rubbed his Tawny Head against me, which, he coming-up to the Level of my Bosom, was a delicious Sensation. We were in a woodland Glade, such as has been so well represented by *Stubbs*, and it is not False, even if it may be Foolish, to say I was expecting Zebras, Antelopes, etc. to stroll through the Clearing in the Moonlight, when a sound of Angry Shouting started up, a Shot was fired; and the Felines scattered at speed, so that I was alone again, but this time with two Men closing in on me, in white Tie and

Tails and with Carnations in their Buttonholes. 'Silly Girl!' *says one* as he Runs-Up; 'you could be Eaten by now'; and together they led me back to the House, where a Band was playing in the Hall, and showed me to the Assembled Guests as a miraculous Survivor of the Lions. 'Your face has been Scratched,' *says one of the women*, and more People Crowded round to See, which made me quite Faint, for fear the old *Marquess* was among them and would tell some Story that he had caught me Stealing, or the Like, and that I'd received my Wounds trying to escape him, for it was indeed he who had Mauled me. 'Come to the Nursery,' *says* this kind woman, 'we'll get it Seen to' – and I went off, glad to hide my Face, if the Truth is to be Told.

In some instances of Tales of the Nobility, there must be a Lack of Credibility, for it hardly seems Likely that they would Act the way they do: let it be said, however, that at no Point have I made up or Embroidered my Accounts of them: that I followed the friendly Woman through antechambers, in one of which the old *Marchioness* stood on the stone hearth talking to a Circle of Friends; and if it is said that there is nothing Unusual in that, I can only add that the Dignified Old Lady was Peeing as she Stood there, and a circle of golden Liquid spread out from under her Long skirts on the Stone, which none of her Friends affected to Notice or Care About. There was a Grand quality in the Way the Noblewoman wouldn't deign to go to a Loo, or Crouch, even, as Girls are taught to do; but I remembered then that she herself had told me to use a *Pot* if I needed to Go, and that it was Possible there was no Bathroom at all at L—, for all its two hundred Rooms, and that they had never Got Round to Putting in New Plumbing, since Jacobean Days. Whatever the Reason, I was soon out of the antechamber and in the Nursery Wing, where my kind Friend bathed my Face and put on Cream; and all this while an old woman who had been addressed as *Nanny* sat on by the Fire; this last remaining silent so long that it came to me she might be Dead, and kept Stuffed by her Loving Charges, who would most certainly have Felt more Love for her than for their Distinguished Parents.

Now I was Patched Up, I was determined to Dance; and to make the Best of my Misfortunes, which Attitude I am Glad to Say has saved me from much Misery. With this in Mind, I asked my Friend for directions to the Kitchens, set off there, and found Lord C— M— without Difficulty: we then went Upstairs and joined the Throng on the Ballroom Floor, and were soon giving our Exhibition Dance, which drew great Applause and Admiration, as it did wherever we went. We spun faster and faster, and ended, as we were wont to do, with a *Scottische*; and all the while I prayed these Wealthy People would throw Money down; for it was the only Way that was open to us to Get Away, and I thought I could rescue Lord C— M— from his Drudgery and Myself from a Fate worse than Death on the Gratuities of the Delighted Audience. Fate, however, had a better Tale to Tell; and no Sooner had we finished our Dance (and with Few Tips in our Cap, for I fear that most of the Guests at L— considered themselves too Poor to give to Others) than a Hand came down on my Shoulder and I turned to see the Fine Gentleman, whom I had last seen walking from his House by the River in *London*, and who now said to me that I was the best Dancer he had ever seen: 'and you are *Robina*,' *says he*, to my Astonishment, 'for that is the Family Tartan,' and he says our Name, so that I was nearly Overcome with Happiness, that this was my Elder Uncle indeed, that he sent me the Silk Tartan in which I had brought Honour to the Clan, by Dancing so well in it. 'I'm not Allowing a Dispute in the Family to stand between us,' *says he*, both Grave and Laughing at the same time, so that I felt instantly *At-Home* although this was the first-time I had met him. And let it only be said that my Elder Uncle told me he had had a Dispute over Land with his younger Brother, my Uncle who had raised me on the Farm; that they had not Spoken for many Years; that my Elder Uncle had thought often of me, and whether I should turn out to be as Pretty as he expected me to be (for he had seen me as a Baby) but I was even Prettier; and a thousand other Things, so that I was Bursting with Impatience to ask him about my Mother and Father, and told him too that I was Destitute and that Lady S— of B— had Abandoned us in the Palace and I had no Roof over my Head: in Short, 'You will come back with me to *London* tonight,' *says he*; 'and you shall stay with me in *Chelsea*'; and he said too that my Ball should be given there and he would be only too happy to Bring Me Out in style; so my Happiness knew no Bounds, and in particular when my Elder Uncle told me I should have as many New Dresses as I could Wish For.

*

If the Journey to *London* was long, I was hardly the one to know it; and in all my Transports of Delight that I should be Rescued at Last I saw little of the Fields and Parkland of the Great Estate of L—, but saw only the kind Countenance of my Elder Uncle, who was as Well Pleased, or so it seemed, as was I, by my Appearance in his Life: 'I've wondered how you were Turning Out, *Robina*,' *says he*; and I was soon Red in the Face from his Compliments, while Indiscretion followed as Quickly on their Heels: 'Tell me,' *says* my Uncle, who was as Fine Near-To as he was Far-Off, and his Car very Magnificent, 'Tell me,' *says he*, 'how is my Brother's Temper these days?' And then, 'Is your Aunt as *Mouldy in the Face* as she used to be?' And what with asking of the Economy of the Household, and whether we had enough *Bran* to eat, and that he had just purchased a Machine for Sawing an Egg in Six Parts, which he proposed to give to them, I laughed and forgot myself entirely, so that I told of my Aunt's Savings and my Uncle's Stern Moods without a thought of the Real Worth of these good people, who had reared me without Nature ever intending them to. So it is that Charm, which my Elder Uncle possessed in Abundance, can drive the Sober Lessons of a Lifetime into a Duststorm; yet my Elder Uncle was so Concerned for my Future and Present Happiness that I consigned my Humbler Scottish Relatives to one side and thought only of the Glorious Opportunities that lay ahead for me: and indeed my Elder Uncle was always Generosity Itself, it being no fault but that of my own Innocence and Ignorance that I knew nothing of Strings Attached, while my Uncle and Aunt in the Borders knew no Strings other than Purse Strings, and how to keep these as tightly fastened as they could. 'You were Sensible to run from the L— Family,' *says* my Uncle when he had been silent awhile, breaking his silence only to say a Name, which he said was the name of a Young-Man who might be *Suitable* for me; 'for the L— Family are feather-brained, as you saw, and besides they have no Money.' 'How is that?' *said I*, and told of the Precious Stones in the Form of Birds and the Great Possessions everywhere, but my Elder Uncle smiled and shook his head at me: 'They can't Touch it,' *says he*, and left me as we drove on in darkness to wonder at his words; for there was a Silk Rope across the Rooms when the house was open to the Public, it was true, and the Treasures were Untouchable; but at other times, and in particular at the time of the Ball, they had been freely Available, or so it had appeared to me. 'Don't think of them,' *says* my Uncle; and he went on to tell me of his house in *Chelsea*, which I had lately glimpsed, and how he had enjoyed my Dance, as had his companions. 'And if I'd known it was my Niece,' *says he*; and he then went on to Turn my Head the more, so by the time we were in *London* I fancied myself the first *Princess* in the country (which my Elder Uncle had said would not be so Unlikely to me). I was, in short, as silly a Goose as ever walked up the steps of a house in *Swan Walk* (for this was the name of the street where my Elder Uncle lived); and if I was to be thinned down rather than Fattened up for the Slaughter, Stuffed full of Nonsense I was certainly about to be.

*

Yet there was a great-deal to account for my Illusion, for to be in a Fine House by the River at *Chelsea*, to enjoy the kindness of my Uncle (for the Uncle who had reared me in

Scotland I now named my Younger Uncle) and to receive all the Attentions of Society was to be my Happy Fate; and if those Days could have Lasted Longer I might have Forgot the outside World altogether: for, as we came into the House I felt so much *At-Home* there, and was so kindly welcomed by my Uncle's Maid, who was from *Italy*, that all Thoughts of Other Days disappeared on the Instant: 'You must eat,' *says* this Charming Creature from *Italy*, who said her name was *Joia* and I should know her as *Joy*; and she proceeds to bring Great Bowls of *Pasta* and Sauces of *Walnuts* and *Basil*, so that my Uncle was Laughing at my Fine Appetite. 'I'll show you the House,' *says he* when I had eaten my Fill, tenderly helped by *Joy*, who was the Maid, also, she told me, of a Beautiful *Contessa*, a Friend of my Uncle (and as I discovered from her, the Woman with the Face of *St Anne* whom I had seen when I danced with Lord C— M— outside the House). 'But she's no Saint,' *says Joy*, laughing and speaking very Low at the same time, for my Uncle walked ahead, and stopped here and there to show his Treasures, which were Arranged in each Room: 'she's away in *Rome* but when she returns you'll see what kind of a Woman she is,' *says Joy*; but the Maid's eyes were so full of Good Nature and Sweetness that I thought only of the Fine Season that lay ahead, with the *Contessa* and my Uncle and no doubt as many Balls and Parties as there was Time for; and in many Ways I judged well to think in this Way, though in others it could be said that I was a Fool and too Obedient to the Desires of this Charming Couple. However that may be, I was soon taken into the Drawing Room on the First Floor of the House, which had Tall windows that looked on the River and the Old Physick Garden: 'We can go in the garden whenever we wish,' *says* my Uncle, 'for I have a key to the gate;' and he held out a Great old Key: 'there are herbs there that haven't been grown for hundreds of years in this country,' *says he*, 'and we shall go and pick some later', etc., but all in such a profound Tone that I must wonder what he said, though I was to find out, indeed, later, not knowing then the Definition of the Word when he said it, which was *Aphrodisiac*. He then showed me his Collection of Chinese Porcelain: 'This is *Tang*,' *says he*; 'and this is *Sung*,' etc., and in particular a Jade Bowl, which he said had been in the Summer Palace at *Peking* and was without Price. 'My dear *Robina*,' *says he*, 'I shall do all I can for you here,' and he says there is a Conservatory and a Ballroom at the Back of the House and my Ball shall be Held there; and that the *Prince*, who on seeing me at the Palace had been overcome with Surprise and Pleasure (for in the *Bag O' Nails* he had considered me a *Tart*) had asked after me and would most certainly come to the Ball, and very Likely be Round before that time. 'The *Prince* has Certain Difficulties,' *says* my Uncle, 'and you will help him to Overcome them'; but as I couldn't know what these might be, and as I was also Eager to speak to my Uncle at last concerning my Parents, I spent less time than I should in pondering these Matters. '*Robina*,' *says* my Uncle, who looked Grave on hearing me ask him of my Father: 'there are Men who are born with every Advantage; with a Silver Spoon in their Mouth, and with every Privilege to Look Forward to, from Doting Parents'; and at this my Uncle looks very Sad and cast down his eyes so I durst not go-on and ask him more: 'Yet they are Traitors,' *says* my Uncle on the sudden, and he says that my Father went to *Cambridge* and got-in with a Set that were Against the Ways of Thinking in this Country, which have always been Right and Proper; that they did all they could to bring Strife to this Nation, by calling on People to Rise Up, who had been well Satisfied before; and in Short that they were Scoundrels of the First Order and my Father had joined up with them. 'But where is he now?' *say I*, and I own I could hardly keep from crying, for I knew the Answer in my Heart and wanted only to Hear it from his Lips and keep it in my Heart after that Forever. 'Your Father went to *Spain*,' *says he*, 'and he joined a War there, on the Wrong Side, for he was against the *Monarchy*, and we've not Seen or Heard of him Since,' *says* my Uncle. 'And my Mother,' *say I*, but then *Joy* comes in and says the Dressmaker is in the Hall and has brought swatches of stuff for me to see, for my New Dresses; and I own I was Distracted, and so said nothing more, when my Uncle told me that my Mother was a Selfish Woman, very Full of Gifts but none for Mothering, and that she had gone off Abroad without a Thought for me, for her only interest was in Herself. Indeed, I determined not to Anger my Uncle more, by talking of these Matters, which clearly Displeased him; and I confess I went with Speed to meet the Dressmaker, who was from *Paris* and bore no Likeness to the Little Woman my Aunt had taken me to see.

*

And thus in Gratitude at the Favours Received from my Uncle, who was as fine in his Manners as in his Looks, and was as concerned with my Happiness and Prosperity as my Parents should have been and my poor Aunt and Uncle most certainly were not, I lost all sense of the Need to Make My Own Way in the World: losing also the Desire to study History of Art or to learn more of the Meaning of Life: and thus, as I say, I was soon little different from a Kept Woman, in that I wanted all Chores to be done for me and all my Expenses to be met; but I was ignorant still of the Price that must be Paid for this, for I was hardly more than a Schoolgirl, remember, and fresh out of *Scotland* at that, where the ways of my Uncle's Household would have appeared libertarian in the extreme. However that may be, I *blossomed*, as my Uncle was kind enough to say it, in my first days in *Chelsea*, my Hair being Dressed each morning by the Royal Hairdresser, who was a FRENCHMAN, and my Ball Gowns fitted on me twice in each day. There would be no need to Dwell Further on a List of Such Vanities, except to say that one of these, viz. a long-skirted Gown of Blue Organza (which was the colour of a Violet) was the Cause of my Beginning to Understand the Plans my Uncle had for me. *Joy*, coming down to me as I sat with my Uncle in the *Conservatory*, said my Fitter was here, and the Red Dress being finished (for there was also in the Making a Dress of Red Taffeta, which would go with my

111

Hair, or so my Uncle told me), I should start on the Blue Dress straight away. I went up the stairs after her and into the Place that was put aside for these Fittings, which was a Form of Alcove on the Landing (this House being one of the oldest in *Chelsea*) and with Deep Landings where my Uncle placed his Collections of Chinese Treasures; or, in this case, had made a Small Room with *louvred* Doors which could open out or close when Wanted. There was a Mirror here, and the Fitter being Ready to see me, she greeted me with the Respect which I was alas! coming to Take for Granted (and which in its Turn came from the Belief of all who met me that I was an *Heiress*, my Uncle being Famous for his Money and Possessions). She then held out a whalebone Bodice and required that I should strip off altogether, for if the Dress was to Succeed, it must be a Very Tight Fit. How I wished then that I could refuse the Fitter, for I have always Disliked to Undress before any Person, as has been told. And I wished soon, too, that I would never hear of a Fitting again, for it began to appear to me that I was to be Fitted Up in one way, to Accommodate another Kind of Fitting later; and had I known this I would have prayed for my *Circular Baize Skirt* and my *Black Top* and gone straight back to *Carlisle*, to beg my Younger Uncle for any kind of Humble Labour on his Farm.

With the Blandishments of *Joy*, who told me that my Ball was only a Week away and that I would look more lovely than any other of the Girls in my new Blue Organza, which she said would make me *Queen of the Night*, and other such Compliments (all of which Turned my Head exceedingly) I was soon stripped to the Buff, and Suffering the cold Fingers of the Fitter. 'We shall need to Raise you hardly at all,' *says she*, and pushed with the Flat of her Palms under my Breasts, which were small and white as Snow, and which at her Prodding soon showed Rosy Nipples Standing Up, a Sight I had never seen Before Me, in the Glass. 'And here,' *says Joy*, who stood behind me and could be seen, as could I, three times over in the Mirror for it had Two Panels at the Side;

'here you won't need to build out;' and she gives my A—s—such a Squeeze as nearly to Make me Faint; 'She is Perfect,' *says* the Fitter, who made out she knew nothing of this, and was moulding the Whalebone Corset round me, so that my Breasts were filled with Blood from the Exercise and Blushed like Daisies. 'And you shall be the Belle of the Ball,' *says* the Mischievous *Joy*, for she had always a strong vein of Jealousy towards me, I think, being no older than I, and in no way Fitted Out to catch a Husband, but consigned to the kitchens and to the works of *Mrs Beeton*, where she is told she must first catch a Hare.

However that may be, I was not too proud of my own Reflection (and indeed I tried to pull fragments of the Organza over me, particularly my Private Parts, which anyone might say blushed too, except they were by Nature Red) to see that *Joy*, still jocund with me, had slid up the *Louvres* in the doors; and that Eyes looked in; and I had nowhere to turn, as you might say, when I heard a Man's Voice that was most certainly not my Uncle's, and a Woman's Voice, also, this being a Voice I had never before heard in my Life. '*Joy*,' say I, 'what is this?' But then the *Louvres* closed again and the Voices sounded some way off, on the Stairs. 'Is that the *Contessa*?' *say I*, for the Woman's Voice had some *Italian* in it, like her Maid's. 'It is, *Robina*,' *says she*, making out very abashed, but laughing really, as I could see. 'And who else?' *say I*, very much alarmed now at what lay ahead for me at the *Contessa*'s return. 'Ah,' *says Joy*, 'you'll see;' and she goes on to say that I shall be one of the richest and most beautiful women in the land, and she, *Joy*, will come with me wherever I go, and especially *Abroad*, for she has good reason to suppose I will be offered a *Yacht* and a villa in *Corfu*. '*Piange troppo qui*,' *says she*, and saucily tweaked at me again, where the hairs pulled; but by this time the Fitter had taken offence too and was pulling cloths over me, so I was like a Statue that was about to be carried away from a Museum. *Joy* then folded back the doors and led me out on the landing again, as if nothing had happened. 'You'll be the Belle of the Ball,' *says*

113

she and says she'll wait up all hours for me to come home so she can hear the tale of my Triumphs, and wait up she did, but not for this reason, I could swear.

*

Lest it appear that I seek Favour, or Sympathy at least, from the Reader, I must say here that I was Barely Surprised by the Peeping; and that I was much Enraged and Afraid excuses me little; for I had seen my Uncle with his Gallant Ways, at the Balls we had attended, and had seen him take Girls Young Enough to be his Daughter into his Room Late at Night; and in all Honesty, whether I felt Gratitude that I wasn't Chosen by him (for he had another, Higher Aim: I could warrant otherwise that my Uncle had no Scruples in this Line and my Younger Uncle I had seen often enough at the Farm with his Gander up, yet not seeing I saw it; while my Father, I must think, would very like Seduce his own Flesh and Blood if he was Willing to Betray them in every other way); whether, as I have told, I was simply grateful to my Uncle and was thus determined to show little surprise at his sending a Friend Spying, I will never know; but I knew too that in *Swan Walk* few Cries for Help would be heeded; and in-fact I had seen my Uncle go-in his Room with *Joy*, he then calling out to me to come in and see them, which I would not.

However that may be, I was as I say only too unsurprised by the Eyes in the Shutters and while I had cried out very earnestly to *Joy* to close them (which she promptly did) I confess that my Blood was Up and I knew for the first time that my Beauty could bring me to Ecstasy, as doubtless it could to many Men. Yet I wanted only the Right Man, who had not Shown Up at all the Parties my Uncle so kindly Escorted me to; and I can only plead my Innocence and Ignorance that I was all this time unable to see what my Uncle wished for me (for why should he have Put himself Out in this way for a Niece without Hope of Return?) and I fully Deserved What was Coming to Me; yet at the time I was so Taken up with myself that I thought my Uncle would have given a great Wedding for me if I had married the *Dustman*: here, however, comes the *Contessa*, and after shaking me by the Hand and saying what a pretty Girl I am, we went down to the Conservatory, where *Joy* had laid out the bone china and the Tea.

*

If I had known what it was to fall in-love with a Woman, as I know now that I did with this charming creature, herself more beautiful than Leonardo's *St Anne* and more graceful than the Venus de Milo (but as full of mystery also as *La Gioconda*) I might have spared many hours of suffering; and many Crimes, indeed, which were committed for Men or to Spite them, when the love of a *Madonna* was all I truly sought in my Existence. But I thought I saw her only as a Friend, and she was so Much with my Uncle, also, and holding his hand and laughing (though she took my hand often too, and in my Youth and Folly I felt my Blood Up, but considered this to be the Rightful feelings of an Orphan too long deprived of its mother and knowing for the first time the ecstasy of filial love) that I vowed then and there to do and say what the *Contessa* asked of me, so rapidly did she take my Heart and my proper Sense away from me. '*Robina*,' *says* my Uncle who was happy at the *Contessa*'s return, 'shall we tell you the plans we have for you?' 'Why, yes,' *say I*, for I was certainly curious to know if I could stay in the *Contessa*'s presence, this being all that was of any significance to me. 'You'll wear your Red Dress with the Rose tonight,' *says* my Uncle. 'Yes,' *says the Contessa*, 'I've heard it suits you to perfection.' 'And you'll meet a certain gentleman,' *says* my Uncle. 'Let him pick your Rose,' *says the Contessa*, laughing very much now, but always in a voice of such pleasantness, and always with an expression of such grace that I, poor Goose that I was, knew only complacency at her mention of my Red Ball Gown, which was indeed very fine. 'We'll come back here, as our Guest wishes to see my Collection,' *says* my Uncle. 'Yes, and

115

he has some of the manners of Her Majesty *Queen Mary*,' *says the Contessa*, with more laughter, 'for whatever he demands can hardly be refused him.' 'Some treasures are beyond Price,' *says* my Uncle, and I saw he gazed at his *Jade Bowl*, while the *Contessa* looked very eagerly at me, so eagerly indeed that I must wonder if I too am not collected by my Uncle and to be sold or exchanged in part value to the highest Bidder. 'There are the *Sung* and the *Tang* vases,' *says* my Uncle, 'and he will certainly want one of those. And the *Famille Rose* Dinner Service. At least he shan't have the most Precious thing in the house,' he goes on; 'Not without paying a considerable sum,' *says the Contessa* still laughing, and squeezing my hand until I thought I would swoon, to be accorded the friendship of so wonderful a being; 'she is all too important to me, to let her go: indeed I shall change my mind and stop her from going to the Ball.' And so on, so I hardly knew if I was on my head or my heels; and through all this *Joy* stood smiling in the door of the Conservatory and bursting into chuckles sometimes, as if I were the subject of an Auction, and a comic one at that. 'Do you know of the tight-fistedness of some members of the Family?' my Uncle *says* then, for it was clear that the *Contessa* liked to hear of anything to do with him, and even more now to do with me, for I was foolish enough, with her loving glances, to believe I had supplanted him in her affections. 'Don't tell me they've been mean to my lovely *Robina*,' *says she*. 'Why, they have been monstrous, her money's in Trust and they won't break it for her,' *says he*. 'But that's a Crime, at the very time of her Life when she needs to travel,' *says she*. 'And to buy new Clothes,' *says* my Uncle in an innocent voice, for he knew no doubt that I must express gratitude to him for my new Gowns, which I did. 'You should send them your mother's Collection, to spur them to a generous act,' *says the Contessa* (and I must say here that even in my ignorance I was surprised at the rapidity of their talk, for it was they who were like Comedians, with their Patter; and had I known more of the theatre (I had been only once, in Edinburgh, to a

116

Panto and had gone home in Tears, much distressed by *Mother Goose*, as well I might be) I would have known they spoke so much together and told so many items to each other that there could be no such thing as a Secret, divulged for the first time in front of me). 'My mother,' *says* my Uncle, 'was a Collector too, but an Eccentric one,' and as his friend the beautiful *Italian*, took my hand and pressed it warmly in the excess of her mirth I must laugh too, for my Uncle brought out as we spoke and placed on the floor a great crowd of *Glass Jellies*, which were most horrible and putrid in appearance, like frozen jellyfish and causing even *Joy* to leap back in fright at the sight of them. 'They were for Pianos to stand on,' *says* my Uncle, when he got his breath after his own Gusts of Laughter; 'for in her day the Pianos wore skirts.' 'And knickers,' *says the Contessa* and strokes my knee very fondly, remarking that I should have no need of knickers under my Red Dress, for she has heard that it's so tight a Fit that Pants would be seen to Ride up under it. 'And they stood in the Jellies, these Pianos, so that they shouldn't go through the floor,' *says* my Uncle. 'With shame, for fear someone would peep under them and play them,' *says the Contessa*. 'Yes,' *says* my Uncle, 'I think we'll send them to *Carlisle*,' and then we all laughed when we thought of these *Jellies* on the train and the face of my poor Aunt when she was told to come and collect them. 'But it's late,' *says* my new friend and Mentor, and waves to *Joy* to take me off and dress me: 'for we all go to dine at Lady Y—'s before the Ball,' *says she*, 'and we shall be late.' So it was that I learnt of Plans afoot for that night; and so it was also that in our Haste we left the *Jellies* underfoot, with dire consequences, as we shall see.

*

Lest it comes to mind that I had no-one to thank but myself for the *fiasco* of that night of the Ball, I must here say that I was led with my Eyes Open into Compromise and Corruption; that however quick was my Conversion to the Ways of the World, my Guides, in the form of the *Contessa* and my Uncle,

117

were three times more quick; and that they led me with such ease to the Sink of Iniquity, Cupidity and Indulgence shows only that I was bred and brought up to obey my Elders, as my poor Aunt had told me, and had she desisted from this path of instruction I wouldn't have gone with so little Resistance into a Life of PROSTITUTION (for that, at least, was what it seemed to me that my new Protectors were demanding of me); and, which is worse and lay ahead for me although I had no way of knowing it, another Fiend, more powerful still than the Charming Couple, waited in the Wings to finish off my Coming Out, all of which very nearly succeeded, once Out, in me being Put Away. Of that, however, more in its time: for that night, when I dressed under the hand of *Joy* and came down in my Red Dress, I was still Pure as the Driven Snow. 'You're very pretty tonight, my dear,' *says* my Uncle; and the *Contessa*, in her great Beauty (for her Gown was all stars and moons in silver and gold, on pearl satin) did me the honour of remarking that even in *Rome* or *Venice* where some of the greatest Ladies lived only for their *toilette*, I would Stand Out.

If only for the reasons of the above Compliments, and my excessive Vanity, I must give here an account of this Dress (also, lest it be thought that it could in any way resemble the Gowns in which I had begun my Season, I will confess that its Cost was ten times that of the Gowns the Little Woman had Run-Up, all of which may show how Vulgar I was already become, that I counted Money like my Uncle, and began to know the Cost of Things: but also, as I grew each day older, it came clear to me that there were in the World two Levels, in every way: for at the Parties where my Uncle escorted me I saw none of the Faces I had seen when I was at the Balls chaperoned by Lady S— of B—; these people were finer-looking, for Beauty makes its own Price, and they wore Dresses and Suits that were Cut with greater Finesse: 'This is Society,' my Uncle told me, 'the Rest are Hicks'). To continue with my Red Dress, this was from the Greatest House in *Paris* and was of Red Taffeta, as has been told, Cut on the

118

Bias and with a Full Skirt which Flared out at the Hip, but not before receiving, pinned low on the Stomach where the Material was Stretched excessively Tight, a Red Rose such as only the *Parisians* can make, of a fine Cloth, exquisite with petals and Foliage, and sewn on firmly, being arranged there so that the Stem, which was of wire covered in green cloth, should not Stick Out as I danced and thus Castrate my Partner, or lead him to think, at least, that he danced with a Man all along, feeling the Protuberance. (Here I must say that in all the Nobility I never met a Man who would have turned a Hair at being told his Partner was of his own Sex: indeed it happened at some of the Low Dives that the world-renowned CAROUSEL was there, in Drag and more Lovely than any Woman and the young Lords danced with her Happily, which can be ascribed only to the wicked Public Schools in England, where the model of *Alcibiades* is more acceptable than that of King *Henry the Eighth*.) Suffice it to say that my Stem was well tucked in under the Rose and fastened to the Dress and that the Creation did indeed make me a Beauty, if only in my own eyes and in those of my Escorts; yet I must also own here that many Heads turned when we came to the Ball, and not only to Gaze (or Star-Gaze the fine Night Sky of the Gown of the *Contessa*) but most certainly at myself: 'Who is the Girl with the Rose?' came many Voices; and my Confusion, I am sorry to say, was quick to melt away and to be replaced by Complacency and Vanity, for I was now among the Highest in the Land and Universally Admired, the dinner having been at Lady Y—'s, who was a Lady of the Bedchamber, and the Ball, which my Uncle and the *Contessa* had innocently forgotten to advise me, being at the Palace and our gracious Hostess Her Majesty the QUEEN.

*

The Palace was so fine, and the Beauty of the Women and the Good Looks of the Men shown up by the Chandeliers, all of Drops of Glass; and the Footmen so Numerous, that I thought myself to have walked into Another World, or the Arabian

Nights at-least, for my Aunt and Uncle in *Carlisle* had told me always that the Nobility was impoverished by Taxes; and Royalty in a Struggle to Open Hospitals with so small an Allowance; when all I saw was Magnificence, and not the lesser part in the Jewels at the necks and heads of the Titled Ladies and the Princesses and Royal Duchesses; and the QUEEN herself in a great *Parure* of Rubies and Diamonds that might have come from the *Tower of London* to be placed on her, save for the fact that the Jewels in the *Tower* are fake, in order that the QUEEN may wear the Real Ones. However that may be, I was, as I say, so Dazed by the Riches and the Soft Lights (albeit the Loudness of the Voices much counter-acted the Dulcet Tone of the Evening, for the Nobility is Prone to Shout on all Occasions, in order, it appears, to have its Will done—and it is done quickly, for fear the Din will start up again) that I had time to note little of my Neighbours or Surroundings, other than to see with Pleasure the great Popularity of my Uncle, who was several minutes with the QUEEN MOTHER and longer dancing with the Royal Prin-cesses, who were all Agog at his Wit and Charm, or so it seemed to me. I had then the Honour to be presented to the QUEEN MOTHER, who smiled at me very kindly: she was attended by Lord J—, very quiet-spoken as a Courtier must no doubt be, for when she had taken my hand (and hers had many fine Sapphires on it) she said to Lord J— that she would like a Favour of him: 'Yes, Ma'am,' *says he*, 'any Favour I can perform will be more than a favour, it will be an honour,' etc. when *she says* to him, still quite loud, 'Well, Lord J—, will one old Queen get another Old Queen a Glass of Champagne?' and was then laughing Fit to Bust, so I had no idea where to look, while Lord J— laughed as daintily as he could and made a signal to a Footman and a tray of Glasses of Champagne was brought.

In other rooms I had hardly time to stop, so anxious were my Uncle and the *Contessa* to introduce me to the Greatest People in the Land; once my Uncle pointed out to me an old man with a Long Nose and, 'He is Mr Herbert H—, a famous

Bore, my dear,' *says he*; 'keep well away from him,' and I did indeed see some poor misfortunate woman at the side of the Bore, and he hitting out at her sharply when her Attention wandered away, so that she gave out cries of pain at it; while in a further Room, which was hung with Tapestries, a Stern-looking Woman came up to us and said she was a friend of my Aunt's and she was surprised to see me here and with These People (and she looked Daggers at my Uncle, as if he had brought me to a Low Den and not the London home of our most gracious *Sovereign*.) '*Robina* is with us for an evening,' *says* my Uncle and goes away at a pace, with the *Contessa* at his side, but not before telling me that this is Lady E— D—, who takes my hand in a very strong Grip, and who, as my Uncle says in a low Voice, is the daughter of the tenth Duke of D—. 'I'll tell your Aunt I saw you,' *says her Ladyship*, still very severe. 'Don't tell her I have this new Dress,' *say I*, not thinking, but very embarrassed that since all my poor Aunt's effort to clothe me with the Little Woman, etc. I was found in another Gown altogether. 'This one costs more Money,' *said I*, and was every minute more of a Goose, for Lady E— D— wasn't in sympathy with my Embarrassment seeing doubtless only my Disloyalty. 'It will be hard for you, *Robina*,' *says she*, 'for we are brought up to expect no Money, as the Estate must be Kept up, but with Trade and Industry it's different, and certainly your Uncle thinks of little else.' 'Trade and Industry?' *say I*, for I was too dull to know what she talked of and that I was in the process of receiving an Insult. 'Yes,' *says she*, 'that is how your Family Fortune was built.' But she then, as if to Recompense for the Hardness in her, said I should come over to the Table and see her Aunt, Lady *Blanche*, who had known my Father when he was young and before he had Disappeared and my Mother bolted, for this was the way she put these Unpalatable Facts. I was then taken to the table without further ado; and Lady *Blanche* smiled up at me very sweetly, but by a chance of Time the Footmen were serving Soup in the Room and a Plate was set in front of the Venerable old Sister of the tenth Duke of D—

(whom I was to see later and in very different circumstances, I regret to say). 'My dear,' *says* Lady *Blanche*, 'you are very pretty.' And she goes on to say that I resemble exactly my poor mother; it can't be said, however, that I was concerned long with the sorrowful sentiments these comments were bound to provoke, for Lady *Blanche*, on looking down at her Soup Plate, lifted it up to her Bosom (I had perceived this custom among the Noble Ladies at the Ball at L—, it coming from the Piercing Cold in Country Houses and the Need to warm the Bare *Décolletage*, thus Raising a Warmed Plate to the breast): on this Occasion, however, at the Palace, the Plate was filled with a white Soup already and Lady *Blanche* hadn't seen it, being partly blind perhaps, or Blind Drunk (for I can't say her Remarks on my Ancestry were other than Garbled) and thus Tipped the Contents of the Plate down her Front, making her Blanch all over. (Also, let it not be said that severe Ladies do not come to the Aid of their Relatives when in Danger or in any kind of Plight, for Lady E— D— was a long time Mopping and calling for more Footmen in her strong Voice); and this, I must confess, I took as a Way to run from the Room quickly, and go in search of my Uncle and the *Contessa*. These I found in conversation in the *Throne Room*, and with the *Prince* whom I had last seen when I performed my curtsey in this very Room to the MONARCH, and when I had been under the chaperonage of Lady S— of B—; all of which *His Royal Highness* was kind enough to remember.

*

If I had lost all knowledge of my Aunt and Uncle who reared me in Carlisle, who were now as far from me in my thoughts as my own father and mother; and if I'd not waited for Lady *Blanche* to recover herself from the Spillage and tell me more of my Parents, it was for the Reason, as has been told, that I considered my Uncle and the *Contessa* to be truly my Parents now: I was obedient in every way to them and would go to the Ends of the Earth for my beautiful new Mother, who had only to take my hand (as she did when I came up to them in

122

the *Throne Room*) for me to Burn with Love for her and to beg her for any Instruction, however humble, which, on this occasion, took the Form of asking me to stay awhile with the *Prince* as she and my Uncle had a Conversation due Elsewhere; and so saying, and squeezing my hand so I nearly fainted for Desire to please the lovely *Madonna*, she went from the room at speed with my Uncle and I was left alone with the *Prince* (the ROYAL DUKE).

My Natural Shyness was at first hard to overcome, for the Room was so Awesome and the Portraits of the Kings and Queens on the Walls so forbidding in Expression, that I was at first Tongue-Tied: furthermore I recalled quite well the Night of the *Bag O' Nails*, when the ROYAL DUKE had been sporting quite merrily with the *Tarts*; and to see the face of QUEEN MARY, painted in her *Toque* and staring down at us was disconcerting in the extreme, and not only for the reason of seeing this distinguished Escort apparently Frowning at her Successor, but also bringing to mind the words of my sainted mother the *Contessa* that the *Prince* couldn't well be refused what he demanded, which I feared in this case lay not far from him, viz. under the Rose, with which he at-once began to play and Fidget, in the most Exacerbating Way.

'Robina,' *says he*, when he has looked round and seen that we are indeed alone in this Room which has seen so many Ceremonies of Crownings; and he then pulled me on to the *Throne*, which was wide enough for both of us, if a Tight Fit: 'My pretty little *Robina*, you are a hundred times more Pretty than when I last saw you,' etc.; while I was red with Shame that such words should be spoken in this Sacred Chamber, and to a Commoner who had the Cheek to occupy the Royal Seat. 'I believe we met when there was a Power Cut at a certain Establishment,' *says the Prince* laughing heartily; and as I could give only a demure sign of Assent, for the Throne was too High for me and I was slipping down off it, while the *Prince* knelt now on the floor by the Royal Hassock, as if he were about to anoint me, which I very much feared he might. 'My Power wasn't Cut Off, I can assure you, when it comes to getting In to a lovely Girl like you,' *says* the DUKE; and then goes on to say at great speed that his Cousin, who had lately been on the *Throne of Greece,* had a Villa in *Corfu* and we can go there together: 'You'll get a Tan,' *says he*, 'you'll be Rosy Red all over,' and then as I started to slide faster down off the Throne, he *says* his Cousin was pushed off his as well, and a good Life can be had nevertheless; and all this as I recalled I had no Knickers On, for the *Contessa* had said the Dress would Ride Up if I wore them, and I was now, or the Rose at least was, no more than an inch away from the *Prince*'s grasping Fingers. 'Don't be Bashful,' *says he*, 'for I've seen you before, *Robina*, or shall I say I've seen your Before from Behind!' And he laughs so much as I slid down and he had the Rose between his Teeth; while I thought for the first time, such a Fool I was, that it must have been *His Royal Highness* who had been shown me when I had my fitting, and I'd heard a Man's Voice and then the *Contessa*'s, and I wondered then if I could love her still, after landing me in this Pickle, which she had surely done, for now I saw it clearly. 'Yes,' *says the Prince*, inasmuch as he was capable of speaking, with the Rose in his Lips like a *Señorita*; 'a Red Rose in a Red Bush;' and with that he Bit Off the Flower, and even its Stem, and applied his Teeth and Lips to my Naked Self, which was Palpitating: 'a mossy Mound,' *says he*, and worthy of a pretty Rose,' etc. etc. but I was on the floor and the Dress had Ridden Up, as had been Feared, and even without the Pants to make it do so.

There can be few Times in a Girl's Life that she can look-back on with Greater Clarity than her first Deflowering; yet, having Bit off the Rose, the *Prince* was stopped in his Efforts by the Door Opening and a Shadowy Figure coming in at the end of the Room, and with a Groan he pulled himself to a Kneeling position, to give the Air, no doubt, of a Man who worshipped the MONARCH to an extent bordering on Idolatry, for he directed his head to the Portrait of QUEEN MARY and closed his eyes, though he was also I believe in Great Pain, for the Swelling in his Groin was Plain to See, so I must hope the visitor not to be the precursor of a great crowd, a rush of courtiers maybe, preparing for a ceremony; and the scene was all the more Unsuitable in that I was half-naked and still under the Throne, with the Dress as obstinate in its place over my midriff as a Horse that Refuses a Fence. Fortunately, however, the Interloper was alone: he made his way to a Table of Canapés and Other Royal Titbits that had been Laid Out, and Stuffed a Large Number of them in his Tails, before Going-Out and leaving us alone; and fortunately, then, too the *Prince* was too Deflated by the Interruption to Go-On. So it was, with the *Prince* following the Emaciated Man out of the Room (and I was to see him later, my Uncle telling me he was a *Romanoff* and very Badly Off, so I must be grateful to a RUSSIAN for the saving of my Honour) that I was once more my own Mistress, and with a Great Effort pulling down my Dress went out by the other door, behind the Throne; where I rejoined the Ball, and received from some of the Young-Men a good-deal of Merriment, for they were all quick to see that the 'Bush had lost its Rose'.

*

In so great a Palace, where the Highest in the Land were gathered about their Sovereign, and where claret and burgundy was supplied, or so my Uncle said, by the Duc de C— who was an Old Flame of the DUCHESS OF WINDSOR; and the Hock by Prinz von T— und T—, who had been, said the *Contessa*, Not On Our Side in the Last War but was a Cousin of the QUEEN; in this Wonderful and Magnificent Dwelling, as I say, it was of much Concern to me to discover a Sort of Person I wouldn't have thought to see there: namely *Felons* and *Sons of Suicides, Slave Owners* and *Courtesans*; and it was through the *Contessa*, who was always motherly with me, that I learnt these Facts of Life; that to find Crime it is necessary to seek it in the Highest Places. It is to my eternal discredit, alas! that I went into this Life without questioning; and it may have been that the *Contessa* took away all those moral qualities my Aunt had tried to implant in me, or it may

125

be that I was born without a Sense of Right and Wrong, as my Aunt often told me; and in that case the Blame must lie with my Parents, who hadn't given a thought for me: whatever the Cause, it never came to me that I should apportion Blame to myself, or change my ways, as we shall see.

'That is the old *Marquess* of J—', *says the Contessa*, for she led me through these Halls, where the Mirrors and the Candelabra gave a dazzling effect: 'He's just out of Pokey, y'know,' and she laughed exceedingly, relating that the old *Marquess* had been at the H— P— Hotel and had sent for a Jeweller of great Fame to call on him there with a Case of Diamonds aand the like, 'and then Coshed him on the Head,' *says the Contessa*, but laughing so charmingly that I must join in too, while I stared too in horror at the old Jailbird, who was as Complacent as the Morning Sun. 'But why is he here,' *say I*, in all my innocence and ignorance, but 'Shhh . . .' *says the Contessa*, 'here comes Old *Splicer*, as the Eleventh Duke of P— is called, and that he has a Castle so Vast that there is a Train in the Basement and the Servants load it with Food to take along to the Dining-Room; and that they have lived with their Families on the Estate so long they have no Idea what Government is in, or how to Vote, which Old *Slicer* does for them, thus ensuring that his Son, who is second only to the Royal Fog in his Thickness, may stay in as *Tory* M.P., which indeed he does. 'But that's no better than Serfs,' *say I*, for my Aunt was always democratic, and told me all men were equal in the sight of God, though she made no mention of Women, it's true, and it may be that I sought happiness and Wealth for myself without the Labour from which this must result for this reason: that I was both above and below the Common Man, for I wasn't one of them. However that may be, I looked on old *Splicer* with disdain and Fear, for he walked in a Stumbling Way, as if he were more used to being conveyed on a Train than on his own Feet; and he was Shaggy too and Muttering to a Younger Man who walked very quietly alongside him: 'That's *Splicer*'s nephew, who will Inherit,' *says* my Companion; 'his father was next in Line, but last week he shot himself, which we heard of in *Rome* and it was very Amusing.' 'But how can it be?' *say I*, for I was afraid now that the lovely *Contessa* had taken leave of her Senses. 'He had a great Shoot at his Estate in Northumberland,' *says she*, 'and at the end of the Shoot the birds were lined up in the Hall, as is the Custom, y'know, and then he picks up his gun and shoots himself so he falls in line with the rest of the Bag!' 'I'm surprised he didn't Miss,' *says* my Uncle coming up, for he had finished his business with the Equerry and the Gentlewoman of the Bedchamber; 'he once shot a Bumble Bee when he was staying with me and marked it in his book as a Grouse;' and 'that is amusing,' *says the Contessa*; but then up-comes a man with a Ferocious Scowl, who asked me if I would give him the pleasure of dancing with him, and following straight behind him was a woman of outstanding refinement, whom my Uncle said was Mrs P— C— who was the most famous Courtesan of her Day. 'Is her day then over?' *say I*, for the Scowling Man (who was the tenth Duke of D—, my Uncle said, and the Father of the Severe Lady E— D— who had Looked Down on me for my Genealogy) was eager to Take me In to the Ballroom while the Lady behind him was Angry, or so I could see, at his Preferment of me. 'Yes,' *says* my Uncle *sotto voce*, 'her Day is nearly done.' 'The Duke has given her an Immense Fortune,' *says the Contessa* and I confess that it was then that it came to me that I could be Rich and Admired and have no more to do than Polish my Nails or order Stuff for a Dress. 'She's had her Womb out this year,' *says the Contessa*, and it seemed that in Polite Society any Subject could be Brought up; that Likewise with People, viz. *Criminals*, *Ponces*, etc. amongst the Highest, so it was with Topics, which my poor Aunt had told me should never be talked of in Public, or at a Dinner: *A Lady's Insides* being one of the first of these. 'Yes, she's had the Factory out but she's kept the Playpen,' *says* the tenth Duke of D—, who was sweating, with Fear it turned out, that I would refuse his offer to dance (which I was indeed about to do, but my Uncle saying that the *Duke* had never been

127

refused anything in his life, that he had the largest Estates in England and Paintings and Drawings of Great Value, I pitied the man and accepted him); also I saw the *Royal Prince*, with his Hair Combed down since our Encounter, coming up on us, and so I went at speed with the tenth Duke of D—, but that I was going out of the Frying Pan and into the Fire was sadly the case, as shortly we shall see.

*

The Floor of the Ballroom being very full of People, the tenth Duke of D— soon found reason to implore me to sit with him, at the side; and this I did, but I was still afraid of the *Royal Duke*, who danced with the *Royal Princesses* in turn but had always his eye on me (and I was rightly afraid, for my Uncle, I knew, expected that we would all return to the House in *Chelsea* together and I could see no Way Out of this predicament, particularly as I owed so great a debt to my kind Uncle and to the *Contessa*). For the *Prince* was old and Ugly in my eyes; though not more so than the tenth Duke of D—, who was now *propositioning* me, which I scarcely knew, I must say, as my mind had wandered off to the lack of Romance and Happiness in my Life.

'*Robina*,' *says he*, 'you are the prettiest girl I've ever seen,' etc.; 'and what would you like most in the world? Tell me and it shall be yours, my darling,' and so on, all of which, as I say I was at Pains to hear, for the *Prince* was dancing ever closer to where we sat, and with the QUEEN in his arms this time, which was a great embarrassment to me. 'You'll come with me to *Ascot*,' *says* this Dreary Duke: 'there's a fine Horse I'll give to you, she's a grey Irish Mare.' And he goes on to say he has great Estates in Ireland too and a Castle there and I shall visit my Horse whenever I wish; 'and you'll have your own Colours,' *says he*, and then very wistfully asks me if I am 'Red everywhere', which as I say shocked me always with the Nobility, that they have no Delicacy and are always talking of Private Parts or Privies (for they like to talk of Lavatories, and this may be for the reason that they still have Old Bogs in their Houses, but I cannot say). '*Rubra*,' the tenth Duke of D— *says*, squeezing my knee now, and looking down for the first time at the Place where my Red Rose had been stitched and seeing the absence of Something, for there were Threads pulled and a fragment of Leaf and Stem. '*Rubra* shall be the name of your Mare and she'll win all the Races for you,' *says he*, all the while pulling at the thread as if he thought he could get to the part below: 'it means Red,' etc. and his fingers clawed into the stuff of my poor dress so I must fight with him to stop disrobing me there altogether, and before the eyes of our gracious *Sovereign*. What was worse, was that the *Prince* watched these antics and his face became grim, so that my spirits sank correspondingly, seeing he was bent on taking me tonight and hadn't the good sense to forget our Entanglement, which had been Fruitless, for all that the Flower had come away in his hand. I was close to weeping, indeed, for my Uncle had said I should be at the House in *Chelsea* at Midnight; and never did any *Cinderella* wish less to return home: I reflected, also, that little *Cinders* had slept alone and undisturbed in her Rags by the Fire, after the Exertions of the Ball; and I wished myself in her place, which I had never thought myself likely to do, for I must return home and find the *Prince* there, and I would be in Rags too, if the tenth Duke went on with his Pullings and Fumblings.

'*Robina*', *says he*, as the *Prince* circled the floor and turned to come down on us like a Huntsman, so that even the Duke of D— saw it; 'tell me you'll come out with me now to the Club.' And, as may be surmised, I saw little choice but to go with him, though I hoped ardently that it wasn't the *Bag O' Nails* that he had in Mind, for fear I would see my poor Lord C— M— there, if he had escaped from the kitchens at L— and come to *London* to look for me (as was indeed the case, but I was too Lost in-Love by then to care for his Feelings, I regret to say). However that may be, I thought then that I wanted only One Thing, and that was to get-out of the Palace and so I said that I would go with the Duke: soon we were in a Great Car and going away from the Lighted windows and

Merriment of the *London* Home of our Reigning Family; and it wasn't until later that I learnt of the Power they Possess, in chasing and following whomsoever they please; for the *Prince* had no intention of letting me Slip Away for the Rest of the Evening, and Royal Detectives came after us to the *Faro Club*, as it was called; but this, as I say, I wasn't to know until later, and by then I was in-love, and with a Young-Man with Golden Hair and Blue Eyes, as fresh in his Wit as in his Countenance, all of which brought a greater air of age and Weariness to the Complexion of the tenth Duke of D—, while a later Meeting with the *Royal Prince* appeared now quite Impossible.

*

If the World had appeared to me by then as a Strange Place, where there were many Economies made by the Gentlewomen who had Girls in their Charge, and where the Rich and Landed took Care to hide their Possessions and to enjoy them at the same time, keeping the Jewels in the Vaults of the Bank and wearing Imitation (with the exception of the QUEEN) so they could in so many Words have their Paste and Eat it; if I had found the Manners of the Great Families coarse in the extreme, for these noble Bumpkins behind their Walls had missed the Enlightenment and had not even woken to the Democratic Government seeing all Those Outside Their World as Foreign; if, as I say, I had come to know the Ways of Men and their Impetuous Desires, I still had never seen the like of the *Faro Club* and its denizens, which, to spare the feelings of the Reader, I will dwell on only briefly and with Tact.

The Interior of this Magnificent Building was all in gold and red, and Gaming Tables took up the *piano nobile*, whence I was escorted by the tenth Duke of D—, he first stopping at a Desk and buying a *Plaque* which he handed to me straightaway and which had printed on it £1,000, the *Plaque* itself being frosted and Pink, but apart from this I may say that it was not the beauty of the Object which held me, but the

Value, which was more Money than my Poor Aunt had ever let me Set my Eyes on, and which I knew (for it was a great-deal then) would set me free. For I was a bird in a Cage, however Gilded, with my Uncle, and I dreamed of Independence; but we must learn too late that this Quality is come by Hard Work and Endeavour, and not by the simple Stealing of a *Plaque*, which was alas! the first thought that came to me, and thus was my Introduction to my next Crime, which was LARCENY. 'We'll play *Chemin de Fer*,' *says* the Duke, who had caught no trace on my Features of my wicked Ideas; he stops on the stairs to kiss me and say, 'What are my Chances?' so I must make out I knew nothing of his Meaning; and then he tells me as we entered the great *Salon* the names of the Gamblers, who were many of them *Earls* (and one to be a Wife Murderer but missing his Prey killed the *Children's Nurse*, all this in later times) and a young Mr V—: 'He's lost his Estates in Yorkshire at the Tables and now he's playing for his Woods in the South,' *says* the Duke; and a *Greek Shipowner* of a most fearful Countenance, but hung-around with Pretty Girls, English and Greek: 'They do Exercises,' *says* the Duke, 'to keep the *Shipowner* amused,' and he goes on to tell me that these Women, and counting also the Wife of the *Rich Greek*, practise at picking up silver spoons with the muscles of their C—nts, 'though you won't need to do that,' *says* the Duke in an eager tone; and it may be surmised as to the horror I felt at the Company I was in, which was a Company of *Thieves* and *Tarts*, but all sanctioned by Money, which I saw was all and nothing, for my Spirits were low despite the *Plaque* and my wicked Schemes.

Were it not for the appearance of Mr W—, I daresay I might have seen the Folly of this Way of Life and gone directly to *St Pancras* and North, and thrown myself on the Mercy of my Aunt, who had no Thought of course that I was fallen in such evil hands; but I reflected that I must leave behind the *Plaque* to do this and that I had no Money with me otherwise, for the *Contessa* had said it was Common for a Lady to carry Cash in her evening Bag; and that at *St Pancras*

I must Reverse the Charge, which would indeed be the case, that my poor Aunt would find her Charge coming back to her, and she no doubt as unhappy to receive me as to accept to pay for the Call. So I hung-back; and Mr W— came up as the Duke was at the Roulette Table, and all this within a very short while of my Coming, so that it's true to say that Evil waits on no man; that Satan will find work for Idle Hands, and that it follows that good Impulses, rare as they may be, should be acted-on immediately. It was too-late, however, Mr W— had come up to me; and he told me I was looking for a Game and he would show me Poker, and he led me to a Room where a small company were sitting, and all the while he taught me the Rules of the Game I kept my eyes on him; for Mr W—, who was in no way like Lord E—, of whom I still thought fondly, yet was more fine in looks than the North Briton, and it was because he had *Scandinavian* Blood, or so he told me, but was of an old English family from the South of England, though he might have more the air of a *Viking*. *'Robina,' says he*, for he could see I was stricken with him, and I think he was himself much taken with me: 'you see I know who you are, for I asked as-soon as I saw you come up the Stairs, and you live with your Uncle in *Chelsea*, amn't I right,' 'You are,' *said I*, for I must confess I could see him in my Bed already, after all the times I'd heard of or seen the Act that is called Love. 'I'll take you there when we end the Game,' *says* Mr W—, and I must say his smile was Wide and his manner very Open, so that I wondered how he came to be in this Den for Rich Villains. As I have said, it was unnatural, or so I was fool enough to think then, for a Young-Man of the integrity of Mr W—, to find himself in with this Lot; and no sooner had I thought this than I determined to Save him, as women will often try to do when they are in-love, and often to no avail, for a Rake will go back to his Pleasures when the first Happiness of the Bed has gone; indeed, I saw no Difficulty in thinking one minute that I would give myself directly to Mr W— when we were in *Chelsea* (for I'd forgotten there were my Uncle and the *Contessa* there and I was

Blinded by Love, I think); the other minute in thinking that I would rescue Mr W— from such a Life as this, which he must lead because he cannot find a True Love (but now he has, etc.); and the next minute, in saying to him that I would go to the End of the World with him; for Mr W—, saying he had no Ready Cash on him (and even this delighted me, for it showed me we were the same, as Lovers yearn to be, I having no Cash either as already told), Mr W— saying to one of his Companions, who was a Swarthy Young-Man that he knew who lived in the *World's End*, which was near *Chelsea*, that this Companion could take us home, and it being clear that Mr W— was as eager to be Alone with me as I with him, I thought myself quite happy to go as-far with him as he desired. So we rose to go; and I can say only that *Cupid* must bear the Blame for my actions: I was in-haste to hold and be held in the arms of Mr W— and I had no time to go to the tenth Duke of D—, who was wandering miserably in the Gaming Rooms; and seeing also two men in the Livery of the Palace come up the stairs, I knew the *Prince* and My Uncle were after me; so, as I say, I left very rapidly and by an Iron staircase out of the window at the back that Mr W— pointed out to me (for he was apprised of the wishes of my Uncle and of Royalty to keep me a Prisoner, and in this way I had spoken of it, without the Loyalty which I owed to my dear Uncle and his Friend). However that may be, I was glad to hear Mr W—'s words: 'It's not midnight yet, *Robina*,' *says he* and on the Iron Staircase kissed me very tenderly, so I thought I might Faint Away, so long had it been that I had gone without Love; 'we'll go-back to your house, for my Flat is being Decorated at Present;' but I was too much of a Fool to see that I walked into a Paradise fit for Fools like myself, with Mr W—, that I should have asked him where he lived, and heard his Answer, if there was any; and it went the same with me that I was glad to give Mr W— the *Plaque* that had been given me by the tenth Duke of D— (and this in the Cab that took us to the River, where I might as well have Thrown myself, for I gaped like a Fish in wonder at the Honesty and Valour of Mr W—): 'I'll take this directly to the Duke tomorrow,' *says he*; and he says that he'll put it in a Sealed Envelope, 'for the Duchess doesn't like him Gambling and taking Girls,' *says he*, and thus gave me to think he knew all these People well and could Move in these Circles, always keeping to himself his Reputation as a man of Incorruptible worth; but these were his Blue Eyes that proclaimed it and not the Facts, as we shall see: indeed Mr W— was a very Great Scoundrel and I, on the very night of meeting him, already his Partner in Crime.

*

If Mr W— gave me every reason to Hope that Romance could come for us and make us Rich in Happiness, he was eager also to tell me of the Fortune we would enjoy together, once I was his: 'My Uncle is Rich, and I'm his Favourite,' *says he*; 'He is a Director of *Sotheby's*' (which was I knew the Famous Auction-eers, where Thousands of Pounds flowed in and out, and Jewels and Antiques of Great Value awaited the Tap of the Hammer). 'He wants me to follow him in the Business, but he has also amassed a great Collection and a great-deal of Wealth'; and he goes on to say that his Uncle's house in the *New Forest* would one day be his, with his Collection of Fine Paintings and Furn-iture by *Kent* and *Chippendale* and Carvings by *Grinling Gibbons*; and this, I am sorry to say, led me on to boast of my own Uncle's great Collections, and the Trip he said he would make soon to the *Far East* to bring back more of the *Oriental Art* that I confess now with a heavy heart I did Claim would Come to me, and not at his Death either but much sooner. Alas! that Lovers must vie with each other to give tokens of their Sameness, for Mr W— cried out in Astonishment at my words, and said his own Uncle had just lately begun on a Collection of *Sung* and *Ming* and he must put our two Uncles In Touch, so they could bid for each other's Gems: 'And no need for the Auction then, when we are all friends,' *says* Mr W— who was so keen a Fellow, but with so sweet a smile and such a Candid look in his Eyes that I was close to Swooning, at the Bliss that lay

134

ahead for us, and the Convivial time that would be had by
our Uncles, whereas, as the Reader shall see, it was indeed a
case, for my poor Uncle's finest Pieces, of *Going, Going, Gone*;
and all at the hands of the Rascally Mr W—; but we will come
to it in our own time. At that hour, as has been told, I was as
Blind to the Real World as if a Potion had been Slipped me;
and I thought I was rich already and Mr W— and I about to
take our Honeymoon in the *New Forest*, when there was no
Reason whatever to believe this, and I was exactly as I had
been before the Ball at the Palace and the visit to the *Faro*
Club, viz. penniless and with my Uncle in *Carlisle* holding on
to my Trust: yet of him I never spoke to Mr W—, though my
younger Uncle came to hear of Mr W— soon enough and
with disastrous Consequences for my Trust, as will be clear.

In my Blindness I saw only dimly Mr W—'s Companion,
who was at the back of the Cab and in the Gloom: indeed,
he was so hideous a man that no greater Contrast could
be found than that between him and Mr W—; and to make
matters worse, the Grotesque Creature (for he was malformed,
horribly Black in the face and with a Leer that sent Shivers
down my Spine) leant forward in an Interlude, of which
there weren't many, of Mr W— pressing my hand, and
bringing his leg sharply up against mine, so that I felt the
cut-off Stem of my Rose stand straight on the Lap of my
Dress; in one of these Gaps, when the Cab rounded a corner
and Mr W— and I were thrown together once more, this
Gargoyle says to me that we are Cousins and not far-off
Cousins either: 'I've been waiting for a Card to your Ball,'
says he with a Twist to his Lips, 'but one hasn't come yet.
You may tell your Uncle that I am keenly expecting one.' 'Of
course you shall have one,' *says* Mr W—, although as far as I
knew Mr W— was not on the List himself, and it may have
been that he was *Not Safe in Taxis* or that the Snobbery of my
Uncle and the *Contessa* (for this I regret to say was already my
Way of Thinking, having learnt Disloyalty and now adept at
it; (yet to exonerate my wicked Thoughts I must also say that
my Ball, and all the Thousands of Pounds which my Uncle

135

liked to say it would Cost him, for there were to be Chandeliers and an Aviary built on, would hold no Meaning for me without Mr W— and I could only thank Heaven that I had made this Encounter before the Ball, and so could Enjoy Myself to the Full and run no Risk of Wasting my Uncle's Money). Yet it was not to turn out so; and I do believe that I would have directed Mr W— to take me in the Cab to the *New Forest* (where I was Fool enough to think he was Welcome) rather than to *Swan Walk*, had I known the Attitude of my Uncle towards Mr W—, which Attitude drove a Wedge between us I fear, this Wedge being far from the least Factor in the Succeeding Change in my Fortunes. For the time, though, I was happy to be thrown in the arms of Mr W— as the Cab carried us to *Chelsea* and I took care not to hear the words my 'Cousin' uttered, for these were as ugly as his Face, and yet served only to make the Kind Promises and Sweet Phrases of Mr W— more Alluring. 'Tell your Uncle,' *says* the Cousin, 'that if I don't receive a Card for your Ball I shall expose my Findings on his business dealings to the Public'; and on my asking him how he should imagine I could speak in this way to my Uncle: 'He'll like to Save his own skin,' *says he*, 'for I've been Digging and Delving and what I came up with ain't a pretty sight.' 'Come, come,' *says* Mr W—, for he saw my Discomfiture and was always attentive to me, so that I felt as Safe as Houses with him, whereas I should have been better served to step out of the Cab on to the Embankment and into a Houseboat half-slipping down the *Thames* than to trust my Safekeeping with this Villain, 'Don't go on in this way. Surely we're at the World's End now,' *says he* (and a drab place it looked to me, though I was glad to be there, so long as Mr W— would ferry me to the Other Side; but the Wretched Man showed no sign that he would Leave Us Alone, so we could indulge in more Fondling and Petting, which was on both our Minds and no Mistaking it for anyone with Eyes in his Head. 'I'll come on to *Swan Walk* with you,' *says* my Cousin, 'and speak to your Uncle directly. He cheated me in the Trust and now he's taken over my

Shares in the A— Estates; he shall Pay Up tonight or Answer for it.'

Now my Shame and Fear were great indeed, and Little Wonder; for I had Escaped my Kind Uncle's Protection (and might go to Gaol for it, as I knew, for no Guest can depart from a Ball at the Palace until the QUEEN has taken her own departure, and I had readily done this, so inviting, or so I thought, a Warrant Out for my Arrest); I was bringing an Evil Cadet Branch of the Family right into the Home of its rightful Head; and then, too, as if I woke from the Dead I saw that the Hopes entertained by Mr W— and myself to Kiss and Make Vows was Unreasonable, at the very least, for my Uncle had said he would go-back to the House with the *Prince*. My Alarm was worse when I implored Mr W— to stop the Cab at-once, and that I would walk back the last way myself: 'No, No,' *says* Mr W—, thinking no doubt I was too much dis- appointed that my 'Cousin' should stay with us, 'we'll be there soon, my Beauty,' etc.; and although the Drug, or whatsoever it may have been, of Love, had Worn away and I looked in despondency at the Embankment as we passed it and turned by the River into *Swan Walk*, Mr W— held me so Close with his arms that I couldn't see what his Feet were doing, namely kicking my Kinsman and so forcing him to half-open the Cab Door in his Agony, which measure sent him flying into the air, and then into the *Thames* for a loud Splash came up to us. 'It's All right,' *says* Mr W— to the Cab Driver, who now showed his Alarm, 'It's a Dive for Charity, to take place at Midnight as you'll see it is.' The Driver being mystified by this, he drove on despite my Cries of Stop! and this was in all Probability for the reason that a great number of Cars came down the Road at that time and a Black Car as long as a Royal Barge among them, which Convoy came to a Halt by my Uncle's house, my Heart lower every minute to see my Uncle and the *Prince* come out of it, which they did. 'Please let me go alone now,' *said I* to Mr W—, for my Desire had quite gone and I wanted only to save myself, I'm sorry to say. 'Your Uncle will be glad to see me again,' *says* Mr W—,

137

'it's a while since we met.' 'And my Cousin?' *say I* in Trepidation, for I saw a Horrendous Face with Dripping Hair pull up above the Parapet of the Embankment: 'What will you do with him?' 'I'll save your Uncle from his Attentions,' *says* Mr W—, but for all his Reassurance it was too-late: the party by the House, where the *Contessa* also stood, had seen me far-off; the Royal Escort was sent away; the *Prince* came towards us at a Brisk Trot, and the Cab drove off and left us on the Sidewalk, where I recalled so well the *Scottische* and Highland Fling I had danced with Lord C— M— for the entertainment of my Uncle, now wishing I had done No Such Thing and had stayed in peace on my poor Aunt and Uncle's Farm in *Carlisle*. 'Good evening, Sir,' *says* Mr W— as Bold as Brass to the Royal Personage as he came up; and 'Good evening Sir,' again to my Uncle, who was most Frosty to see him there and immediately ordered him to get-off. 'But can he come to the Ball?' *say I* to my Uncle, with all of us standing in the Road and no doubt making a Commotion, for the window of the Bedroom of the old Earl of H— next door went up and there was an exclamation of Annoyance, though whether this came from the Din we made or the sight of a *Hanoverian* in the *Royal Borough of Chelsea* it was hard to say. 'You'll go now or I'll call the *Police*,' *says* my Uncle; and I must say he was a Fool to speak in such a way, for I was more in-Love with Mr W— after my Uncle's treatment of him than I had been before; and it must be said that if Guardians and Fathers wish to Warn Off Unsuitable Suitors they should adopt a cunning pleasantness that the Girl may Go Off the Prospective Lover rather than Go-off directly with him, which I then vowed to myself I would do. Besides this, the *Prince* was an Old Man for one so young and Hopeful of Love as I, and he Ogled in a way that made me Sick to the Stomach, particularly as he held a Great Key to the Physick Garden, where my Uncle said we would all go and pick the Herbs to make an *aphrodisiac*. I went with no great alacrity in the footsteps of my Uncle: indeed I ran back once as the Prince put the Key in the Lock of the Garden Gate and kissed

Mr W—, for we were in the shadows. 'I'll Shin Up your Pipe tonight,' *says* Mr W— in a whisper; 'And what of him?' *said I* very low, for my wicked 'Cousin' was now walking along the Embankment with a staggering gait and dripping wet all over, so hideous in appearance he could be the Ghost of Banquo. 'I'll take care of him,' *says he*; and went off to take this Apparition into his own Custody, and I must say that I felt the greatest Pride in Mr W— then for his perfect Aplomb, and disliked my Uncle for insulting him; and I thought even that my Uncle was perhaps a Shark, as our Clansman had said, and had deprived him of his rightful Inheritance; and knowing of my Grievance with my Aunt and Uncle in *Carlisle*, who wouldn't Break my Trust but kept the Revenue to themselves, that the same Ruthlessness might obtain in this case, and our Cousin have had Shares Siphoned Off and nothing further said of it. Thus it was, in my Ignorance and Folly, that I turned in my mind against my only Benefactor and gave assent to Mr W—'s Dangerous Plan for later in the Night: yet I had to Live, I had had the Prince groping me one time already, and his Breath, furthermore, was a great-deal more powerful than it had been earlier, this stimulated by the Fine Wines and Champagnes of the Palace, I have no doubt, but causing me half to Faint when I was led into the Garden and fondly kissed by him, while my Uncle and the *Contessa* followed and stood by the Lavender, laughing and Talking as they always did, and Mr W— and his Terrible Charge went up the Road and past the Gates of the *Royal Hospital*.

*

The ingredients of the Love Filtre which was now truly in preparation, and which the *Contessa* picked, were *Gentian*, *Camomile*, etc. and *Ladies' Purse*: 'That I'll fill tonight,' *says* the *Prince*, squeezing me; *Cowslip*, *Solomon's Seal* and a flower that was even Blue in the light of the Moon, *Lithospermum*: 'That's what I'll fill it with,' *says he*; and a secret ingredient which can be told to no-one or so said the *Contessa*, and I

139

could swear she was a Witch that night and the name of that herb I will never dare to say. For all that, I wondered at my Uncle's amusement and his lack of Care for my Discomfiture: indeed he called *Joy* out to the Garden and there was *Slap and Tickle* all round, and this I suppose was to *titillate* the *Prince*, who was showing the signs of his night's Drinking all the more gravely as time passed; and with my Melancholy to contend with also, my Uncle must have thought himself a poor Pander, for all his going with *Joy* into the Bamboo in the Gardens. 'We'll go and dance in the House,' *says the Contessa* when she has done Plucking and across the road we went; but it must be said now that for all the gratitude I bore my Uncle I vowed I would never go to-bed with the *Prince*; that I waited for Mr W— with a Passionate Desire that had grown all the greater since receiving the Kisses of the Royal Halitosis; and that despite all the kindness that had been shown me I resolved to Trick my Benefactors and so I did: 'Uncle,' *say I* when we go-in to the House and we are alone together a short-while, 'may I be left with the *Royal Duke*, in your opinion?' 'Left with him?' *says* my Uncle, who was delighted but surprised too, I must say; 'Yes,' *say I*, and the *Contessa* coming up then with the Potion in a Glass she hands it to me and I drain it down, for it seemed to me that it could only bring me Benefit later, when Mr W— came; and so I determined I should enjoy myself, if my Views of my Uncle and *Joy* in their Ecstasy or the Sad Memory of Lord E—'s Thrusting was anything to Go By. 'I'm in-love with the *Prince*,' *say I*, 'and he's Shy: can't we go alone to the Conservatory?' 'Why of course you can,' *says* my Uncle who had drunk down the Filtre too and even though a prickly Borage stuck out of it, so he forgot his Surprise in the Pain of it. 'When is the *partouse*,' *says the Contessa* coming up to us, and she goes on to say the *Prince* is a very Difficult Man when it Comes Down to it; that he needs Constant Stimulation, and that we have an Orgy planned that will surely whet his Appetite. 'No, no,' *says* my Uncle, 'you can turn them away at the door, my dear; *Robina* has fallen in-love with the *Prince*

140

and all will go smoothly.' 'In-love already?' *says the Contessa*
who wasn't so much of a Fool. 'Yes,' *says* my Uncle, 'it's a
Miracle,' and he took me in his arms and kissed me very
fondly, the during of all of which taking place while the
Royal Duke was in the *Loo*. 'I'll send them away then, for I'm
not in that mind myself tonight,' *says the Contessa*, and
saying she was tired she went to direct *Joy* to turn away the
Guests, many of whom came Naked under their Coats in
Readiness for the F—ing but were too much in-awe of my
Uncle to complain when they were banished from his House
and told the Party was at an End before they could get their
End Off. 'One thing you must know,' *says the Contessa* when
she has led me to the Conservatory and quite Innocent
arranged me there, pulling up the Skirt of my Red Dress so I
might have been no more than a *Tart*, and letting down my
Red Hair so it tumbled as far as my A—e; 'and that is that the
Prince is a *Jack Rabbit*.' 'Why, what's that?' *say I*, for I was
afraid now that my Royal Suitor would come out of the Bog
translated to a Hare, or some such thing, all of which could
be believed after the drinking of the Potion and on a night of
Full Moon with *La Strega*. 'He Comes too Fast,' *says the
Contessa*, 'and he looks for Virgins to Cure Him of it.' 'Comes
too fast?' *say I*, for I began to understand my Wicked God-
mother's Meaning and had more Fear now, that I wouldn't
get-away in time from the *Prince* and he would Cover me
with Shame, which Mr W— would no-doubt Upbraid me for
if he were to sense it there. 'But here he comes!' *says the
Contessa* so I thought in my Alarm she saw the *Prince* appear
round the Corner already spending himself; 'I'll leave you,'
and she went out into the main part of the House so I was
alone in the Gloom of the Conservatory and my Heart in my
Mouth I must confess, for I had lost my Rose to him and the
Contessa had half-exposed the Red Bush beneath; and for all
my Screams there would be no Help available, my having
said (in my most recent discovered Crime, DECEIT) that I
was in-love with the *Prince* and wished only to surrender to
him. 'Why, what's up, *Robina*?' *says he*, seeing I was alone

and so placed to show myself to him as much as a Baboon in the Zoo, or so it seemed to me in my Confusion; 'is there no Party for us here?' And he comes up to me quite gentle, as if he had no Intention of grabbing at my Parts, which of course I knew he had. 'We're to sit together in this Romantic place then?' *says he* still very calm; but I had no time to Pity him, for I saw his Eyes go Narrow at the Idea that a Slit was on Offer to him, and now he came very Fast over the Parquet Floor to the Conservatory; and for the rest I must be forgiven, for I was a Young Girl with no Resources of my own, remember, and newly in-love, after my great disappointment with Lord E—; furthermore I fought for my Independence and had a Dread of being a Concubine of the *Prince*, wishing rather for a life of Hard Labour and Just Reward until such time as my Trust could be broken for me. For the time, however, it was another Part that the *Prince* had it in mind to see Broken, and it was for this that I foiled him and so can't be judged, in my eyes at least, too Harshly for it.

In the Dark, and with his Flies now undone and a small Pr–ck sticking out, the *Prince* now came at Full Speed (fearing perhaps that his Staff would Outstrip him) and then Fell, Cursing and Groaning, and then I'm sorry to say Screaming in Fear which wasn't Manly (for a male Member of the Royal Household must set an Example to his Subjects and in the Case of War must be ready to lead them into Battle without Timorousness), none of which the *Prince* showed on his Coming Across the *Glass Jellies* I had placed in his Path, all unseen by the *Contessa* and glistening there with the Moon Coming in through the Roof of the Conservatory. The Cries for Help all coming from the *Prince*, Help was quickly available; *Joy* and other Servants ran in with Candles and Torches; and I must beg Forgiveness once more from the Reader if I say that I went with a Light Heart and my Melancholy quite disappeared, up the Back Stairs of the Old House to my Room, before I was seen by a Soul; indeed the Filtre I had Drunk had Filled me with a Radiant Happiness and a Longing for Mr W—'s Visit, and my Ears were Deaf to

142

my Uncle's Exclamations of Horror, at his Royal Patron being Sprawled there on the Parquet and all round him my Grandmother's Collection of *Fantastic Jellies*.

*

Without *Joy* I can't say that I'd have lived to the Day of my Ball: for I slept hard that night, the Love Potion taking me sooner to *Lethe* than to *Eros* (and this gave me cause to wonder if the *Contessa* had not wanted me drugged asleep in readiness for the *Prince* and had mixed in Deadly Nightshade or some such Herb to ensure that I was in no fit state to repulse him); however that may be I was soon asleep and still Hungover in the morning when *Joy* brought my Coffee in to me. 'He didn't come up your Pipe,' *says she* when I told her all of my exploits of the last evening; and sits down on my bed, which is how we would often pass the morning I'm sorry to say, with nothing to talk about but Ball Dresses and Men; 'I thought he would,' *says she*, talking of Mr W— and making me uncomfortable, for I thought so too and was sad to miss him, for it was the same with me always: if I wanted, he did not, and no need to pull the Petals from a Daisy to find that out, better indeed to obey my dear Uncle's wishes and join a Daisy Chain than place any trust in the affections of fine Young-Men, whether North Britons or from the South. 'We'll have to find him,' *says Joy* for she saw me pale, and she hated me to be unhappy I think, though much of her Advice I should never have taken, and if I hadn't I'd have less to be Repentant of, and there's no doubt about it. 'I found this Card,' says the maid from *Calabria* (and it was true that she had in many ways more native cunning than her mistress the *Contessa*); and she shows me the invitation Card to my Ball, which were in very great demand I know, for my Uncle was very fascinating to Society and the Royal Family were coming to the Ball, etc., and I believe he had hired Bouncers, to keep out such Undesirables as my 'Cousin' and Mr W— or so my Uncle gave me to understand and in no obtuse manner. 'We'll find Mr W— and give him this Card,'

143

says the wicked Joy, 'and then you'll have everything on earth that you want, *Robina*. And I shall come as your maid when you're married,' *she prattles on*, and I was too taken with the idea to refuse her, though how I could afford a maid when my money was in Trust another four years and Mr W— was penniless I didn't consider at the time, nor did I know that Mr W— had Nothing: I had seen him got-up very fine, and if there were Problems, a sense of which had reached me, I thought he had perhaps been Cut-Off until such time as he should Settle Down, and his inheritance would be let loose like a dammed stream when it was known that he had married the niece of my Famous Uncle, and therefore there was no need for Anxiety on that Score. How wrong I was must be told to its dismal tune, but this being more of a dirge than a Wedding March, I'll speak of it only briefly, a slide downhill being by its Nature an event that doesn't go at a measured pace, but gathers speed in a way horrible to behold; and it will be seen too that I gathered no Moss as I went, and was indeed more in danger of losing my Marbles; and my Uncle's *Ming* too, as we shall shortly see. '*Joy*,' say I, 'I'll get dressed and we'll go and find Mr W—.' 'Wear your Lilac Linen,' *says Joy*, for she had given thought to the matter and feared too that Mr W— had not Fancied me enough; 'it's so good with your red Hair,' *says she*, and then, 'You're too pale in the face, *Robina*,' and she starts to put Rouge on my cheeks with a Sable Brush and then takes out Lip Salve and puts it on my Lips, so I look the most natural, bonny girl you ever could see, just down from the Lochs by the Looks of me and ripe for Seduction, for I wanted it now and was in a fever to find Mr W—, as I have related. 'One more place,' *says Joy* as I was ready to fly out the door, and she pulls open the bodice of the dress and exposes my Breasts, putting there dabs of Rouge, which movement made the Nipples stand quite erect and I looked to have two Flowers there, blushing awake in the stamens. 'He'll see that through the dress,' *says the sensible Joy* (for it was true that the dress was partly Transparent and had a Slip which she forbade me to wear

144

with it); 'now we'll go with our Card and he'll want to Come, I'm sure of it.' 'But where does he live?' *say I,* for *Joy* had buttoned me up and we went out on the Sidewalk, being careful not to be seen by my Uncle, who might ask where we thought we were going with my face so red and my Breasts as Visible as a Mermaid, at the height of the Morning. 'He lives in Mayfair,' *says Joy.* 'He must be rich then,' *say I* (and for all my Resolutions I kept in me a Curiosity for Money, so I do think that if I had been given a great Fortune by the tenth Duke of D— as the Great Courtesan had got, I still would have Gambled it all away and wanted more, or Speculated sadly with it, this Propensity coming from my Family and insuppressible, though I had from my father I think a strong sense of Justice and Equality and would give much away, being *Robina* as *Robin Hood.* 'He is in *Mount Street,' says Joy,* and so we walked there from *Chelsea* which on a fine summer day was a pleasant walk, with Heads turning at my appearance, and we were several times Followed, I'm sorry to say.

Mr W—'s Flat in *Mount Street* was on the First Floor of a great Building: the Hall Porter was Tipped by *Joy* to let us upstairs, all of which she accomplished with ease and Grace, and we were soon at Mr W—'s Door, while my Heart was Pounding, as needs no describing, and the Saucy *Joy* was down on her knees with her Eyes to the Key Hole, though I might have Fainted Away altogether if she had told me she saw Mr W— F—ing Another in there. This was not the situation, however: 'The Flat's Empty,' *says she,* and proceeds to take a Hairpin from her Bag. '*Joy,* what are you doing?' *say I,* though I could see perfectly well, and in truth had no Objection to be found by Mr W— in his Bed when he should return from his Outing, so keen was my Appetite for him. 'We'll leave the Card on his Mantelpiece,' *says Joy:* but first I must say we stood astounded when the Glory of the Flat was shown to us with the opening of the Door; and I can say only that the Furniture was Gilded, being *Boulle,* the Cabinets were inlaid with *Mother-of-Pearl* and there was a *Chinese Chippendale* Mirror over the Mantelpiece, which was packed with Cards already, to my Dismay. 'Never mind,' *says Joy* leading me up to them, 'they are most of them not Engraved,' and she runs her finger over the Lettering, like a Blind Man; 'they are printed and there isn't one that has Decorations on, like ours,' *says she*; and the impish Girl set the Card in Pride of Place under the Mirror, where I stood Reflected and very Pretty I Must say it myself, when we see the Door open also in the Reflection and Mr W— comes in and stops dead at seeing us there and without a Kind Smile at first on his Lips I fear. 'Why *Robina*,' *says he* very low; and then bursts out in a Great Laugh and comes Swooping down on us and throws an arm round each, so *Joy* is laughing and cooing like a Turtle Dove, so I began to think she wanted Mr W— too and this was why she had found his address, stolen the Card, etc. 'I couldn't have a better Surprise,' *says* Mr W— and we laughed more at his wonderful Gaiety; 'I thought I'd see a *Dun* and saw a *Robin*,' and many Fooleries I could barely understand, but by this time we were in Mr W—'s Bedroom, which was as Splendid as his Drawing-Room and on a Canopied Bed, with *Joy* squealing like a Pig and me only too happy if she would run off now to *Chelsea* and leave me alone with Mr W—. '*Joy*, you have the Food to Prepare at Home,' *say I*; and then had committed the crime of ARROGANCE, for I wished to show Mr W— that *Joy* was only a Servant, to forestall him seeing us as Equals; and I hoped she would run off now with her Tail between her Legs, whereas the Reality was that she had her Tail in Full View to us now, having pulled down her skirt, that was made of some rough Italian material and lying on the Bed in a Provocative Pose, Face down and with her A—se rising and Falling so that only a Simpleton could have mistaken her Desires in this Direction. 'My, my,' *says* Mr W—, who was enjoying himself Hugely (and I saw to my Mortification that he had a Great Lump in his Trousers), but accordingly and at no Bidding from myself my own Tits went up, which Mr W— now saw and Grabbed Hold of, so the Dress split open and I had no Idea what I could say to the *Contessa*. 'Well, well,' *says he*, 'which of you shall I have first?'

'Io,' *says Joy*, or some such Nonsense: 'Yes,' *says* Mr W—, 'You're no more than a Little Sheep, and we know what the Shepherds in the *Abruzzi* do to their Sheep, but I won't B—ger you today,' and so saying he unbuckled his Trousers and began to beat poor *Joy* with his Belt, which to my Astonishment she Wanted More of, for the Redder her Behind became, the more Cries of Pleasure she gave out. 'As for you, *Robina*,' *says* Mr W— when he had done and *Joy* had stopped her Moaning and lay Still, 'you and I will get Married and then we'll Have Ourselves a Ball, and it will be after your Ball that we'll do it,' and he kissed me on the Nipples many times so I was Swooning for him: 'We'll go to *Gretna*,' *says* the Wicked Fellow, 'and we'll be there at the Anvil to be Spliced in the Dawn.' As may well be thought and with no need of expounding the Reasons, I agreed to this at-once: I gave not so much as a Minute to the Considerations that my Uncle would Cut Me from his Affections altogether; that my other uncle would Tie up my Trust so no Fingers could ever Unknot it, nor that *Gretna* was so near to my poor Aunt and Uncle's land that they might well Catch us, if they were up with the Late Lambing, or some such thing. None of these Dangers presented themselves to me in the least; and I prayed only that *Joy* wouldn't Split it another way, viz. tell a Secret where it would most be Welcomed, viz. to her Mistress the *Contessa* and so I now must promise the Minx that she could come and be our maid when Mr W— and I were married, which Proposition was most Disagreeable to me and of which Mr W— Cared not at all, Either Way: but even then I wasn't alerted to his Cunning and saw him a Knight in Shining Armour, who would take me up to the Border to be his Bride.

*

You may be sure I behaved with a due Sense of Impatience in the days before my Ball: my Life was to begin a new Phase and I could barely wait for it; and my poor Uncle all the while thought I pined for my Coming-Out, and thinking even that

I pitied the *Prince* and felt true Repentance for my wicked Trick, *says*: 'Robina, you won't be too sad when I tell you the *Royal Duke* is unable to come to the Ball; he's with his Stallion' (and he spoke the Name of a Famous Horse that had won the *Derby*) 'he's Lame,' *says* my Uncle, 'and that's the Sad part of it, I saw him Hobbling at Ascot yesterday, but he bears you no Ill Will'; and I being astonished that this Horse should have any Feeling toward me, then perceived that it was the *Prince* who was Crippled and by his Fall over the *Jellies* no-doubt, so I said, and not for the first time, how much I regretted my Foolishness, etc. and that I would be happy to see the *Prince* when he could dance again, for I knew he wished to dance with me. 'Quite right,' *says* my Uncle and seeming much relieved at my Change of Heart; 'he'll be recovered by the time of the *Highland Balls* and asks you to *Balmoral* to stay for the Scottish Season'; and I must smile and accept with a glad Smile, when I knew that I'd be in *Scotland* afore ye, and getting Wed too, though I had all the time in the World later to Repent that I refused the High Road, that my kind Uncle and the *Prince* offered me, and took the Low Road with Mr W— instead, which led me to the very Gates of Hell.

Blind Love must be, however, and I went again to Mr W—'s but this time alone, and found the place abandoned and empty; and in the face of all this even then I could accept nothing of the Truth concerning my Hero: 'He's a Crook,' *says Joy* laughing very much (for I was disconsolate and thought Mr W— had gone Abroad, with Another very likely, and Prettier than I). 'He moves into Flats and borrows Great Furnishing and Pictures through the Use of his Uncle's Name, who is the Famous Auctioneer, saying they are for some Rich Person and he represents them and these Fine Pieces are On Approval and then they're all brought back in, when the Tradesmen learn they've been Duped; but our Mr W— will have sold some of them Overseas by then you can be Sure.' *Joy* was (in her jealousy and Mortification, as I believed then, at Exposing herself Shamelessly to a Young

Blood who was in-love with me) happy to Goad me further with the stories of Mr W—'s malpractice: 'You can believe your Plaque for a Thousand Pounds wasn't returned to the Duke,' *says she*; 'he'll have gone to the Club and cashed it in; and the worst of it is that he uses that vile man, your "Cousin" to do all the dirtiest work for him, so he's often not seen himself at the Scene of the Crime.' And *Joy* goes on to say that the tenth Duke is coming to my Ball; that he will speak of the matter to my Uncle and I will be in Trouble; and I confess my tears flowed, but my Blindness was still with me and I thought Mr W— much maligned; I prayed that he would come to the Ball and carry me off with him; in short I cared for nothing else, and I was hard pressed to pass the nights and days before I should see the Gallant Mr W— again.

On the night of the Ball my Uncle was good enough to call me to him: 'Here, *Robina*,' *says he* and he hands over to me a Leather Box, with a Ruby and Diamond *Parure* inside, on velvet: that is to say a Tiara, a necklace of great Magnificence, and Drop Ear-Rings; 'I've had a Clip fastened to them,' *says he*, 'for your ears aren't Pierced yet;' and in so many ways did he show his Regard and Concern for me that I was unable to speak for all the Gratitude and Tenderness I had towards him, and in particular that I wouldn't see him again after the Ball for I'd have married Mr W—, and my Uncle would find the Bird had flown the Nest, which I was sad to reflect on, the Bird being as I knew likely to be considered a Magpie, with such a quantity of Jewels in its Beak. 'You will be the Belle of the Ball,' *says* my Uncle, and he *says again* how the *Prince* has heard that my Nickname is *Rubra* and it's for this that my Uncle bought the Rubies, so the *Prince*'s fondness for me would return, when he next saw me Red from Head to Toe, and my Uncle laughed a great-deal and said I was a Good Girl and the *Prince* had forgiven my High Spirits, but he wouldn't eat Jelly again, and so on, so we both laughed and I went off very happy with my Fine Jewels and all the more Impatient that Mr W— should see me in my Splendour, for certainly the Red Stones in my Hair were a Sight that would attract a Crowd of Admirers, as indeed they did.

If I pass at speed over the Matter of my Ball, it is perhaps because Disaster casts so great a Pall in looking backward: Let me say only that the Ballroom was Grand, the Chandeliers with a Hundred Candles Apiece in rose Glass that was *Waterford* cast a fine Hue on the Guests and especially on my Tiara and my Hair and my Complexion which was that night *Carnation*, and an Aviary with many Tropical Birds gave out a sweet sound that was Refreshing to the Senses in the intervals from the Band Playing. All this aside, it suffices to say that I was much Praised, and so was the House and the Contents; my Uncle's Collection was well Lit and Mounted, and the *Jade Bowl* in its Place; the Air was scented with Night Stocks; and the Bouncers working to keep the Unwanted Guests from the Door, for there were many of them, and among these Gate-Crashers, I am sorry to say, was my 'Cousin' who had Mr W— by the Arm and wouldn't let him go. 'What's this?' *says* my Uncle, much alarmed that his Ball should have an Unpleasant Incident; 'I didn't ask these Gentlemen' (and by this, you may be sure, he also meant Mr W— for he had no Idea of the Tricks *Joy* and I had been Up To, with delivering a Card). 'Oh let them in,' *say* I, for I was overcome at the sight of Mr W—; he was in an Abundance of Good Looks and I was Swooning to be taken in his arms, for he was as fair as Young Lochinvar and had come to the Feast to rescue me, or such was my Fancy then. 'Very well,' *says* my Uncle, for he wanted only to give an Agreeable time to all, and he signalled to the Bouncers to let my 'Cousin' go, which they did. 'Ha,' *says* my 'Cousin' by way of thanks to my poor Uncle, and walking up to him administered a Slap to his Face, which drew a Gasp from the Guests, 'you Swine,' *says* my 'Cousin', 'you cheated me of the Property Trust and the A— Estates,' etc. and my Uncle turning on his Heel and going out of the room the Band struck up a Lively Tune and there was Dancing and Supper, which was Salmon and Strawberries, but my Uncle had gone and there was no Finding him.

If I had some Guilt at this, for I had persuaded my Uncle to admit the Monster, all such Feeling was dispersed when Mr W— took me in his arms on the Dance Floor where we danced very Close together a long time, despite the Waving of the *Contessa* from the side of the Floor, that she wanted me to get out and mingle with the Guests and in particular to dance with a Lord B— she had saved for me for the evening, the *Prince* Being too Crippled to attend. I paid no attention, however, and danced with Mr W— as if I were in very Heaven: 'When do we leave for *Gretna*?' were the only words I could address to him, and these with difficulty, for he held me so close to him there was barely any Breath left in my Body. '*Robina*,' *says he*, 'I've something to tell you.' And he goes on to say that we're not going to *Gretna* tonight: 'You came to my Flat,' *says he* (and it was *Joy* who must have told him this, though I had no time to reflect on it), 'you saw that it has been Ransacked and Pillaged; in short that it's quite Stripped of everything now and Uninhabitable.' 'I did,' *say I*. 'I am under Attack from the *Russians*,' *says he*, 'they are threatening the Freedom of the West and I am fighting for it; I am in Constant Danger and yet I'll Fight to the Last for our Rights,' etc. so I hardly knew how to answer him, for he was asking me all the time too if I didn't think it right that we should postpone our Wedding when the Future of the Country was at Stake, that there were Higher Things than the Pleasure of One Couple in the World, that he was in Hiding since the Russians had destroyed his Flat and he was going to *Hungary* tomorrow to fight in the Uprising there and I could on no Account come with him, as it would be too Dangerous. 'But,' *say I*, and I cried so my eyes were as Red as the Rubies on my Head, 'how long will you be in *Hungary*?' 'I don't know,' *says he*, 'as long as the Injustice of the *Russians* goes on,' and he says it's bitterly cold there and he hopes to survive it, but he may not and I must Be Brave about it. 'Tonight we'll go to a Place on the River that I know,' *says he*, by way of Consolation for me, and when I then looked up at him, for we still danced but at a Slow Pace, he laughed and said he would be Fine and I wasn't to Fash Myself, which was what people said in *Scotland*, and sure enough we'd be there together by the end of the summer and would exchange our Vows with the *Russians* well Crushed by his efforts. So I could be in some measure cheered; and so it was that we went out unobserved by the Wall at the back of the Conservatory and left for the country, where Mr W— said there was an Inn, *Skindles*, that waited for us with a Bottle of Champagne; but not before I had been to fetch my poor Aunt's *Fur Coat*, which I gave on Loan to the Rascally Mr W—, to keep him from the cold in *Hungary*. If I'd known then that my Uncle also would depart tomorrow morning for the *Far East*, which he hadn't wished to tell me till the end of the Ball for fear I was sad to hear it, I would have stayed in *London* and pledged my Obedience to him, and put Mr W— from my mind; or at least I think I might have hoped to show Loyalty where it was due; but unknowing and Foolish I went to *Maidenhead*, to lose mine, and was the poorer as well of my Uncle and my Lover by Morning.

*

I could enlarge here much on the Method Mr W— took to make his life passable and easy and mine a Bed o' Nails; but it is too long and the Articles are too trifling: I shall mention some of them as the Circumstances I am to relate shall necessarily bring them in.

After we had gone from the House in *Chelsea* we arrived at the *Faro Club*, where Mr W— said we should Gamble for *Hungary* and took Credit out on my Name, which the Chief *Croupier* believed was Good for a good-deal, for I had told Mr W— in my Foolishness that my Uncle was about to pass down his Fortune to me; and this, you may be sure, had been told by Mr W— to every Shark and Mountebank in London, so that one consequence for me when Mr W— was gone was to be Pursued by Fortune Hunters and to have to Lie Low with *Joy*, which cut the Enjoyment from our life considerably.

152

However that may be, Mr W— Raised Five Thousand against my Name and we went to the Roulette Table and there were many Eyes on us I may say, for I was Aflame with the Prospect of a Night with Mr W—, and was Crowned with Rubies also, which I must say did Show my Beauty to great Advantage. 'Robina', *says* Mr W—, 'put it all on Number Seventeen, that is your own Sweet Age.' This I did and I watched the ball roll with Trepidation, yet I thought still of myself and of my Future with Mr W—, Fool as I was, and when Number Seventeen Came Up and there were Groans and Cheers and Champagne summoned, I was the last to see or hear it, so great was my Thrall to my New Life, as I saw it. 'Now we'll go to *Maidenhead*,' *says* Mr W— in a Low Voice, 'and you'll take the money for me tomorrow to Cardinal M— for the Relief of *Hungary*,' and the Young Blade embraced me with such Zeal that the Crowd burst out laughing, to see us Young and Happy and Rich.

Yet there is an Evil Streak that will show itself at the Gaming Tables, and often to the most Innocent among the Group; and I must say in my full Repentance, which, as shall be told, I have the Leisure a-plenty to endure, that it was to me that this Evil Genius came, for-all that I had everything in the world, my Uncle loving to lavish gifts on me and a Lover as Fair as any Northern Man to Call My Own. 'No,' *say I*, 'let's go on and we'll make more.' And I said to Mr W— that the *Russians* would be Defeated by our next Great Win, and we would buy an Army with it, for we had eighty thousand pounds in Chips on the table before us, Remember, and there were more Eyes on that Pile now than there were on my Pretty Face, a fact that there can be no Denying. 'Why not?' *says* Mr W— and he calls to poor Mr V—, who had lost his Woods and Estates and was now Down to his Last Tied Cottage, which would go tonight doubtless and leave a poor Family Out in the Street, though I have never known the Nobility to be mindful of such things. 'Come and watch us win,' *says* Mr W— to this Unfortunate, 'you'll pick up *Robina*'s Fortune.' And it's true that there then was a Stampede for all the Gamblers to touch me, though whether it was believed that I was indeed *Lady Luck*, or whether these Rogues thought they would get my Uncle's Fortune off me if they made my Acquaintance it is hard to say. 'I'll put it on the Number Three,' *say I*, for I had a Feeling for that Number since I was a Child; 'No, no,' *says* Mr W— laughing all the more, 'put it on twenty-one,' and he says that's the age of my Majority and we shall all have a Great Ball on that day, though I think he looked ahead to the Vast Sums he imagined were settled on me to come free at that age, at the hands of my Uncle, and would less likely say the number if he'd known of my Small Trust and that this was all that would ever Come to me. Alas for Good Resolutions, however: the Number was wrong to me and yet I put the Full Sum of our Winnings on it; the ball rolled and landed in Number Three and a Groan went up, for I believe we were popular that Night and they wanted us to win, being about to be Lovers. 'We are bound to borrow more now,' *says* Mr W— who was not at all abashed by this: I couldn't stop him from going up to the *Caisse* and taking another five thousand on my name; to be Brief this happened twice more again and I was swooning with Fear, while a great number of Onlookers gathered round to see me play, or so they imagined, with my Uncle's Fortune; and when we were Twenty Thousand Down I was pale and trembled so much I must be carried to lie on a *chaise longue*, for Mr W— was doing all the Gambling now and I couldn't bear to see the Chips go to the Bank and leave us Destitute. '*Robina*,' *says a Voice* near my shoulder as I lay there helpless: 'You are in-trouble certainly'; and this was the tenth Duke of D—, who said he had come from my Ball, which was still in Full Swing, that I was much missed there, as my Uncle had Vanished too, since being Insulted, and the Duke had come on here in the hope he would find me. 'You owe me, my pretty *Robina*, a thousand pounds, don't you?' *says he* and he spoke of the Plaque he had given me some days back and that I had handed over to Mr W— in the Cab, which I saw was a Mistake on my Part for Mr W— had not

154

returned it as he said he would, to its Rightful Owner. 'We must repay our Debts in this Life,' said the Duke and he ran his hand with speed up my skirt so I gave a gasp and was about to fall from the *chaise longue*, 'we'll do it tonight and at my house,' which he then proceeded to say was in *Mayfair* and only a stone's throw from the Club; yet my heart sank so low at the idea I must lose my all in *Mayfair* and not *Maidenhead*, that I went more White than before, and a Footman was sent for Smelling-Salts, which they kept in good Supply at the Gaming Club and little wonder at it. 'You'll come,' *says* the tenth Duke of D— and his manner was solicitous for I think he was afraid I might die in the Act and leave him with the Dubious Pleasures of a *Necrophiliac*; 'you'll make me a Happy Man tonight, won't you, *Robina*,' etc. Oh that I had gone back to my own Ball then and tendered my Apologies to my Uncle for all my Behaviour, and danced with the Young-Man the *Contessa* had singled out for me, namely Lord B—; but I had no Knowledge then that the *Contessa* and my Uncle would be gone by morning and I would be left with my Guilt and Grief; I thought only of the next hours with Mr W—, and so I fell into another Crime without Care of it: 'I'll come with you,' *say I* to the Duke. 'Hooray, I can't believe my Luck; indeed you have brought me Luck,' *says the poor Man*. 'But if I can Gamble one more time,' *say I*, 'for I need to win my Money back'; and so the Duke, who was ready to believe I was addicted to the Tables like everyone else in the Room, was Indulgent to me and laughed and pulled me to my Feet and we went to the *Caisse* where he purchased a Plaque and gave it to me: 'Here's your last Thousand, *Robina*,' *says he*, 'and don't be too long over it.' And he led me to the Tables, still chuckling away to his Heart's Content, while I had committed, as I well know, the Crime of PROSTITUTION and worse than that still, for there was also FALSE PRETENCES to be taken into consideration. For I saw Mr W— and I ducked away from the Duke by saying I needed the *Lavatory*, and Mr W— and I together went into the street by the Fire Escape which was I think better known to Mr W— than the Front Entrance to the Club. Now we were indeed a Couple of Criminals, yet it was I who would suffer the most ghastly consequences and Mr W— none at all, for I was of that evening a Debtor to the tune of Twenty Thousand Pounds and I'd heard it said that the Proprietor of the Gaming Club gave High and Low alike no longer than a full Day and a Night to Pay.

*

If my Spirits were lowered a little by the Great Loss, I was still glad to go to *Skindles*, where indeed a warm welcome awaited us and a Private Room set for Supper, there being a Bottle of Champagne and Strawberries, so that Mr W— in Full View of the Waiters shared the Luscious Fruit with me Lip to Lip and then hung Cherries from my Ears: 'No Fortune is more priceless than your Beauty, *Robina*,' *says he*; and then has me swear I'll keep myself for him while he is in *Hungary* and not to let the tenth Duke of D— after me, or any such thing: 'You are mine now, *Robina*,' *says he*, and has all the Waiters laughing at the droll Method he has of pouring champagne in a Goblet and drinking from one side and I from the other: we were as merry as a pair of newly-weds, in short, and I gave my vows on anything he pleased, though there were Black Clouds on the Horizon, of that you can be sure. '*Robina*, my pretty darling,' *says* Mr W— when we had drunk and supped at the Fruit, 'look what we have here,' and he goes to draw back a curtain which shows there is a Bed in the form of a *Gondola* and very fine, of Gilded Wood, at least to my eyes for I was untrained, remember, and had given up the Study of History of Art, which Ignorance led me to be as easily dazzled as a Village Girl. 'Come on it,' *says* Mr W— and smiling very much asked me to help him undo my Necklace and he took the Tiara from my head himself, but all the while pressing against my waist and neck and peering down at my breasts so that even the waiters were laughing as they cleared our plates and filled the bucket with another Bottle, I regret to say. 'More rubies there,' *says* Mr W— for my

156

nipples blushed without need of Rouge from *Joy;* 'my sweet girl, let Nature be all you need and give your Jewels to the Needy.' And he goes on to say the *Hungarians* shall have my Rubies for we no longer have Money to give them; and I assented, I fear, for I was weak with Desire for the Villain; 'Tell me, *Robina,' says he,* when he has closed the door and pushed away a Lad or two, who wished I think to see me naked, 'tell me where we shall live when we are married.' And with this Mr W— slid off my dress entirely, this being no Light Task owing to the Whalebone with which it was made up, and a task he was well accustomed-to I daresay, but I thought little of it at the time. 'Why, in the *New Forest,' say I.* 'No,' *says he,* 'we don't want to live with my Uncle surely, we must have a House of our Own,' and then takes off his Trousers and Shirt, but had no Erection I'm sorry to say and still I had no idea of his Meaning but lay on the Bed as a Lamb to the slaughter, with all my Body open to him, and a waiter making Sounds behind the door, for they were Peeping Toms at the Inn and were *Italian,* I believe, so that the sight of the Mound of Venus with a Fiery Bush above was as Thrilling to them as a view as *Mount Etna.* 'A *Manor,' says* Mr W—, sitting astride me now like a Horse, 'we'll buy a *Manor* near *Oxford';* and he says he likes to be near *Dons* and *Philosophers* and we shall entertain there, in the *Manor,* and be entertained too: 'for we mustn't be Bored with each other, my darling,' *says he.* 'But how shall we buy the *Manor?' say I,* for I was afraid now that I wouldn't satisfy Mr W—, for his Staff was at-last growing Thick and yet I could give him only a Thin Answer. 'I have Twenty-five thousand In Trust,' *say I,* 'and it's my Uncle and Aunt in *Scotland* who Handle it for me' (and I knew my Melancholy would come on me once more, which it did then, for Mr W— had no Money, and what I'd suspected was indeed true, that he had thought me a Great Heiress, and now he knew the Truth had dwindled as fast as his Expectations of my Fortune; so that he was all-at-once shrivelled and invisible). 'Never mind, *Robina,' says he,* 'I love you for all that,' and then he laid on top of me and wept that his Love was so great for me, and we drank a further two bottles of Champagne while he continued to protest how he did love me, and all the while we were more and more Drunk, so I couldn't rightly say when he came into me or how, but it was a *Fiasco* and no doubt about it, though my love for Mr W— was unabated. Indeed, I blamed myself for the size of my Fortune when Mr W— would have done better to castigate his own Shortcomings; however it was, we slept at last very uncomfortable in the *Gondola* and when I woke there was Dawn in the room and Mr W— had departed, taking *the Plaque* and the Rubies with him, as hardly needs the telling. Now I must make my way to *London* in my Ball Gown (and I had also to face the Anger of the Inn for Mr W— had gone without Paying): I cried, I must confess, and repented too late my Hasty and Foolish Actions, and the Inn-Keeper asking me to write out a Promissory Note, he offered me a Ride in the Vegetable Van back to the City: thus I arrived in *Chelsea* as the Sun was Up, and was delivered at my Uncle's door with as little concern as a Sack of Potatoes, so far had I sunk from the Fine Young Lady of the Night Before.

*

Troubles come not in Twos but in Threes, and after I was stripped of my Heirlooms and my Virginity and Cast back on the River *Thames* at *Chelsea*, I had short time to think of that stretch of Water Further Down where I had lost all to Mr W—: indeed, I had no more than the Forenoon to reflect on it, for when *Joy* had helped me to Bath (and I must say she tried me sorely, for she would make out I had enjoyed a Night of Passion and was filled with Envy of it, so she ran into the Bathroom every minute with an Italian Pepperpot and demanded to know if Mr W— had been of those Dimensions; while I had too much Pride to disabuse her); when the Forenoon was gone, as I say, the Dreaded Summons came, in the Guise of a *Beadle*, or a Man dressed up as such to intimidate the Clients of the *Faro Club*, and this man requested in no uncertain terms to see my Uncle, and on being told he had left to the *Far East* (as too had the *Contessa*) he told *Joy* he must therefore see me at-once and receive the Twenty Thousand Pounds that were owing to him. Alas! Let no-one who ever had a Dream of a Win at the Tables forget my Predicament: I feared for my Life, at the least: 'They will Carve up your Face,' *says Joy* in a tone that Curdled my Blood, and well I believed her, for *Joy* was from the *South of Italy* and she knew well the Methods in comparison with many of which I would rather die. 'What shall I do?' *say I*, and I was the most perfect Wretch you ever saw, for the Swarthy Man waited at the door and I had no-one in *London* to turn-to now, it being a great-deal too late to go and find Lady S— of B— and Ask Assistance, as my poor Aunt had told me to do if I should find myself in Difficulties. It was the End of my Peace and Happiness that I saw, and I'd rather Prison to the Handling of the Steward from the Club: 'Tell him,' *say I*, 'that he must give me to this Evening; that is only Fair,' etc., though I had no Notion of how I could extricate myself from so Dismal a Situation by the Evening or indeed Ever. 'Courage,' *says Joy*, who went down very stalwart to the Vile Creature and let him pinch her A—se I daresay, in return for a few hours more of Freedom, and then she comes running back up to me and says there are two Monsters at the Doorstep now instead of one, and we are Trounced for certain, and we must try and run out the Back Way, which led to *Paradise Walk* as it would most definitely prove, if we could reach it. But *Joy* had no Key to the Back Door; my Uncle had taken it to the East with him, for fear of Robbery of his Collection, which was housed in the main in the Conservatory at the Back of the House, and we were Sunk without Trace, as far as I could see. 'I've laid my Eyes on one of those Gargoyles,' *says Joy*, for she was in my Room again and peering down at a Corner in the Curtain; '*Robina*, come and look! And you may know him, I'll say you do, even if he ain't half as pretty as your Gallant Mr W—.' Her words alarmed me, and I went to the window, for *Joy* was full of Mischief and I feared the worst, that the tenth Duke of D— had come to collect his Debt in turn, so that I'd spend the rest of my Days repaying my Creditors, which was an Idea so Dreary that I swore I'd get to *Carlisle* and never come South again if I could only escape the House, and would climb over the Roof at night if it was Required of me. 'It is he,' *says Joy*, 'it is your "Cousin", *Robina*, he has come to save you,' and being *Italian* the Foolish Girl bursts into Tears, for the *Italians* believe in the Family above else, which is not true of the English, certainly, and not of me then, for I loathed and despised my 'Cousin' and held him Responsible for the Spoiling of the Ball on which my poor Uncle had lavished so much Money; and that he should arrive at our House was Trying in the Extreme. 'The Collector has gone,' *says she*; and looking down I did perceive my 'Cousin' who waited on the Door-step with a Hideous Grin on his Face, like a Corpse brought back from the Dead, which he most closely resembled. 'Bring him in,' *say I*, for I had no other Kin, it was true, that I could go-to, and False Kin was better than none, or so I thought in my Youthful Folly and Ignorance. 'We'll see what he can offer us.' Thus it was that I entered on the last and most Shameful Phase in my Life; but my Hopes were Shattered, Remember, and I was Penniless and in Debt, which is a good time for the Devil to walk in the door, as was well known by my poor Aunt in *Scotland*.

*

A Catalogue of Disasters makes Dismal Reading, yet for the sake of Clarity, so the Reader may understand the Terrible Inevitability of Crime, once it is set in its Course, some such Outline must be given, viz. it seemed as Nothing to me that my 'Cousin' should take my Uncle's Jade Bowl from its stand: 'I have Instructions from your Dear Friend and mine,' *says he* (and I hearing him speak of Mr W— had my Heart Flutter again, so great a Goose was I, the greatest that ever flew upstream to foul its own Nest, of that you can be sure); 'he said that if you were in-Trouble, *Robina*, you should go to his Uncle, the Auctioneer, and he would help you, so we'll go together with this Fine Piece'; and the Vile Creature cackled with Pleasure, yet I was without Feeling now and thought only of the *Beadle* from the *Faro Club* and prayed for my Release (and not knowing then that another form of prison lay in-store for me and another Escape would need the finding, viz. that I was with-Child by Mr W—, for Nature is no Respecter of Pleasure and would as gladly pollinate on a rainy day as a fine one: all this, as I say, was to discover itself to me as an item in the Catalogue of Doom, and without *Joy* I'd be at the bottom of the river, I've no doubt, and not with my most kind Relatives and with prospect of Marriage, Comfort and Security. 'I'll take a Commission on it,' *says* my 'Cousin' and he holds the Bowl up to the light so we can see it is very delicate and his hands, which are as big as an Ape's, might crush it: 'Never fear, *chère Cousine*,' *says he* (for the Monster was affected, as Upstarts are inclined to be): 'you shall carry it to *Sotheby's* in your own fair hands'; and with *Joy* we all went off together, my Spirits rising, I'm sorry to say, that I would be freed soon of my Debt and could wait in Peace for the return of Mr W— from *Hungary*.

How Life, like the Wheel at which I lost my *Integrity*, can deal a Number long thought *extinct*, is known to all but Fools: yet I was a Fool indeed and went smiling into the Offices of the Auctioneer ('The Auctioneer will Value it for us and then we'll go and sell the Bowl in *Bond Street*,' *says* my Rogue 'Cousin', who I must now acknowledge as my Flesh and Blood, for we were Partners in Crime, and I bore more resemblance to him than I did to my poor Uncles); I went with a Light Heart, as I say, into that Venerable Building, which is the Repository of all the Finest Art of this Great Nation, and there due to Excesses at the Tables or in the Beds of Courtesans, on the part of the Nobility: I walked with my Cousin to the Table where the Catalogues of Past Crimes and Plunders of the Aristocracy were Laid Out: viz. Pendant, Yellow Diamond, Gold Mount, *Property of a Lady*; and Fragment Poseidon 6th Century B.C. By Direction of the Estate of the Right Honourable the Earl of P—; and my Cousin asked that he might see Mr W—'s Uncle on Important Business, while I stood behind him with the Bowl, which I had borne with care from *Chelsea*, and looked all about me, as I say, at the Magnificent *Oils* and *Splendid Furnishings* of which the Nobility chose to Divest itself; yet when I then looked at the Table and saw that it was my Old Enemy *Annie* who sat there I was struck dumb with Disbelief, so many Turns of the Wheel, as I have said, had gone by in my Life since I was at *Mlle Weiss*'s and studying History of Art. '*Robina*,' says Annie and laughing as if we were Old Friends, 'well Fancy that,' etc.: 'So what brings you here?' And then she sees the Jade Bowl and lets out a Whistle at the sight of it, for it was very fine, and all the more so for *Annie*'s knowledge of its worth, provenance and so on, doubtless, for she had had many years at *Mlle Weiss*'s studying History of Art, which I had not. 'So how is it that you can sell this?' *says Annie*, whose Eyes were bright with Mischief, while I pulled at my Cousin's sleeve, to tell him we should walk out of *Sotheby's* at-once; whereas he, it goes without saying, was delighted that I should meet a friend at the Table, who would make our Passage to the Office of Mr W—'s Uncle all the more Smooth. 'This belongs to Mr A—,' *says Annie* and says my Uncle's Name, so I was Red with Shame at our Misdemeanour: 'it's a Famous Piece,' *says she*, 'and hardly needs another Valuation, for your Uncle was in with it before he left for the East' (and by this time my Cousin shows his Mortification also, and begins to Back Off): 'It's at-least twenty-five thousand Pounds,' *says the Minx*, keeping a very Sharp eye on me, and taking in *Joy* too, who was in a Cape and looked the Perfect Criminal's Maid, I regret to say. 'Well, he asked us to come in and obtain yet another Valuation,' *says* my Cousin the Ass, and with that he Bolts out the door into *Bond Street* and *Joy* and I go after him; but my Spirits were again Dashed by this, for I saw Annie stare after us; and for-all that we sold the bowl in Ten minutes to *Wildenstein*, and for Twenty-Five Thousand Pounds: 'I'll take Five Thousand as my Commission,' *says* my Cousin, 'and it's rightfully mine, for I've been Cheated long enough by the Family'. For all the Relief that I could now send *Joy* to the *Faro Club* with the Rest of the Money, which I did, I knew my Deserts were coming to me, and I think I can say in all honesty that I had never a moment of Enjoyment since, until at-last I reached the fresh air and pure atmosphere which in my wretched life I had so long been lacking.

*

If Fortune Hunters, Young-Men-About-Town and the Like had an Idea they would come and pay Court to me, that the *Mice would play while the Cat was away*, etc. they were certainly Mistaken; for *Swan Walk* had now the *Royal Duke* very many hours each day at his Position at the Gate of the Physick Garden, and the tenth Duke of D— at the Turning into *Chelsea Embankment*, so I was Caged-in as a Prisoner: I couldn't venture out for fear they would Accost me; and it's true, as has been told, that I was Sick in the Mornings and began to fear greatly that I had missed the Curse, which I couldn't remember the Day of, as I have been always bad at Counting, despite my Scottish education (which is known to send Bairns out to make Capital in the world). 'It is Late,' *says Joy* (who was kindness itself and had lost her Envy for me entirely, though she took some Satisfaction perhaps from my *Interesting Condition*): 'Here you must drink this,' and she hands me a bottle of GIN; 'I've run a Hot Bath,' *says she*, 'and you must drink the GIN in the Bath,' to which I agreed for I was Desperate now, and wondered too, as Time had gone by, where my poor Mr W— could be, if he was dead in a Corner of a Foreign Field and whether this was to be the last of the Disasters, though there were more to come, as we shall see. 'Come, the Water will get Cold,' *says she*, for she saw I was Brooding, and put this down too to my State, though I'll never know if I was indeed with-Child, or if it was *Joy's Italian* love of *Opera* that made her tell me I was, and I was Suggestible then, with the Lack of Exercise, and the fear my Suitors would break in and claim me each day. However that may be, *Joy's* Medicine worked Wonders: I was no sooner in the Bath and drinking the GIN, which gave me at first Happiness and then Melancholy, than All Went Well with me. 'The Redcoats have landed,' *say I* and laughing, I regret to say, and coming down the Stairs with the GIN in my hand: '*Robina!*' *says Joy* but too-late, for I had too much Spirit in me to Heed her; and indeed I ran past the Woman in Tweed who was at my Bedroom Door and Cast myself down on the Bed, singing and bursting into Fits of Merriment that one at-least of my Troubles was at an end. '*Robina,*' *says* this Woman, when my Laughter Dies Down on seeing it is my Aunt from *Carlisle*, 'I have Bad News of you.' And she looks round the Room and says the Curtains and Valances are Very Common, which I have often seen in these People, that Bad Taste is a greater crime than any other, and it did indeed give my Aunt, who had never been in the House in *Chelsea*, more Cause for Disapproval than my Roll Call of Dishonour, viz. LARCENY, PROSTITUTION or OBTAINING MONEY UNDER FALSE PRETENCES and most latterly MURDER, if I had indeed been with-Child as *Joy* assured me I was. 'A friend of yours by the Name of *Annie* was kind enough to Get in Touch with me,' *says she*; 'and you'll get dressed now, My Girl, if you don't mind, for I have a Cheap Day Return to *Carlisle* and your poor Uncle has had to Dip into His Funds to buy your Ticket;' and then as I get up and still Giddy, I confess, she says my Uncle has heard of the Reputation of Mr W—; that he is a *Charlatan* and my Uncle has put my Money in Trust until I am Thirty; 'which is for your own Good,' *says she*; and she says also that she is most concerned to find that Lady S— of B— Brought Out none of the Girls entrusted to her, that it was all Money Down the Drain as far as she could see, and that I would go to my Great-Aunt's Summer Ball at *Berwick*, where my Aunt and Uncle expected me to meet a young Kinsman of my Great-Aunt, who was *quiet* and *sensible* and had a *Rod and Tackle* Factory in *Jedburgh*; that I am bound to like him, in short; and so saying she sweeps up my Ball Dresses and says we'll take them North for they'll Come in

Handy for her Patchworks, and we can't wait any more for fear we'll miss the Train.

The Reader may well imagine the Relief and Gratitude on the part of so Absurd and Vicious a Girl as myself, that there is so much Forgiveness and Charity in the World; and I daresay we'd have gone quite happy to *Scotland* if there hadn't been a Commotion on the Stairs and *Joy* runs in White in the Face and tries to Bar the Door, but to No Avail; for in-runs not the *Royal Duke*, which was my greatest Fear, as has been said, (and Compounded by the fact that my Aunt, for all her Puritan Zeal, keeps still a picture by her Bed of the *Old Pretender*) nor the tenth Duke of D— who would Appear at-once to my Aunt as he actually was, which was a Dirty Old Man; but Mr W— Himself, all Aglow with the Glory of his Campaign and wearing my Aunt's *Fur Coat*, which was the worst of it. 'Good afternoon,' *says she*, very Stiff, and turns to me: 'That is my coat, *Robina*, I believe?' 'Yes,' *say I*. 'It's a Brave Coat,' *says* the Foolish Mr W—, 'it's been in the Wars,' and he holds out the Sleeve, which has indeed a round Hole in it, but which I know was made by the Mouse biting through, though the Cause was of little interest to my Aunt. 'Take it off at-once,' *says she*; which he did; and so it was that I saw my last of *London*, and of the Gallant Mr W— and went North once more, with my Aunt very Cantankerous all the Way.

*

In my great good Fortune here I can tell only of the Kindness and Bounty shown me by my Aunt and Uncle, and of my Hopes for the Ball at *Berwick*, which is to be in a *Marquee* with a Band of Bagpipe Players; and to give my most Sincere Pledge for the Future, that I will live for my new Husband, help him all I can with his *Rod and Tackle* Business, and that I won't look South of the Border even once, but will Remember as-long as I live that my Repentance is only the Consequence of my Misery, as my Misery was of my Crime.

165